Trouble Brewing

For Vince

Trouble Brewing

This one's on me ...

Paul

Paul Carroll

Matador
9 Priory Business Park,
Wistow Road, Kibworth Beauchamp,
Leicestershire. LE8 0RX
Tel: 0116 279 2299
Email: books@troubador.co.uk
Web: www.troubador.co.uk/matador
Twitter: @matadorbooks

ISBN 978 1788037 327

British Library Cataloguing in Publication Data.
A catalogue record for this book is available from the British Library.

Printed and bound in the UK by TJ International, Padstow, Cornwall
Typeset in 11pt Minion Pro by Troubador Publishing Ltd, Leicester, UK

Matador is an imprint of Troubador Publishing Ltd

For Sabina

AMUSE-BOUCHE

Brian Parkin had given considerable thought to how he might commit suicide. He'd spent hours on the Internet typing in a succession of search combinations without quite stooping to the obvious, 'best way to take your own life?' Brian was surprised to learn that lack of exactitude in his research was no hindrance to getting to the heart of the matter. He was soon immersed in a sea of advice promoting various ways of saddling the pale horse, each detailing the different scales of agony and speed of demise to be expected. All of which were leavened with entreaties to either call the Samaritans or to 'stop bleating and get on with it'. He worried that in even using the search function on his computer in this way some do-gooder, or even the police, would be alerted and suddenly arrive at his doorstep.

But now he was ready. He carefully checked the ingredients arrayed before him on the kitchen work surface. Each item meticulously apportioned and waiting to be pressed into service – olive oil, butter, cornflour, milk, plain cream cheese, eggs, basil, Gruyère cheese, cream. He took a bowl of mushrooms from the fridge and set them down. Now, finally, the preparation of his last supper could begin.

Despite his nickname of 'The Barnsley Chop' Brian was fastidious and precise when it came to cooking. There was no bish, bash, bosh about his approach in the kitchen. A place for everything, and everything in its place. It's what had made him the most famous celebrity chef in the country. Once.

He ran his eye over the table setting laid out in the corner of the kitchen. White linen tablecloth, best bone china dinner plates and sterling silver cutlery, the latter a hitherto unused gift from his agent. The bottle of Brunello di Montalcino he'd opened some two hours before breathed easily in the cosy domesticity of the setting.

He turned his attention back to the ingredients assembled in front of him and picked up one of the mushrooms. It was six inches high, and quite unlike any fungi he'd ever cooked before. Olive-brown in colour and with a cap around five inches in diameter, it gave off a faint odour of roses. Inverting the mushroom, Brian could see the wave-like edge of its radiating fibrous tissue and its crowded white gills. *Amanita Phalloides*. The Death Cap.

Brian knew exactly what his demise would be like. He had done a course on mushroom hunting once and knew what to avoid, and why. Shortly after eating the mushrooms the alpha-Amanitin toxin would set to work ushering in stomach pain, vomiting and diarrhoea. But that was nothing – it was the irreversible disintegration of his liver and kidneys that would kill him. Normally, one mushroom could be lethal and death could take days. Brian had six mushrooms, one for each ramekin of fatal fluffiness, in order to hasten the rapid onset of heart failure.

In the end, it was cutting in the Sunday Splash that made up his mind. He would poison himself using the very craft, experience and knowledge they now derided. He'd show them. He'd show them all. His ex-wife, who dropped him as soon as the money dried up. His agent, for whom stabbing him in the back once wasn't enough. The television producers who had all looked the other way. The media who had mocked his misfortunes. The public, the bloody, fickle public. Soon they'd all be sorry.

Brian had made his signature dish of double-cooked mushroom soufflé many times before – he'd even led thousands of aspiring chefs through the recipe live on air for his TV programme *Four Gas Rings and an Oven*. But that was a few years back now, when his name was in demand to endorse everything from Aunt Bessie's to Zabaglione. Now there were no cameras, overhead or otherwise, to grab the close up of the saucepans and no need to think about the one he'd prepared earlier. He was on his own.

Momentarily, he gazed out of the window of his Surrey pile to the paddock and the sixteen acres beyond. *His* paddock and *his* sixteen acres, purchased on the back of all his hard work and sacrifice. White cumulus clouds cushioned the sun against the blue sky on this finest of May afternoons. It looked as if God was in his heaven and all was right with the world. Well, maybe the world of the new owners who were moving in next week.

Brian extracted from his wallet a smudged newspaper cutting and began to read. Over the past few days he had read the same piece a hundred times. Repetition hardly weakened its sting.

Who's Smiling Now?

When does a TV chef become a former TV chef? That's a question I asked myself when I discovered by how far Brian Parkin, 'The Barnsley Chop' as millions knew him, had passed his sell-by date. 'Is he still alive?' you ask. Barely, is the answer.

But first the good news — Parkin is still involved in whetting the nation's appetite. Not as the stellar celebrity renowned for his 'no-nonsense cooking with a twist' but as the face of a series of two-minute recipe films on the website of a Yorkshire cheesemaker. The title of the series? Why, 'Say Cheese' of course.

Where did it all go wrong for Brian? Being accused of improper sexual advances towards a supermarket delicatessen employee started the rot. The girl, somewhat besotted by Brian's beefiness, was proven to have made up the charges — she'd never actually met him — but that didn't stop one red top precipitously using the headline, 'Celebrity Chef sticks his sausage in bacon slicer'.

Settlements aside, and an apology on Pg 15, the attendant ridicule signalled the start of the slide for Parkin. As work offers dried up his wife decided that her husband's plain fayre couldn't compete with the nouvelle cuisine being served up by Brian's agent. A lengthy and costly divorce later and Brian was as relevant to today's TV as Love Thy Neighbour.

The moral of the story? The fame banquet doesn't last forever, which is certainly a lesson some present-day disciples of drizzle would do well to heed. Never mind, Brian. It was good while it lasted. At least you made it to the cheese course. Don't forget to smile for the webcam now …

Bastard, thought Brian, before folding the cutting up and reinserting it into his wallet.

CHAPTER ONE

'So this is what all the fuss is about.' DeWayne Talley III of Kokomo, Indiana, framed his half-pint glass against the etched Victorian pub window and surveyed the distinguished golden colour of the ale within. The late afternoon May sun pouring through the dusty pane into the gloomy interior of the inn imbued the contents with celestial effulgence. 'Let's put it to the test.'

Before he could take a swig of beer a flat, booming voice from the other end of the bar splintered the reverence of his act of worship. 'I thought you Yanks thought big? Why settle for half a miracle when you can have a full one?' Godfrey Dransfield, 'Sir Godfrey' to everyone in town, harboured a disdainful disregard for anyone who drank halves, women included, and was fed up of tourists ruining his favourite pub. And he should know as he spent most of his waking hours in the Fountain Head.

'Sorry?' came the confused response from the hapless American visitor who still had to cross off 'Sample Brim beer in Brimdale' from his Day Three itinerary.

'Sorry? For what?' deadpanned Godfrey. 'Maybe if you drank a pint you might be able to speak proper English afterwards. That'd be a miracle.'

'That's enough, Godfrey,' snapped Peggy Weatherill, the landlady of the hostelry in which this touching example of the two countries' special relationship was playing out. 'I think it's high time you were getting yourself off home.'

'I'm only being helpful to our transatlantic visitor, Peggy. But if that's how you feel, I'll take a *rain check.*' Turning to the hapless tourist Godfrey added, 'Unlike you, *I will be back.*' Chuckling at his own wit Godfrey whistled his Border Collie, Bouncer, and headed unsteadily for the door.

'Sorry about that,' Peggy said to the visitor. 'We do have some colourful characters around here. It goes with the territory.' She was used to intoning this standard apology to passing patrons. It went with her territory more like.

'Our guide gave us the heads-up on these Yorkshire characters,' said DeWayne. 'They *"say what they like and they like what they say"*, is that right?'

'Something like that,' smiled Peggy, resisting the urge to be drawn further on such an incendiary subject.

'Is it true that your beer is like Champagne? That's another thing the guide said. Guess that's why we're here.'

'It's like beer, mostly,' Peggy corrected. 'I think what the guide meant was that we're trying to protect the Brim name, like Champagne does so no one else can call their wine Champagne. We want to make sure Brim can only be produced here in Brimdale.'

'So you can get Brim beer made somewhere else? That would knock the tourist trade right off.'

'It's not so much the tourist trade as much as the beer

2

itself. There's a brewery in Leeds selling something they call Brimmer ale, which they say is like ours but it's full of artificial rubbish. But if the public is confused Brim loses out, and so do we, so we're trying to put a stop to it.'

'I s-e-e,' summarised DeWayne, who by now thought it more prudent to get on with the actual sampling. 'Well, here goes – again.' Clutching the dainty half-pint in his boulder-sized fist he raised the glass of Brim to his lips and cautiously tipped a thimbleful into his crater of a mouth. A quizzical look swept his face as he tried to capture the experience. Finally, 'Gee. That's so warm you could take a bath in it!'

Peggy, now ruing the fact that she'd sent Godfrey off for early ablutions, simply thrust a leaflet into the American's other baseball mitt of a hand and said, 'You can read more about it in this pamphlet.'

Early next morning, the dawn sunlight finally penetrated the dark and knotted unconsciousness of the chef who had once held the whole world in his ladle. Brian Parkin blinked painfully before screwing his eyes tight shut against the growing, dazzling light. *Where am I?* A sudden thought struck him. *Am I dead?* Slowly he opened his eyes again to take in his surroundings. He recognised his garden. After a few more seconds of orientation he realised he was spread-eagled on top of the compost heap. *Had he? Was he?* He was confused. *What am I doing here?*

As he struggled to his feet he felt his head banging and his stomach churning. Could they do that at the same time? He remembered with a start what could be causing this condition. The Death Cap. So this is how it fitted.

3

He abandoned the effort to get to his feet and let his bulk subside, none too gracefully, back on top of the rotting vegetation. He noticed an empty bottle of Brunello di Montalcino strewn casually on the grass next to him, but couldn't locate immediately an accompanying wine glass. His memory flickered – yes, the wine. He'd drunk it all. In fact, he distinctly remembered drinking two bottles. And some Cognac too. As his senses began to clear he caught a whiff of decomposition – was it emanating from him, or from the decaying matter that had been his pillow for the night?

Overcoming his queasiness, he made a further attempt to rise and this time managed to totter six hesitant steps towards the fence separating the compost heap from the rest of the garden. He slumped heavily against the wooden rail as he tried to reconstruct what had happened over the past few hours. He was going to kill himself. Why wasn't he dead? Had he eaten the malignant mousses? He knew he felt ill but harboured a suspicion that his ailments possessed all the hallmarks of a killer hangover as much as anything else. His mind was a blank. He knew he had to get back to the house to jumpstart his wits.

Not without a struggle he negotiated his way towards the rear kitchen door. As he approached, he noticed it was wide open. Loud music was emanating from the building and as he got closer he could pick out Elton John singing crazy nonsense about butterflies and sugar bears. As the chorus faded there was a brief three seconds of silence before the track started up again on a loop. The volume was deafening as he entered the kitchen and he almost threw up as he dashed across to the offending speaker dock to turn it off.

He looked around, beseeching his memory to share the joke with him – what, exactly, had taken place? On top of the hob he espied the golden-brown splendour of his double-cooked mushroom soufflés. Wait a minute. There were only five. Where was the sixth one? An involuntary wave of nausea broke anew deep in his stomach and he retched inelegantly, producing a pitiful braying sound akin to a donkey being thrashed by a brutish owner. Desperately, he rushed to the peddle bin located in the corner of the kitchen – was there any sign of the missing ramekin there? No. He looked next in the refrigerator. Nothing. Frantically, he pulled open the door of the dishwasher – maybe his fastidiousness had seen him tidy up, even if he wasn't to outlive the wash cycle? Again – no sign.

He needed more clues. Keep calm, and *think*. On the kitchen table sat an envelope. That hadn't been there before. He reached for the cheap looking buff-brown enclosure and pulled out a single A4 sheet. Had he written it, or had it been sent to him? The letterhead revealed the sender as the Brimdale Beer Association. Did that mean anything to him? No. And then, suddenly, a flood of recollections from the previous twelve hours beset his brain, like shoppers charging the doors at the Harrods New Year Sale.

He'd been saved. A miracle had stayed his hand from stamping his own exit visa – an eleventh hour reprieve. The letter confirmed it – Brimdale Brewery had invited him, The Barnsley Chop, to line up alongside them and front their campaign. He was wanted. He still commanded respect. He wasn't a has-been. This wasn't the end, it was a new beginning and life could resume again. Brian could hardly contain himself at the realisation that he'd been saved in the nick of time. Now he remembered how he'd celebrated this last-minute pardon, carousing the night away in a celebration of drinking and singing. A party for one, but joyous all the same.

But how had the letter got there? His hand shot to his mouth as he remembered how this unexpected tiding had reached him in the nick of time. The letter had been borne to him, quicker than the good news from Ghent to Aix, by his former agent's secretary who had called in on him unannounced the previous evening. As Lily knocked ferociously to announce her arrival, Brian had at first crouched behind the door. Fortunately, she'd been persistent and, in any event, knew he was in there. Such small margins make the biggest differences. Imagine if he'd kept hiding? What if she'd come half an hour later?

He allowed himself a sigh of relief, and then realised that if he'd not eaten the contents of the sixth ramekin – good God – Lily hadn't helped herself had she? She had been most complimentary about the gorgeous aromas emanating from his kitchen and was delighted to see he was still working hard at his cooking despite all the bad luck he'd endured. Now she was going to die a horrible death and he would be responsible for it as surely as if he'd plunged his 20cm Sabatier Cook's Knife into her heart. His reckless selfishness. He must telephone her but as he frantically looked around for his phone he saw he was mistaken. There, on the back wall of the kitchen, forming a huge exclamation mark on the white plaster, was the remains of the missing murderous mushroom. A large brown stain stretched from eye level to the broken shards on the floor below, exactly where he'd thrown it in jubilation the night before.

Brandon Todd was in two minds. Should he really get a local train from Leeds City Station up to Brimdale, or should he hail a taxi to take him there? After two hours on the train from King's Cross the prospect of a local connection to his destination hardly filled him with good humour. He'd had to get up early too, but then that was something people had been saying about him most of his life.

Checking the travel instructions from his secretary, the next leg of his journey was determined – *whatever you do, don't get a taxi from Leeds – it will take longer.* One judgement call made but it wasn't the only thing Brandon was undecided over. Why was he trekking up north for this meeting anyway?

An hour and a quarter later Brandon walked into the reception area at Brimdale Brewery. If he'd entertained doubts on the train up from London these misgivings had only increased as he rattled through six local stops to get to this small Yorkshire mill town. Ten years ago he might have made a trek like this but now he had people to do this sort of thing for him. As one of the few PR faces the man in the street could actually recognise and name, Brandon didn't need to chase business anymore.

One of Brandon's pet theories was that you could divine the true nature of any business – where it was going and what its culture was – by assessing its reception area. He peered around the dimly lit atrium, made all the duller by acres of dark oak panels, and took in the haphazard pile of magazines on the coffee table. A stack of cardboard boxes tottered at an angle against a huge cast iron radiator while above it a large display panel promoted Brim's sponsorship of the national bog-snorkelling championship. Brandon couldn't help but notice the poster was two years out of date. His heart sank.

The young girl on the reception desk seemed very pleased to see him though, squealing excitedly when he approached her to announce his arrival. 'Oh, Mr Todd. We thought you must have been kidnapped. Now, tea or coffee before I get Mr Backhouse?' Somewhat disarmed by this welcome, and amused a few moments later when the receptionist asked for his autograph, Brandon allowed himself a smile for the first time that morning.

Simon Backhouse, managing director of the Brimdale Brewery and the seventh in a long line of Backhouses to steer the family-run firm, appeared in reception to greet Brandon. He wasn't at all what Brandon was expecting from the managing director of an old established brewing firm – he was wearing jeans, trainers and a t-shirt proclaiming *It's only rock 'n' roll but I like it*. Brandon, bedecked in a £1000 suit he'd had run up on a boys' trip to Bangkok, wondered momentarily if he'd over-dressed for his appointment. The thought also struck him that Simon couldn't have been born when The Glimmer Twins first espoused the sentiment adorning his chest.

On following Simon into his office Brandon was no less curious to discover accoutrements one didn't normally associate with the station of a high-powered executive. One wall contained a huge collection of vinyl LPs that, even on cursory inspection, the visitor recognised were arranged in alphabetical order. A turntable, tuner and amplifier sat on a shelf flanked by two enormous speakers and the musical theme was continued in the shape of a customised Martin acoustic guitar nestling in its stand. A dartboard dominated one corner of the office with four beer crates laid out in line on the floor beneath to create the oche. A gigantic stuffed bear stood to attention behind the desk, seemingly guarding the single silver laptop that stood marooned in the midst of a vast expanse of green leather.

'Interesting office,' ventured Brandon.

'Thanks,' replied Simon. 'It's a great space for thinking.'

Brandon noticed right away that while Simon had a Yorkshire accent, his was far softer and more seductive than the ones he'd been trying to tune into for the past hour or two. His ears relaxed a little. He sat down, as invited, on a gigantic cracked leather Chesterfield settee and surveyed Simon who, eschewing his desk, had plonked himself on an identical seat opposite him. Brandon followed Simon's example in balancing his mug of tea on the arm of his couch. In truth, he had been forewarned by a client who had bumped into the brewer at a digital conference to suspend all preconceptions about Simon until he'd met him. *'Brandon – don't ask any questions, don't delegate it, just get yourself up there. You won't regret it.'* Intrigued, Brandon had done just that.

Simon didn't bother with small talk much. 'Thanks for coming, Brandon. Basically, we need your help, big-style. I've done my homework and I'm not planning to talk to anyone else.'

Brandon was used to flattery and immediately adjusted his fee expectations in the same direction he'd travelled that morning. While the PR supremo had spent an hour or so mugging up on Brim, he still needed a specific brief. 'That's very kind of you to say so, Simon. Maybe you'd better outline your priorities?'

Simon was succinct. 'Basically, we're up shit creek without a paddle if we don't get a favourable EU decision. You have to make sure we win that ruling. That's the brief.'

'I see. Well, I like clarity, and there's no grey areas with that,' said Brandon.

'No, there's not. Four months to do it, that's all.'

Brandon knew about Brim's application to the EU to stop other brewers using the Brim name. Nevertheless, he could see an immediate drawback to Simon's petition. 'But hasn't that bird already flown? Brexit and all that? Will it matter in the end anyway?'

'I think it will matter even more. It's going to take years to sort out the fallout from the referendum, and probably a century to reverse any EU ruling we receive now. We can't get a similar protection with any teeth from the UK – it's now or never.'

Brandon admired Simon's optimism. He knew only too well the trouble Brexit was causing for many of his other clients – as well as creating extra work opportunities for him. 'Of course, the Europeans may not be so keen on giving you a helping hand, seeing as how the UK has given them a slap in the face.'

Simon had clearly agonised over this point, too. 'We've come too far to stop now. It's business as usual as far as were concerned and we've no reason to believe our friends at the European Commission office will say 'no' to us just to pay Boris back. We're in the finishing straight – we just need to get it over the line.'

'Four months doesn't leave much time.'

'That's why you're here,' replied Simon. 'Everything depends on us getting the nod from Brussels and stopping others cashing in on our name. It's make or break time.'

Even from Brandon's cursory research he knew that the bid had been ongoing for years – and blanched at the thought of the fees he could have made from the brewery in that time. 'It may have been better to have called me in earlier, perhaps? I'm not saying I can't help but we're going to be up against it timewise?'

'Granted, but there's more to it than a short-term job for you here – this is a massive opportunity for you longer-term. If the EU ruling is favourable, I know for a fact that there are around six UK companies who have similar applications at different stages. You help us, and they'll be queuing up for you.' Brandon's eyes grew slightly wider. 'Then, and this is the biggie, if we win, I've lined up a major product diversification programme into different ale, natural water and health product markets in this country and worldwide. Our spring will be at the heart of all of those ranges. That's what I've been mainly doing over the past three years – planning the future. Brim's going to go global and you'll be in the box seat for that work too.'

Brandon had stopped getting carried away by promises

of 'jam tomorrow' from clients some time back. 'But first, you have to get a positive ruling and to do that you'll need to throw some resource at it. I mean, what sort of budget do you have?' Brandon may not have hailed from Yorkshire but he had a direct interrogative style when it came to money; he liked to know what's what. Simon's reply, and the value attached to it, would determine how long this meeting would last.

'We're throwing the kitchen sink at this, Brandon. We've been treading water until now but this is the time we go for it. Most of our support to date has been from the Brimdale Beer Association, a group of locals who've mobilised to promote our cause. They mean well but they aren't too sophisticated. We need to raise the stakes, which is why I've committed a substantial figure for the marketing campaign including contributions from the local council and our trade body. There's a lot riding on it for everyone, not just the brewery.'

As Brandon's eyes widened on hearing Simon's interpretation of 'a substantial figure' matched his own, the brewery boss added his clincher. 'Plus, if you help us to pull it off I'll pay you a bonus equivalent to your fees for doing it. The only condition is we'll insist that you personally lead the campaign, not some minion. I doubt you'll have a more lucrative offer this year.'

As Brandon responded to the news of this unexpected windfall by relaxing still further into the embrace of the settee, Simon's offer appeared to be endorsed by a high-pitched trill of approval from the creaking couch. It looked like they had a deal.

'This is a lot of money for us,' continued Simon, 'and

even for you I venture, but losing is unthinkable. Whatever it takes, Brandon, whatever it takes. This is going to be your show now, on your say-so. Are you up for it?'

'When do we start?' grinned Brandon.

CHAPTER TWO

So this is how culture shock feels? Cora Songhurst was in her second week back in West Yorkshire after living and working in London for the best part of two decades. She turned to the reason for her unexpected return, her mother Alicia, clutching for breath in her wheelchair. Maybe, under the circumstances, a short stroll hadn't been the best idea but Cora was still adjusting to her mother's illness and the restrictions it imposed on her and those around her.

As Cora loosened her mother's scarf and double-checked that the small oxygen canister was attached to the chair she felt a swell of self-doubt dampen her resolve – not for the first time that fortnight. How could she possibly nurse her mother through her debilitating respiratory disease when she'd never so much as looked after a sick kitten? Well, it wasn't a question of choice anymore; it was a question of need. Now she was back. But for how long?

Alicia's thoughts were racing in direct proportion to her breathing. Had she done the right thing in accepting Cora's offer to return home and look after her? Alicia knew her daughter was motivated more by a sense of duty than filial devotion and she could simply have said 'no' to

Cora's suggestion, but the fact was Alicia felt it was her due to accept. Was she being selfish? Yes, but there would be scant time for regret over this final act of indulgence. Why shouldn't she allow her only child to see her through her final days on earth? She had seen her husband Kevin to the grave five years earlier, so now it was her turn.

That Alicia was going to die wasn't in doubt – it was just a question of when the chronic obstructive pulmonary disease closed down her airways for the final time. How crazy she had been to smoke all those years. Various surgical remedies to tackle the disease had been discussed with physicians but Alicia had decided, easements aside, to let nature take its course unimpeded. Cora admired her mother's fortitude and took to wondering if it would be worse to have a sound mind and a serious physical illness or to enjoy rude physical health and lose grasp of one's mental faculties as age settled up life's account?

As her mother's discomfiture eased and her breathing returned to something approaching normal, Cora sat down on the bench next to her and surveyed the landscape of her childhood. The family house, a higgledy-piggledy Grade II listed hall that sounded a lot more impressive than it looked, lay five hundred yards back up the lane, one of only three dwellings in the hamlet of Brim Over that had looked down on its neighbour, Brimdale, for centuries.

Cora struggled to recall much in the way of detail, or warmth, in her upbringing there. Academia was at the forefront of her world back then with both her parents holding esteemed positions at Leeds University and Cora hadn't let the side down, passing through Bradford Girls'

Grammar with distinction and going on to read History at Oxford, just like her mother.

Cora's early years were unremarkable, conspicuous only for her singular, scholarly endeavour. For so long convinced that doing well in her studies was the primary purpose in her life she sacrificed friendship, relationships and other interests to this solitary focus. As her twenties faded and she took stock of her life, what had she achieved? A job as a curator at the British Museum cataloguing the past, and a bedsit in Acton.

Recognising that she was gathering dust faster than many of the exhibits in her charge, Cora determined to do something new and definitive to force her life in a new direction– she decided to write a book. She was an avid enough reader to recognise that the world didn't need another academic tome on the Roman Empire or the Spanish War of Succession so, quite to the amazement of those who knew her, Cora came up with the sensational *The Empress and her L'Eproveuse* (subtitle 'The Secret Sex Life of Catherine the Great'). This historical fiction presented the salacious antics of the eighteenth-century Russian Empress through the eyes of the lady-in-waiting charged with testing out potential lovers before passing them as fit for her mistress. The book, made all the more compelling by the first person narrative technique Cora employed, became a crossover sensation, being read as much for its erotic revelations as its factual insight.

That was just the start for Cora. Over the next decade she continued to select key historical figures (Boadicea, Saint Paul and Cleopatra among others) to give them the Songhurst treatment, racking up hundreds of thousands of book sales, inspiring a number of film and TV treatments and winning an array of literary awards.

Quite how she'd managed to bring it off even Cora didn't know. Nevertheless, despite being blessed with literary success, she remained a shrinking violet when set against the usual 'look-at-me' efflorescence of the publishing world.

Cora didn't have a man or children in her life to distract her from looking after her mother so it was only right that she should spare a few months – it may even be only a few weeks – at her mother's side. After all, Cora had made little effort to visit home regularly since she had become a successful writer. And Cora found herself agreeing with Alicia's observation that she could just as well write books in Brim Over as in London, so she wasn't really taking her away from anything.

Relieved that Alicia was once again breathing evenly Cora struck up a conversation, determined to keep off the subject of health. 'Do you know, Mummy, I'd quite forgotten the views from up here.'

Alicia followed Cora's gaze until it lighted upon a tumbledown pile of stones a further two hundred yards down the path. 'The Priory, you mean? You used to play there when you were a child. Do you remember?'

'Vaguely. I always thought it might be haunted by ghostly monks or something.'

'Nonsense. No such thing as ghosts. It's possibly haunted by the memory of Henry VIII but that's quite a different matter.'

'Yes. I don't suppose The Benedictines have ever quite forgiven him, have they?'

'Benedictines? It wasn't a Benedictine order there during The Reformation – it was a Cluniac order, an offshoot of the Benedictine order.' Despite her illness, Alicia was still a stickler for historical accuracy. As a tutor in that discipline she had always come down hard on sloppy research. 'They had Cluniac nuns too, but obviously not there,' she added.

Cora shrank at being corrected by her mother, something she had experienced all too often in her life. 'Sorry, Mummy.' Dispirited at once more being in the wrong she decided the stroll had lasted quite long enough. 'Ready for a push back up the lane now?'

It appeared that Gary Merriweather was harbouring doubts over the veracity of recent reported sightings of the people's PR champion in his locale. 'Brandon Todd? In Brimdale? Yer pulling me plonker.'

His drinking partner in the Fountain Head, Howard Amos, nodded emphatically. 'It was him all right. At the brewery. Plain as day. You know what this means, don't you?'

Gary, in fairness, didn't immediately gather what Brandon's fleeting presence in their town signified. 'I've not time fer games – spit it out.'

'They're giving us the elbow. Our efforts are unappreciated. They're bringing the experts in.'

'We dunt need a tosser like 'im to 'elp. That's right vexing, that is.'

Meetings of the Brimdale Beer Association didn't normally start quite so acerbically and any casual drinker in the pub that evening would have been hard pressed to spot that the two middle-aged men sat next to the fruit machine were in fact the vital few who would convert the bureaucrats of Europe to their cause's favour. But this was the monthly meeting of the BBA, an organisation that, seven years after Howard had founded it, had now dwindled to an active membership of two.

Howard possessed an unerring sense of duty to the town of his birth – he was a man of action. He had served as a local councillor for twenty-five years and numbered among his finest achievements the installation of dog waste litterbins in the two local parks and on The Stray, an expansive public common on the outer boundary of the borough. An alumnus of the local grammar school, Howard ran Brimdale's only photographic studio and there wasn't a family portrait, classroom shot or wedding album in town that hadn't had his finger hovering over the shutter release.

Gary was a relative newcomer, having lived in Brimdale only twenty years since moving up from Bradford to take a job as production manager at the local fabric-printing mill. That job had disappeared when the mill closed following the transfer of manufacturing to Sri Lanka but Gary had stayed put in town for the sake of his kids. Now he worked for the security firm contracted to keep an eye on the disintegrating Victorian edifice he'd previously laboured in, ensuring the integrity of the steel perimeter fence erected around the site to prevent travellers breaking in and squatting. Gary's primary qualification for serving on the BBA was that he liked beer.

Together, Howard and Gary fulfilled the roles of chairman and secretary of the BBA though in reality 'chief cook and bottle-washer' would have been a better description. Nevertheless, the meagre budget the brewery and the council had earmarked for marketing support via the Association continued to be entrusted to them.

Howard was trying to suppress the feeling of betrayal that had been mounting since he'd been tipped off about Brandon Todd's visit to the brewery. 'I'll call Simon in the morning and find out what's going on. We shouldn't have to discover stuff like this second hand.'

'Too bloody reet,' agreed Gary.

'It would be scant recognition of our efforts over the years if they brought in such a high-profile PR now.'

'A fancy dan, Johnny-come-lately, bloody glory 'unter – that's wot Brandon-bloody-Todd is. Whatever 'appened to local bloody nous?'

Guardedly, Howard felt inclined to agree. 'Yes, Gary. They're still going to need that.'

'Dead reet,' echoed Gary as he stood up. 'Yer want anuther orange juice?' Despite Howard's calling to preserve Brim's very existence, he was a confirmed teetotaller.

'Might as well, Gary. But you'll never guess what else has happened. I was forgetting with all of this Brandon Todd upset.' Gary sat down again, clearly not going to the bar until Howard shared his surprise. 'Remember that idea of getting a celebrity ambassador for the campaign? Well, I've only got our man.' Howard was in no hurry to just blurt the name out – this was an announcement that needed building. Gary vaguely remembered this plan but thought it had been dropped, probably due to lack of funds. Howard continued, an imaginary drum roll accompanying his 'reveal'. 'It wasn't easy I can tell you, 'cos he's a big fish.' Howard again paused for effect, much to Gary's annoyance. Sensing he wasn't going to get anything from Gary, near the mark or otherwise, Howard didn't hold back any further. 'Brian Parkin, the Barnsley Chop himself, is coming on board to back our cause. We're seeing him next week to dot the "Is" and cross the "Ts". I think such a coup will put a stop to any criticism of our endeavours, don't you?'

Gary looked impressed. ''Appen it will.' This is exactly the sort of achievement the BBA was created to deliver. A look of triumph lit up his face. 'Wait 'til Backhouse and Mr-bloody-Brandon Todd put that in their pipes and smoke it.'

CHAPTER THREE

Across the county in the Vale of York Richard Tasker of the Department for Environment, Food & Rural Affairs was being prepped by the government department's in-house marketing manager. He considered this precaution to be largely unnecessary, as nobody at Defra possessed a better command of the Brim case study than he did. After all, he'd been working on it for eight years. The marketing manager – fairly new to the job – was keen to ensure that the shoot for a new promotional film on 'protecting our heritage brands' went smoothly. He had all sorts of advice for Richard before the crew and interviewer were due to arrive.

'I think I know what I'm doing,' said Richard. 'I have been interviewed before, you know.' In any case, he thought, *it's not like we're on national TV. And they can edit it afterwards.*

The young marketing manager ignored his protestations and weighed up the situation. The interviewee thinking he knew it all but deep down nervous as hell, and as televisual as most Defra officers were ever going to get with his sharp features, poor complexion and department store suit and tie. 'It's just to get the emphasis, the nuances, right,' he stressed. 'What I'll do is fire the questions at you in a dry run, and we can work on what to push and what to drop from there. Then we'll get you into makeup.'

The marketing manager may have looked fresh out of school but he knew his stuff. Despite the 'no-pressure' set up Richard felt his stomach knotting at the prospect of doing the filmed interview. Defra Inspectors didn't normally get called upon for media duties but this was a big story for the department, after all.

'Question one. Why is Defra helping Brim beer in its fight to stop rival brewers making Brim-type beers?'

'Well, our intention isn't to stop other producers as much as protecting the town of Brimdale's exclusive right to make Brim Ale.'

'That is stopping other producers, then, surely? Could you say, "Brim beer is unique to the Brimdale area, and needs to be protected. That's where Defra comes in"?'

Flustered at being picked up on question one, Richard nodded his assent. 'It's all about PGI really. I'll start with that, shall I?'

'Not PGI – "Protected Geographical Indication" would be more meaningful. Not everybody will know what PGI is. Spell it out and give the audience a clue.'

'Right, yes. I'll remember that.'

'Thinking about it, "Protected Geographical Indication" won't cut it with anyone either. Could you get straight into some examples? That's what people will get straightaway.'

'I usually use the Melton Mowbray Pies example – that's a good one. Or Cumberland sausage? Or maybe I could mention some foreign ones like Gorgonzola?'

'They're all good. Champagne is the obvious one but hold all of those thoughts for later. Right, tell me what Brim beer has in common with all of these examples so it should be protected.'

'The products have to be distinct and come only from a designated area to qualify – it's as simple as that.'

'So what's *distinct* about Brim beer? Why can't it be made anywhere else?'

'It's down to the water used in the beer – that's what's totally unique. It's from an aquifer – I'll say "spring" there – that contains minerals that have health-promoting properties.'

'Other beers and beverages claim to have health-promoting properties, too.'

'Yes, but this is *naturally* occurring and it's different to water used in other beer and beverage production – we have to remember that many other drinks marketed in this way are pumped full of artificial additives to meet their claims. Competitors can still do all of that in future – they just won't be able to mention the word "Brim" in any way.'

'So what's in this water that's so special?'

Getting into the swing of it now, Richard felt slightly more confident. 'I could bore you with its chemical composition, but I won't. Essentially, the water used in Brim beer contains a trace element of salicin. Salicin is derived from the white willow bark and we believe that a prehistoric forest of white willow trees once stood above the site of the spring.'

'So what does salicin actually do?'

'The simplest explanation is to say that you'll find

derivatives of salicin in aspirin, and the ancient Greeks used white willow bark to cure everything from back ache to fevers, from heart problems to aches and pains.'

'So that's why it's called a miracle beer.'

'We don't go along with that "miracle beer" description. We can't use that. But it is unique to Brimdale and that's why we've backed its cause for some time now.'

'As we speak, the European Commission ruling on Brim's geographical status is only months away. What will it mean for the town if the application is successful?'

'Like I said – nobody else will be able to produce and market Brim-style products or use Brim-like names. That will protect the brand and with it the jobs and the livelihoods of the local people who depend on the brewery.'

'Viewers will want to know how the Brexit vote may affect the application? Should this have been done and dusted before the referendum to avoid any uncertainty?'

Richard bristled. How many times had he had the same thought in the past few months? 'We've been on this for the best part of a decade. We don't make up the bloody rules.'

'Hmmm. Maybe, "It's now more important than ever to secure this protection for Brim's heritage. And that's exactly what we'll be doing." That sounds a little more emphatic, yes?'

Richard squeezed the small stress ball he carried around with him as an executive toy. He did have a tendency to get wound up. 'Yes,' he growled. 'Understood.'

'And, finally, what happens if the application fails?'

'Surely we don't want to go into that in the film, do we? They'd be screwed.'

'They'd be screwed'. Dave Rawson had no doubts, no doubts at all, as he briefed Mervyn Cutler, Vice President of Monumental Breweries Inc. Mervyn was on his annual visit from Milwaukee to its subsidiary, Colton's Brewery in Leeds, and had just asked Dave what would happen to the small Brimdale Brewery if it lost its battle to protect its exclusive right to the Brim name.

Colton's loomed over the River Aire as it loafed its way through the restored heart of the city's Victorian centre, one of the cradles of the Industrial Revolution. Despite the recent clean up of the waterway and the unanticipated bonus of a sublime sunset, the landscape still looked pretty dismal to Mervyn. 'And how can we take advantage of that?' he countered.

Dave Rawson was a man who had looked to chisel an advantage all his life, which is one of the reasons he had been made head of the brewery at the relatively tender age of thirty-four. Rawson prided himself on making things happen and was the prime mover behind Colton's Brimmer Beer launch some nine years before. He promoted Brimmer as a 'vitamin beer' containing a balanced package of nutrients and minerals – any similarity to Brim was purely intentional despite the fact that the prime ingredient of Brimmer was courtesy of the Yorkshire Water Utility Company. The consequences of Rawson's gamble, however, were unintentional. He had anticipated Brimdale Brewery's inevitable threat of legal action for 'passing off', calculating that he could string that out for years with the resources of their multinational owner. What he hadn't reckoned on was Defra coming down on the side of the Brimdale brewery and applying for geographical protection for Brim beer as a way of settling the matter. Interfering busybodies who'd be better off planting trees and stopping outbreaks of foot and mouth disease.

The legal chess game had dragged on for years – the whole episode rankled with Rawson who didn't like to have his well-laid plans thwarted. As far as he was concerned, the Brimmer legal case represented a small blot on his otherwise perfect copybook with Colton's. Now, with the EU decision deadline looming, there was more than the town of Brimdale banking on the outcome.

Rawson took his cue. 'Take advantage? Without a doubt. The way I see it is this: if they lose their EU bid it will mean we can expand our range of Brim-type products and, with the health and well-being market growing like crazy, clean up. Brim would be buggered – it just doesn't have the resources to compete on an even playing field.'

'OK. So how do we make sure we clean up the most?'

'Well, first off, say they lose, then Brimmer is positioned to go mega. Sales have been OK up to now but people still prefer the "real" stuff. Once Brim isn't the "real" stuff anymore, it's the same as ours. Plus, the legal battle is over – in our favour.'

'And if they win the ruling?'

'We come out second best in the courtroom bun fight and it's the end of Brimmer.'

'But you guys have shot yourselves in the foot by voting to leave Europe. So none of this is relevant anymore?'

'No. It's even more relevant. Believe me.'

'But it's still like tossing a coin – the decision could go either way and there's nothing we can do about it?'

'No, I disagree. There is something we can do about it. We've got to buy them. We've got to buy Brimdale Brewery now, *before* the EU makes a ruling.'

'Buy them? You just said they'd be dead meat if they lost. What would we do a thing like that for?'

'Think about it for a minute, Mervyn,' (and Rawson had thought about it for considerably longer than that over the past few months). 'If we owned them and they win the EU ruling, we could take the Brim brand worldwide. We wouldn't need Brimmer anymore. We'd own the spring, the Brim name, the lot.'

'If we bought them. If they win the ruling. I don't like "ifs" when it comes to spending big bucks. You're losing me here, Dave.'

'Because even if they lose, we can still take their brand worldwide before some other competitor decides to do the same. Better than that, we'd trade off their heritage – the 'original'. With money behind the brand we could increase sales a hundredfold, even if the brand wasn't protected. Buying them is a win-win for us, whatever the ruling.'

Mervyn, unusually for him, was silent for a few seconds as he searched for the flaws in his director's reasoning. Rawson could see he'd piqued Mervyn's interest and he'd not even got on to his ideas for launching a Brim natural mineral water and a range of Brim health and skin products. 'So, do I have the green light to open negotiations?'

'Hold on, Dave. These guys aren't going to sell. Why would they sell now? And they certainly ain't gonna talk to you. They win this ruling, they carry on in their own sweet way and we've taken a beating. They lose, OK, we maybe look at picking it up on the cheap at that point.'

Rawson wasn't going to see his carefully laid plan bite the dust so easily. 'We can't afford to wait, Mervyn. If they win – and they might – that's game over for us. It's the end of Brimmer and a big legal bill. That's a "lose-lose" situation for us. If the ruling goes against them, other companies will be after buying them on the cheap and they're not going to favour us in a bidding war after all the bad blood between us. We have to strike now.'

'I see your logic, but I don't see how you could persuade them to sell to you before that ruling.'

'You just leave it to me, Mervyn. Give me the say-so, and I'll make it happen. And at the right price.'

Besides the Brimmer miscalculation, Rawson had not put a foot wrong in all of his time at Colton's and Mervyn reflected that if his managing director pulled this coup off even that would look like a genius long-term strategy in hindsight. 'Well, see what sort of appetite you can rustle up from them and if you can get the price right, then....'

'I knew you'd see it, Mervyn, I really did.' Rawson, who could now wipe the Brimmer slate clean in one fell swoop, banged the table in delight.

Mervyn smiled at the look of triumph now spreading across Dave's pugnacious and ill-assembled face. He was glad Rawson was on their side, not lined up against them.

CHAPTER FOUR

Brian Parkin pulled his Range Rover into the car park opposite the Fountain Head. At least he'd managed to keep hold of his wheels. He turned the engine off and took in the scene. This was it. His lifeline. A chance to shine, an opportunity to show people he still had 'it'.

A week had passed since the near fatal dinner party-for-one and the euphoria he'd initially felt at his reprieve had been severely put to the test in the interim. First of all, he'd moved out of the house and placed what furniture and effects he had salvaged from his marriage into storage. This new dislocation reignited the sense of isolation that had driven him to within a hair's breadth of the most selfish of acts, and threatened to strangle in his throat his new mantra of 'I'm lucky to be alive'. Was he lucky? It was a good question, and one he knew he wouldn't be able to answer definitively for some time, not while *she* was still breathing. She, whose name he couldn't even bring himself to say. She, who delighted in putting the boot in at every opportunity. She, to whom he'd been married for twelve long years.

What had puzzled Brian for some time was why his ex-wife seemed so determined to make him suffer. It wasn't as if he'd run off and had an affair. She'd done that, not him. It wasn't as if he had treated her badly – he was devoted to her and had loved her unquestionably. And he never denied her occasional 'small luxuries' such as holidays, jewellery, clothes and never-ending home improvements, even when he knew he should have railed in her soaring materialistic ambitions.

Yet, when 'Sausagegate' hit the newspapers, instead of supporting him and helping him to fight the wicked allegations she simply packed her bags and left. At first Brian thought it was because she believed the red tops rather than him. That distressed him greatly but not half as much as when he discovered she was seeing his agent behind his back, and the penny dropped that the relationship wasn't in its infancy. Desperate at the thought of losing her, Brian wanted to offer her another chance, to reconcile, to forget the past and move on. In return, she taunted him, telling him he was finished, 'whether you shagged that girl or not'.

During the divorce, which she insisted on, she played dirty, incensed at the realisation that Brian wasn't worth as much as she thought he was, and knowing only too well, as her new partner was uniquely positioned to confirm, that Brian's big earning days were done and dusted. She instigated a reign of terror, dragging Brian through the courts and making him feel like a criminal as her legal team ordered one forensic investigation after another to discover where he'd stashed 'the hidden millions'. The final indignity, and the cruellest blow, was when she spitefully demanded that his first restaurant, The Reluctant Poacher, where he'd made his name and launched his career, be sold off. Now broke, he couldn't even buy her out or make her change her mind. It was another piece of his former life cruelly yanked from under him.

He'd signed over the restaurant that very morning, twenty-four hours after handing over of the keys to his house – surely these were the final acts of savagery? She couldn't do anything more now to hurt him. He was on his own and only too aware that he'd reached rock bottom. Could he now try to start again, and rebuild his life? A week ago, he thought he was finished and had contemplated the coward's way out – surely the only way now was up? He knew he had to believe that. Where there was life, there was hope.

Cora Songhurst sat at her old bedroom desk looking out of the window at the wind-blasted pear trees bending their backs in the orchard below. She knew how they felt. As the weeks progressed Alicia was becoming more and more demanding; Cora was beginning to dread each new day as it arrived. She had to be there for her mother but, at the same time, her normal routine had evaporated along with her equilibrium the moment she stepped back over the threshold of Brim Over Hall.

Despite Alicia's physical ailments there was nothing wrong with her tongue which remained as sharp as ever, issuing instructions, correcting her daughter and providing her with the benefit of her advice. Alicia's code for calling a time out in the rising tension between her and her new carer was to encourage Cora to 'go off and write a few pages'. Cora had never felt less like writing over the past decade but nevertheless withdrew to her room whenever given this get out.

Cora promised her agent she would develop her next book project while she was away, but had barely time to think. When, how, could she develop new ideas under these circumstances? She logged on to her computer to pick up emails and afterwards, rather than go back downstairs to sit with Alicia, began to idly surf the Internet for any fresh reviews or mentions of her books. Spotting the outline of the ruined Priory on the crest of the hill behind the house Cora suddenly thought of her mother's correction the previous week over which order had resided there. She typed 'Cluniac' into her search engine.

Immediately, Cora spotted that the Cluniacs did live according to the rules of St Benedictine, so she hadn't been that far wrong when she thought the Priory was run by Benedictines. Mother could be so pedantic. As she read on she picked up on the key characteristics that marked out the Cluniacs as different to other monastic orders. They had a reputation for wealth and splendour and rarely did any manual work. *Did that really mark them out as different to other orders?* thought Cora. Their roots were in Cluny in the Burgundy region of France and, unlike other religious orders who were subject to feudal patrons, the Cluniacs were beholden directly to the pope – talk about a gold pass. More austere orders thought the Cluniacs considered themselves as a cut above – a suspicion of opulence hung over their reputation. Cora was beginning to like what she was reading. These boys had come out of the cloisters and were the dandies of the monastic world. And that was before she got on to looking up Cluniac nuns. She giggled as she told herself; *Don't go there, Cora. It will only end up like Dan Brown.*

Cheered slightly by this diversion Cora returned downstairs to re-join her mother in the morning room. Jean, Alicia's daily help, was busily cleaning up the breakfast plates and chatting to Alicia.

'I was just telling your Mother about the news in town,' Jean said by way of greeting. Everybody liked a bit of gossip after all. 'They've only gone and got that Brandon Todd in to help save the brewery. He's been spotted there looking like butter wouldn't melt.'

Cora had heard of Brandon Todd, of course, but couldn't quite understand why the Brimdale brewery needed saving. Before she could say anything, Alicia cut in. 'Awful man. A parasite, peddling in other people's misery. Always something to be bought and sold. It's a sorry day when they have to turn to someone like him for help.'

Ignoring her mother's less than charitable appraisal of a person she'd never met, Cora was more interested in the fate of the brewery. 'I didn't know they were in trouble.'

'Ooh, they're in trouble all right,' replied Jean before proceeding to cast the brewery's future fate and all who sailed in her with the same upbeat optimism of the Ancient Mariner.

Cora was surprised at the scale of this local difficulty – she hadn't been aware of the brewery's struggle to protect its name but could see how it was bad news for the town if anyone could hijack the brand.

Alicia, though, entertained no such sentimentality.

'Would be a good thing if it closed down. Dirty, old, smelly building. Would stop those awful tourists clogging up the streets too. Good riddance, I say.'

'Mummy. That's a terrible thing to say. A lot of people in the town depend on the brewery. It would be awful if it had to close down.'

Jean, emboldened by Cora's response, added her voice to the debate. 'She's right, Mrs Songhurst, it would be a bad blow for us all if it went. There's not much work round here. And it's very good for you, too.'

'What utter mumbo-jumbo. A beer that's "good for you"? Tripe.' Alicia wasn't convinced.

Jean stood her ground. 'My sister-in-law drinks it every day for her eczema. Swears by it. Her skin was like a weeping, running sore until she found Brim worked and now it's like a baby's bottom. Maybe you should try it, Mrs Songhurst, for your breathing?'

More used to assessing claims based on evidence, Alicia countered. 'Along with the virgin's tears I already drink, you mean? I think not.'

Cora came to Jean's aid. 'Don't be mean, Mummy. Whatever you think about the health claims it does sound like the brewery is in trouble.'

'It's not our problem and I wouldn't have thought bringing in some *deus ex machina* in the form of Brandon Todd will suddenly produce a happy ending.'

Jean looked confused as to what Alicia meant by *deus ex machina*. Cora inwardly sighed at her mother's enduring belligerence. 'Mummy, we should be proud of the town and help support it.'

'What, like you do?' her mother sneered.

Nobody was ever going to get the last word over Alicia.

Come on, show time, Brian urged as he unfastened his seat belt and climbed down from the car. His meeting with the Brimdale Beer Association beckoned – the future started here. As he strolled over the road to the Fountain Head he noticed the holy cross etched into the windows of the pub. A sign perhaps of somebody up there liking him after all his trials and tribulations? Or a portent of further nails to be hammered into his reputation?

As Brian entered the inn the first person he bumped into was Peggy, sat chipping wax from the candleholders used to adorn the dining room tables.

'You should stick those in the freezer for a bit – wax'll will fall right off. Doesn't half save a bit of elbow grease,' offered Brian.

Peggy looked up to see the bearer of this advice and couldn't quite believe her eyes – the famous chef had arrived, exactly as Howard had foretold. Peggy thought it was a wind-up when she was first told Brian Parkin was visiting her establishment but had been busy all morning cleaning, just in case. She was used to welcoming all sorts to the pub but was genuinely excited this TV celebrity was going to be the latest addition to the Brim campaign. Not only that, this deal was going to be forged on her premises.

'My freezer's not big enough, Mr Parkin,' was the only thing she could think of to say.

'Call me Brian, please,' smiled the newcomer.

'Only if you call me Peggy,' giggled the landlady, her usual no-nonsense demeanour flying out the door.

'All right, Peggy. I'm a bit early, so where do you want me?'

'Howard's not here yet, so why don't you come through to the bar for now?'

Brian beamed. This was a bit more like it. What a pleasant welcome. His spirits had been so low recently he wouldn't have been surprised if a stoning mob had been on hand to mark his arrival. Brian knew it was ridiculous to be so apprehensive but he had to keep his guard up. This was his fresh start, after all.

As Peggy led Brian into the bar she felt a little giddy. How affable and lacking in ceremony her guest was. Just like he was when he was on the television. Peggy knew all about Brian's rise to fame and his recent well-publicised 'difficulties'. People could be so cruel. Well, she for one was glad to have him there in the Fountain Head. This was special.

'Now, what would you like to drink?' she asked.

Brian checked his watch – 11.30am. 'Seeing as how it's a special occasion, better make it a pint,' he said. 'Brim, of course.'

'You won't get anything else here,' tittered Peggy as the colour rose in her cheeks.

At that precise moment the first customer of the day, together with his dog, chose to grace the pub with his presence. Sir Godfrey was in need of refreshment. Not bothering with an introduction or greeting, the ex-cricketer bent his back into the opening ball. 'I know you. You here for t'chef's job?'

Brian was momentarily stunned at this loosener. Was this man alluding to his all too public fall from grace by inferring Brian was looking for a menial job in a pub kitchen, or was he just trying to be funny?

He squared his bat. 'I'm sure they don't need me in the kitchen here.'

'You've never eaten here, then. That's plain,' said Godfrey.

Peggy's bubble well and truly burst, she glared at Godfrey and made the usual apologies on his behalf before more formally introducing the two.

On hearing Godfrey's name, Brian was immediately catapulted back to his youth. There was no doubt about it – there could only be one Godfrey Dransfield in these parts.

'You won't believe this, but I actually saw you play,' gushed Brian.

'Plenty did,' said Godfrey, starting to warm to this cook he'd seen on the box. 'When and where?'

'Shaw Lane, Barnsley, 1975, Yorkshire versus Notts in the Benson and Hedges Cup.' Like many a Yorkshireman, Brian possessed an impressive recall when it came to less than vital sporting statistics.

'Barnsley, eh? It were rare for us to *laike* there. Mindst, bit of a stroll that day as I remember. Won by eight wickets.'

'Well, I'm tickled pink to meet you,' said Brian. 'Can I get you a drink?'

'Don't see why not,' consented the veteran bowler.

Recognising that peace had once more descended on her otherwise empty bar, Peggy excused herself in order to make sure all was ready for the day's trade. When she returned fifteen minutes later she found Brian and

Godfrey, now joined by Howard and Gary who were struggling to get a word in edgeways, getting on like a house o fire.

'Right, Godfrey. Stumps. Brian's got a meeting with Howard and Gary and they've important things to discuss.'

None of the four men demurred – they all quite liked being bossed around by a strong woman. And they didn't come much stronger than Peggy.

CHAPTER FIVE

It was years since Brandon had last drunk a pint of beer and he was feeling a little apprehensive as he prepared for his personal induction into the fine art of Brim brewing. A week and a half had passed since he'd first met Simon but if he was to be the mastermind of Brim's salvation he had to get to know more about the product at the heart of all the excitement.

Normally, when Brandon was on a factory walkabout, he'd pretend he was a member of the Royal Family – nodding his head in silent approval and running through his repertoire of facial expressions to denote surprise, understanding and approval. He could trot out, with ease, stock questions such as 'you must find this work very satisfying?' and 'how long have you worked here?' without ever learning anything. Today, however, he knew he had to be on his toes. One look at Tommy Whitelaw, the head brewer, confirmed that. Tommy had been brewing Brim for forty-five years and looked like he'd spent the other twenty years of his life playing Rugby League.

'Are you a beer drinking man yourself?' Tommy asked Brandon on being introduced.

Brandon instantly understood he was on trial and

wondered how long he could bluff without looking like a southern jessie, a wine drinker, a man who sent his shirts out to be ironed. 'Occasionally, but I rather suspect that will be changing over the coming months,' he replied.

Tommy's face conceded no clues as to what he thought of this most non-committal of answers. Brandon was unsure whether he had passed muster. He doubted it.

'Do you know the difference between conditioned and cask?' Tommy asked next.

'I think I understand the basics, but maybe it would be easier for you to run through it again – so I can be sure I've got it right?'

As the tour began, so it continued, with Brandon trying not to look a complete idiot as Tommy disgorged decades of knowledge and information. Despite his foreboding, the PR guru found himself fascinated. Over the course of two hours Brandon learned about grist, wort and finings while following the production process through mashing, sparging, filtering, fermentation and racking. Tommy was like Oppenheimer explaining nuclear fission one minute, like a sommelier extolling the virtues of a particular wine the next.

'Of course, with all of this going on, Brim would be a very acceptable little ale in anybody's book,' said Tommy. 'But what we have, our secret ingredient that nobody else has, is our water.'

'The water, yes. The Brim water. Fascinating, Tommy. Why is it so different?'

The head brewer looked Brandon directly in the eye to underline the singularity of the answer. 'It performs miracles. As simple as that. Has been doing for centuries.'

'Can you actually say it's been performing miracles, though? What sort of miracles?'

'If you're poorly, this will help you feel better. If you've a pain, this will relieve it. If you've got a skin complaint, this will stop it. It just does.'

Brandon was somewhat alarmed at Tommy's rather unscientific assessment of the attributes of the natural spring water forever turning up under Brimdale's feet. 'But you'd have to prove that beyond all doubt, wouldn't you? I mean, have you got it all forensically certified and backed up by case studies?'

'We know what we know. The people who drink our beer know what they know. It works, alright.'

Making a mental note to study the chemical composition reports, Brandon changed tack slightly. 'So how long has Brim been brewed here?'

'That all depends. The Backhouses set up this brewery in the 1850s but before that there were monks brewing beer with this water back in the Middle Ages. They were the pioneers. They knew it were different even back then.'

They'd moved on by now to the sampling room. Brandon was going to have his first taste of Brim. Tommy slowly and lovingly pulled two pints of the unusually golden hued ale and the guest couldn't help but notice the generous creamy head perched like a clergyman's collar on the top. 'Tell me what you can taste,' said Tommy as he passed Brandon his pint.

Brandon watched Tommy as he upended a quarter of a pint into his mouth in one go. Taste? What was he supposed to taste? He sniffed the beer and caught a faint aroma of woodiness. The glass felt cool in his hand but not cold. He raised the vessel to his lips and carefully tilted the gilded cargo into his mouth. As he savoured the velvety brew he could discern the subtle bitter flavours at work, not harsh but wonderfully smooth in composition. He looked across at Tommy, two curtains of cream hanging a quarter and half way down the brewer's glass, closely surveying him for his reaction. Brandon swallowed and a surge of intense gratification suffused his senses. Had a thirst ever been so perfectly quenched before? 'Wow, Tommy. That. Is. Superb. I'd never have thought it, but that's amazing. What a texture; what a taste.'

Although it was hard to tell with Tommy, he looked pleased at Brandon's response (that for once wasn't being faked). 'Well, you're not the first to say so. A real quaffing ale is Brim.'

'Quaffing?'

'Aye. Easy to sup. Brim's only 3.8% ABV – a real session ale. A man can have the best part of a gallon and still make it to work next morning without any sign of a hangover. Now that's another miracle.'

Brandon took a further swig of the precious draught. His glass appeared to be radiating but he knew that was just a trick of the light. The tour was like a blind date that had turned out to be a huge success – he and Brim were going to be very happy together. Brandon had always thought one beer was pretty much like another but now he knew how wide of the mark he'd been. Brim may contain similar ingredients to other beers – roasted malt, malted barley, wheat, hops – but it really stood out against other ales he had tried in the past. Maybe there was something in the water after all.

Still aglow from his first pint of Brim, Brandon's next port of call was to the brewery museum to meet up with Simon. To Brandon's surprise, the museum turned out to be a long, empty, bare brick room overlooking the brewery yard. Simon, who today sported a t-shirt proclaiming *Get Up, Stand Up, Stand Up for your Rights*, was poring over a number of posters spread out on an enormous table – the only furniture in the room.

'Welcome to the museum,' said Simon. On seeing Brandon's quizzical look he quickly added, 'Well, it will be the museum once the ruling goes through. I want to be able to move quickly – a museum will be a great addition to the brewery tours we're planning.'

Brandon admired Simon's confidence. 'I like clients who plan ahead.'

'I thought it would be useful to run you through some of the new panels we're planning and some of the old ads we've dug out of the archive – part of your Brim crash-course.'

'You should have done that before I had a pint,' Brandon laughed.

'How did you get on with Tommy?'

'He was very informative. I can't believe how much I liked Brim when I tried it. You'd expect me to say that but really, I loved it. I'll have to watch out – I may end up putting weight on before this job is over.'

'I wouldn't worry about that – "Brim will keep you Trim" as it says here on one of our old posters.'

'A beer for weightwatchers? Brilliant. Bet you couldn't run that nowadays.'

'No. But to be honest we've hardly run anything for

the past couple of years. We've been in marketing limbo while this ruling has dragged on.'

'It's not like you've been idle though, is it? You're ready to push on with lots of new products and marketing once Brussels makes its mind up. It will prove to be time well spent.'

'As long as we win.'

Brandon looked at the various panels and posters on the table. 'I see there's quite a bit of science as well as history here. That's good. Tommy's tour was impressive on the brewing and tasting front but it was a little light on what's been proven and what hasn't.'

'Tommy's from an era where they took things on trust. It's a bit different nowadays. I'd hate to think what George Backhouse, who founded the brewery, would have made of Defra. Would have driven him to drink if he hadn't been that way inclined already.'

Over the next hour and a half, with the aid of the panels and posters, Simon explained to Brandon the full history of Brimdale Brewery and the uncommon characteristics of Brim. Simon told Brandon how, in a typical act of Victorian-era benevolence and discovery, his forebears had undertaken extensive research into the origins of the town. There was evidence of a settlement where Brimdale stood from as early as the eleventh century. Little was known about the efficacious properties of the local spring water until the construction of Brimdale Priory in the reign of Edward III. It was the monks who first noticed that the water had a particularly invigorating effect on drinkers, both human and animal. Nobody knew why it had such an effect, but it was hailed as a blessing from

God. For the monks to establish a brew house wasn't that unusual – back then it was recognised that drinking beer was safer than drinking water and the monks themselves consumed most of the beer produced.

'Did you know that it was the Capuchin order that gave its name to cappuccino coffee because of the colour of their habits?' interjected Brandon, showing off his mastery of marketing minutiae. 'What sort of monks were at Brimdale?

'Benedictines, I think. We've still to do a bit more background digging on the Priory and the Middle Ages panels but it's interesting that the logo for Brim is still a cross. The monks marked their barrels with a cross to show they'd brewed it and to denote best quality. Old man George must have picked up on that in the 1850s when he launched the brewery.'

Brandon looked at the by now familiar Brim logo which adorned the brewery signage, pump clips and pint glasses. It featured a distinctive golden cruciform set within a vibrant vermilion shield device. Initially he'd taken the device as a patriotic affirmation of the beer's country of origin – now its inspiration became clearer.

'And people think marketing is a relatively new profession.'

'Hardly. No flies on them.'

'Or on your ancestors by the sounds of it.'

'Yes. They were operators, all right. After the dissolution of the monasteries by Henry VIII beer was forgotten about for a while until old George Backhouse established the brewery here making Brimdale Ale. Before long it was simply referred to as Brim'.

'The Victorians liked anything with a "miracle" in it – that must have helped.'

'It was George's son, Harold, who discovered the history of the spring and immediately saw that they could use that story to distinguish Brim from other beers. Harold came up with the "Brimming with health" line that we used for years.'

'And the rest is history, as they say,' said Brandon, thinking how the monks, George and Harold could give a few ad agencies a run for their money in the present day.

'Sort of. The family grew rich on the back of the brewery and their success helped speed the expansion of the town like it did with lots of other breweries across the country. That golden era lasted about a hundred years until small breweries began to be acquired by larger brewing groups or faced going out of business altogether. Despite that and all manner of red tape, food standards and regular inspections that have come in over the years, we've managed to continue as a family independent. There's not many of us left.'

Brandon's mind was already going into overdrive with ideas for the new Brim campaign. This was as good a challenge as he'd had for a long time. He fully understood Simon's predicament – it wasn't just the future that was at stake – it was the past, too.

Simon brought the conversation back to present-day issues. 'I need to bring you up to speed on something you'll have to factor into your campaign plans. It appears that the BBA boys have signed up a brand ambassador for Brim. He may not fit into your thinking.'

That evening Brandon was due to be meeting the BBA

for an update with Simon at the Fountain Head where he was booked in overnight. He sensed from Simon's tone that this news wouldn't wait until then. 'A brand ambassador? Go on then – let's have it.'

'Brian Parkin, the celebrity chef.'

'The Barnsley Chop? You've got to be joking, Simon. He's a busted flush. Don't you remember the bacon slicer incident?'

Simon avoided answering Brandon's question directly. 'I admit that I'm slightly surprised at their choice.'

'Surprised isn't the word. Apparently the last time he did a public appearance, turning on the Christmas lights in his own village, the crowd booed.'

'I think they were booing the quality of the decorations, not Brian himself.'

'And did you see that hatchet job on him in the Sunday Splash last month? Talk about finished – you wouldn't hire him to butter the bread in a soup kitchen these days. When you say signed up, exactly how signed up?'

'We can clarify all of that tonight when we meet the BBA. But you'll have the last word on this, Brandon. If you're going to give him the chop, so to speak, I won't stand in your way. I'm just asking you to handle this sympathetically with Howard and Gary.'

It wasn't the first time that Brandon had experienced clients trying to introduce their own creative solutions to campaigns but pairing Brim and Brian Parkin together was certainly one of the daftest ideas he'd ever come across. 'Don't worry, Simon. You can trust me to deal with the situation delicately.'

CHAPTER SIX

As Brandon entered the lounge of the Fountain Head that evening a pulsating rhythm 'n' blues beat greeted him from the live four-piece band getting to grips with a familiar sounding 12-bar blues. *There ain't nothing I can do, I got the holy water blues.* He looked around the room to see if Simon had arrived yet. No sign. As he walked across to the bar the guitarist in the band nodded casually in his direction. Brandon did a double take. As well as being a brewery owner and a forward planning marketer it appeared that Simon could also add lead guitarist and vocalist to his CV.

Brandon nodded back and went to place his order. He knew there was only one choice of drink available for him and wondered if Tommy's line earlier that morning, about Brim being a quaffing ale, would turn out to be true or yet another carefully crafted entreaty. Surely they'd drink wine with their meal?

Peggy the landlady had been fussing over him since he'd arrived and swooped over to serve him. 'I don't need to ask what you're going to have, do I, Mr Todd?' she said as she reached for the Brim pump.

'Right first time, Peggy,' he replied gallantly, before adding 'and do call me Brandon.'

'Oh, I will,' she exclaimed, pleased to have such a distinguished guest on first-name terms. She could hardly believe her luck – first Brian Parkin visiting the Fountain Head, and now, two days later, Mr PR himself.

'You've cheered her up a bit. Normally has a face like a bulldog chewing a wasp, that one.' Brandon turned to see where this less than complimentary observation emanated from to find himself looking at a grey-haired old gentleman sporting a blue blazer, white shirt and striped tie. 'Godfrey. Godfrey Dransfield,' the bar-propper informed Brandon before pointing at his feet. 'And this is Bouncer. You don't need to introduce yourself. We know who you are.'

'Pleased to meet you, Godfrey. It's a charming pub, isn't it?'

'Charming? Not the word I'd use, but it does its job. So, what do you reckon? Can you bring it off?' Brandon, unsure as to what he was supposed to be bringing off, looked back inquiringly at his new acquaintance. 'The ruling,' clarified Godfrey. 'If you don't, this lot's buggered so there's plenty riding on you.'

'Ah, I see my mission isn't exactly classified,' Brandon smiled, taken aback at the directness of Godfrey's approach.

'As top-secret as Peggy's love life,' said Godfrey. Brandon didn't quite understand Godfrey's allusion but instinctively figured there mustn't be anything clandestine about Peggy's amours or lack of them. Before he could think of anything witty to say, or even anything at all, Godfrey ploughed on. 'Most reckon bringing you in now will knock our chances, not help them. All I can say is you'd better be half as good as you're cracked up to be.'

At that Peggy, who had been distracted by her bar maid telling her they'd run out of salt and vinegar crisps, launched herself back into the conversation with a resounding, 'That's quite enough, Godfrey.' Pointing at the snug on the other side of the bar she simply pointed and said, 'Off.'

As Godfrey and Bouncer retreated Brandon shrugged his shoulders. 'Well, it's good to know it means so much to the locals. That's important.'

'He's a bloody nuisance at times, he really is, but he does have a point. It is important to everybody here. Not that they're saying you can't help Mr… Brandon.'

'I'll be doing my utmost to win this, Peggy,' replied Brandon. Deep down in his guts the battle drums began to pound slightly louder. He knew he wasn't along just for the ride on this one.

The sudden cessation of amplified blues was followed seconds later by Simon's arrival at the bar. 'I see you met Sir Godfrey,' he said. 'That must have been nice for you.'

'I think he's running a book on whether I screw up or not,' replied Brandon. 'He's certainly a character. He's not a knight of the realm, though?'

'In his own head, he is. He used to play cricket for Yorkshire in the seventies, a fast bowler, and actually played for England once but only as a substitute. He acts like he's the greatest living Englishman alive – that's why he's nicknamed "Sir Godfrey".'

'Obviously bowled googlies as well,' said Brandon. He turned the attention back to Simon, 'Now I understand why you have the guitar in the office.'

'It will come in handy if I have to go out busking,' shot back Simon without any trace of cynicism in his voice. Once again Brandon's sense of responsibility eked up a notch.

At that moment their two fellow guests for the evening, Howard Amos and Gary Merriweather, ambled into the bar to join them. As greetings were made Brandon felt an icy front emanating from the scruffier of the two, introduced as the secretary of the BBA. The chairman on the other hand at least appeared business-like and proper as he said hello. *Mild and Bitter,* thought Brandon.

Simon asked everyone what they were having and Brandon was somewhat surprised to see Howard order a glass of orange juice. Having nearly a full pint still, Brandon passed on this round, only to detect a faint air of superiority from Gary who then rather detracted from his moment of hauteur by calling for 'a pint of Gary Glitter'. Simon elected to have a small dry white wine.

Eventually, having moved to a table in the dining room, selecting their food and ordering a second round (orange juice, small white wine, pint of bitter and a volume friendly glass of red for Brandon), they got down to the business of the BBA. Simon made most of the running, detailing the BBA's sterling work to date. Brandon had already checked up on their activities and knew that their efforts were the usual well-intentioned but woefully inadequate executions of amateurs. That, in itself, was to be expected and wasn't a problem now he was taking over. Still, no one had mentioned the elephant in the room – Brian Parkin.

Just as Brandon thought he should raise the subject,

Howard was off again. 'Oh, I almost forgot, Simon – I bumped into Martha today and she asked me about supplies for the weekend.'

Brandon was curious as to what new and novel promotional platform Howard could possibly be referring. 'Sounds interesting?'

'Perhaps I can explain the background to that,' Simon said quickly, before either Howard or Gary could elaborate. 'Martha Clamp is, well, she's a "friend" of ours who's very keen on promoting the health enhancing properties of salicin, and therefore Brim.'

'Really?' Brandon said. 'How does she do that?'

'Well, in a number of ways to be honest. Martha is very much into healthy lifestyles, homeopathy, that sort of thing,' Simon explained.

'Shizza white witch,' added Gary, helpfully. 'Quare as they come.'

Brim was using witchcraft to promote its wares? 'It all sounds very new age, Simon, I must say,' said the PR practitioner, who could hardly believe his ears.

'Yes, I should have mentioned it,' said a bashful Simon. 'She's not officially sanctioned by us, of course, but she's most active in extolling the virtues and health-imbuing qualities of Brim.'

'In a way that you can't?' said Brandon, helpfully.

'Yes, in a way that we can't,' Simon agreed. 'Martha holds meetings where, among other remedies, she helps people with their ailments using…'

'Witchcraft…' Again, Gary was being helpful.

Brandon was intrigued. 'What exactly does she do at these meetings?'

Gary got in before Simon this time. 'She 'as these 'ealing sessions, 'er and 'er coven, and people turf up wi' all sorts of ailments, and she cures 'em. They bring their pets too, and she fixes whatever's wrong with 'em, an'all.'

'By drinking Brim?' asked Brandon, somewhat bemused.

'Sum drink it. Wi t'dogs and t'cats she normally just rubs it in if they've got mange. She cured my Rosie.'

'She cured your wife?' Brandon said.

'No. Rosie's mi dog. But she cured 'er,' Gary clarified.

'Right. I see,' Brandon said, wondering what he was letting himself for.

Simon was keen to move the agenda on. 'And that brings us pretty much up to date,' he said. 'Well, no, that's not quite right, because I'm forgetting that Howard and Gary have recently been in talks with Brian Parkin, the celebrity chef.' As baton changes went it wasn't the smoothest, but Simon now sat back and picked up his wine glass to signal that his contribution to the meeting was concluded.

'Tell, me, Howard,' said Brandon. 'What's the main rationale behind engaging Mr Parkin? Is he, in fact, engaged?'

'Oh, he signed up in a flash. He's delighted to help, and that's one of the major reasons we've gone for him. He's very keen,' replied Howard.

'But how were – are – you planning to use him?'

'As an ambassador. People will listen to what he's got to say. He's a big hitter. We can use him at the annual Brim Beer Festival and suchlike.'

'E's a big 'itter,' echoed Gary.

'I think it's fair to say though, his popularity is not what it once was?' ventured Brandon.

'Well, I don't go along with that. My lady wife thinks he's the bee's knees,' countered Mrs Amos' other half.

'A Bobby Dazzler,' added Gary. 'E's well liked up 'ere, any road.'

'In fact, he's coming up here again in a couple of days for a proper look round,' volunteered Howard. 'He's staying here. You could meet him then.'

Brandon ignored Howard's last comment. 'It's just that, with a new plan in preparation, we have to make sure he fits in, that's all. We have to be consistent and on-message.'

'Yer wunt get more on t'message than t'Chop,' said Gary, who didn't take too kindly to the BBA's initiative being questioned in this way.

'Would it be possible to let me have sight of Mr Parkin's contract so we can at least be sure of our commitment to him?' Brandon asked.

Quickly skimming the two sheets of A4 passed to him by Howard, Brandon established that Parkin had signed up for virtually next to nothing, plus travel and accommodation costs – a sure sign of desperation for the once venerated kitchen champion. Realising that getting rid of Parkin wasn't, after all, going to be a problem, Brandon handed the contract back. 'I'll see where he might fit in with the new plan I'm drawing up, but that's ever so useful, thanks.' Brian Parkin didn't yet know it, but his train wasn't going to stop at the last station before the terminus any more.

Each of the four men around the table knew that

the business part of the evening was at an end. All they had to do now was endure a main course each from the Fountain Head's somewhat limited menu and they could then return to their various pursuits. Simon, in particular, had to get back on stage. Brandon, invited to stay around for the more up-tempo second set, pleaded the need to retire early and absorb all the thoughts of the day. As he lay on his bed fifteen minutes later all he could hear was the thump, thump, thump of the bass, accompanied by a noisome, bloated sensation in his stomach. This time it wasn't the mounting heat of battle calling to him but the combination of beer, red wine and Peggy's bangers and mash. He couldn't remember when he had last eaten quite so badly. Still, it had been an interesting day of information gathering. He knew Sir Godfrey was right on one thing – Brandon was going to have to be on top form to gain a positive result here.

Back in the bar, away from the band, Howard and Gary were debriefing over a further drink.

'A right pillock if yer ask me,' said Gary. Howard didn't need to ask to whom he was referring.

'He listened well enough, but didn't really say much.' Howard was being diplomatic, as he still hadn't worked out if the BBA would continue to have a role under Brandon's regime. He had been planning to ask Brandon this question outright but had ducked it, deducing Brandon would do the same.

"E dint seem over keen on Martha, did 'e?' Gary said.

Howard wasn't sure. 'It was hard to tell. Simon could have backed her up a bit more.'

"E 'ad plenty to say about t'Chop, though.'

'Yes, he did,' agreed Howard. 'Still, I think we've set him on the right path on how to use Brian.'

'Wot wi gonna say t'Brian when 'e comes back?'

'No need to tell him anything different to what we've already told him, Gary. The show's about to start and he's got a starring role.'

On stage, Simon was thinking E, A and B7.

CHAPTER SEVEN

Less than twelve hours after coming off stage Simon Backhouse found himself in a solicitor's office in Leeds hearing a song of an altogether different tune. Opposite him, over the coffee and croissants, Dave Rawson had just offered to buy Brimdale Brewery. Simon had entertained doubts as to whether he should attend this meeting but had agreed to the invitation, which had emanated via his solicitors, on the assumption it was an attempt at mediation in the two breweries' ongoing legal wrangle. Rawson had soon put him right on that by announcing, before the coffee was even poured, that he wanted to make Simon an offer to buy the brewery. In this case, lock, stock and barrel was an accurate description.

'You think I'd sell the brewery to you?' Simon, who had actually dressed quite smartly in a crumpled blue linen suit and white cotton shirt for the meeting, stood up ready to leave. He was not being ambushed in this way. Rawson's solicitor tried to soothe the situation by asking Simon to at least hear his client out – he could surely do that, couldn't he? Simon's adviser nodded to Simon that he may as well listen now he was here.

'I'll get straight to the point,' said the Colton's MD,

who rarely did anything else. 'Brim's been on hold for years what with this legal case and the EU ruling. If the EU comes down on your side, you win the legal battle and you carry on. But even if you win it'll be a hollow victory because you're in no position to capitalise because you're brassick. On the other hand, if you lose the EU ruling, nothing will save you. And when you lose, you'll have to sell the brewery for it to continue. Or close it down completely.'

'You seem to have a pretty bleak view of our prospects,' countered Simon, who wondered how Rawson had managed to work out their position quite so accurately. 'I don't see it that way at all.'

'No?' Rawson pushed an envelope across the table to Simon. 'You're betting on zero at the roulette table. In this envelope there's a very generous written offer for the brewery. It will make you very rich, and save the Brim name.'

'I'm not interested in your offer. We have no intention of selling and, even if we did, Colton's would be the last company we'd consider.'

'Think about it. Almost two hundred years of history down the pan on your watch. Closure of the factory. Job losses. Decimation of the town. Could you live with that? You've done well to stay independent all these years but you've got to recognise when time's up.'

'I think we've heard enough,' said Simon, who wasn't going to stay to listen to more of this. As he exited the room Simon's solicitor scooped the letter from the table where it lay untouched.

As Rawson bade an ironic farewell to the backs of the

two disappearing figures he summed up the meeting to his legal adviser. 'Good. I think we have their attention.'

In the lift, Simon was less than pleased to have been hijacked in such a way. 'A pre-emptive bid? As if. George Backhouse would turn in his grave if we sold to this lot.'

The solicitor, desperate to know what the offer was, asked Simon if he could open the envelope. On Simon's say-so he unfolded the letter, took in the figure and whistled lowly before handing it to Simon.

Sensing another massive payday if his firm was to represent Brimdale Brewery in a sale, the solicitor offered cautionary advice. 'I always think you should never be too hasty in these things, Simon. Never say never and all that.'

Richard Tasker declined the offer of an alcoholic drink from the trolley and opted for an apple juice. He was flying back to Leeds/Bradford Airport from Brussels where he'd been presenting to the EU bigwigs on behalf of Brim. He was brassed off. After years of compiling reports and arguments supporting Brim's case the panel had once more changed personnel, a regular EU occurrence, and he was virtually back to square one in terms of outlining the justification for a positive ruling. The delegates got his goat, asking questions on issues that had been settled long ago and wanting re-assessments and updated reports on this, that and the other. And they would insist on bringing up Brexit as a factor that had to be taken into account, just to let Richard know who was in control. OK, it was a long haul and he shouldn't weaken near the finishing line but he cursed these career politicians who were intent on chucking their weight around. Especially the French and the Italians who seemed to think their views counted more than anybody else's.

Still, he would have to comply. He knew that. This was his absolute priority. The biggest issue he faced was the demand, from the French representative, for an updated forensic report. He wanted 'absolute reassurance' on the water composition used in Brim and the aquifer it came from in order to confirm its unique attributes and origin. Richard had argued that there was already substantial documentation on this matter, but to no avail. 'It is the central factor in the application and must be verified regularly,' he was told. As he left the meeting he tried to tell himself it had been generally positive in tone – if all they could come up with were double-checks at this stage, then maybe Brim was going to win the coveted status it so desired.

One thing was for sure, though – it was going to mean a load of extra hard work for him. Richard's wife, Debbie, complained that he took work far too seriously and let it interfere with his home life too much – now he'd have to step it up even more over the next couple of months. He would make it up to her and his young son, Ben, when this was finished – the thing was not to weaken now at this critical stage.

He would get on to Simon Backhouse in the morning with an update and the final list of EU demands. Now he intended to have some 'me-time' as the flight headed over the English Channel. Goodness knows he'd earned it. He pulled from his briefcase the latest copy of *Cycling Weekly*. Cycling was his absolute passion in life and he was already looking forward to the weekend and a sixty-five-mile sportive through Swaledale and Wensleydale with his Richmond cycling club. The wheels never stopped turning in Richard Tasker's world. Only when he was whizzing down the narrow country lanes did he feel free of the weight of work and home responsibilities, where he could truly be himself, a charger on a white steed riding to the rescue. Quite what he was rescuing he hadn't quite worked out yet but that was to be no hindrance for now.

'The ball's rolling, Mervyn.' Dave Rawson was briefing his boss on the bid for Brimdale Brewery in a transatlantic phone call.

Mervyn, slightly grumpy at having his breakfast disturbed by his over-keen British factotum, wanted to know how far the ball had rolled. 'And?'

Mervyn had reluctantly signed off the initial bid despite his misgivings that they were opening with their top dollar price. Mervyn felt they had no place to go if their bid was turned down – he always liked to build in plenty of wriggle room in his dealings. Plus, in Mervyn's view, this was a bit of a long shot – he reckoned Brimdale wouldn't bite.

'I suspect that they're giving it some serious consideration right about now. It's not the sort of offer you can dismiss without a lot of thought.' Rawson knew he'd gone for a first round knockout with his offer and wanted Mervyn to understand that his opponent was reeling under the unanticipated onslaught.

Mervyn didn't sound overly taken in by this appraisal. 'What did Backhouse say when you made the bid?'

'To be honest, he didn't say a lot, but I took that as a positive sign.'

'But not as positive as him saying he could be interested? So what happens next?'

'I think we leave Backhouse to stew for a week or so. Let him justify to himself how he could turn down the offer of a lifetime. We sit tight for now, Mervyn, that's my suggestion.'

'Well, in the absence of any other option, I agree with you.' Mervyn was bored now – he had other things to do. 'Keep me updated. Got to go – late for a meeting.' Mervyn set down his phone and returned to his coffee and the Wall Street Journal. Sometimes you had to give people their head, if only to demonstrate that they should have listened to you in the first place.

As Rawson rang off he knew Mervyn was less than impressed – could this bid be another Brimmer-like discredit on his record? He paced to and fro in front of his office window, watching two Canada geese gliding serenely on the canal basin. Rawson knew, like himself, they were paddling like hell underneath. He'd not expected Backhouse to bite his hand off when he presented the offer but he'd been taken aback when the Brimdale brewery boss had left the meeting room in such an abrupt manner. *Very unprofessional,* he thought, but maybe Backhouse was posturing, playing games, to get a better deal? It was possible.

Mervyn also disagreed with him over his grandstanding bid strategy. Normally he would have been of the same mind as his boss, starting out low and aiming to meet in the middle, but his gut feel told him Backhouse would have no appetite for haggling and would respond best to a 'no-brainer' deal. Had he miscalculated that too? Surely, Backhouse must have had enough by now as the last independent family brewer of note still standing? All very noble to hold on, but so very stupid too.

What was really worrying the Colton's chief though was the rumour he'd heard, since substantiated, that Brimdale had brought in Brandon Todd to spearhead its PR campaign. He'd not mentioned that to Mervyn. It was certainly a surprise move, particularly after all of Brim's ham-fisted PR efforts of the past. Rawson couldn't work out what their game was – hearts and minds were all very well, but surely they should be focusing on lobbying the EU and that wasn't Todd's forte at all. It was almost as if Backhouse was planning ahead to capitalise on a favourable outcome. Whatever the intention, it was perplexing from Colton's point of view. He felt considerably happier when Brimdale was bouncing along the bottom looking, for the entire world, like the game was up even if it won the EU ruling. Now they were giving the belated impression that they were getting their act together Rawson couldn't help but feel his hostile bid for the brewery was in danger of not getting past square one. He was going to need to come up with some further persuasion.

CHAPTER EIGHT

Brian Parkin placed his knife and fork in the middle of his plate and looked around. The restaurant room in the Fountain Head wasn't exactly busy. Peggy hoved into view with the inevitable question: 'Everything all right?' One look at Brian's plate, with half of his beer-battered cod still uneaten, should probably have precluded the stock enquiry.

'I'm just not hungry, Peggy, that's all,' Brian said in a gallant attempt to not pass judgement.

'It's so difficult to cook for a chef.'

'I know. But this is my day off, so don't worry,' Brian said graciously.

'How did you get on with Howard and Gary?' asked Peggy, trying to change the subject.

'I was going to ask you about that, actually. Have you got a minute? Would you mind?' Peggy sat down opposite Brian to indicate she wouldn't mind at all as he prepared to share with her the upshot of the meeting he'd had earlier with the BBA.

'Well, they tried to sound upbeat but they were a little unsure as to exactly what they wanted me to do. There's a beer festival in September and they spoke about me doing some personal appearances, but that was about it.'

'I suppose they're waiting to see what Brandon Todd has in mind,' replied Peggy, not totally surprised to hear of Howard and Gary's lack of precision.

'Brandon Todd? What's he got to do with it?'

'They didn't mention it? He's just been appointed by the brewery to get the appeal through. They've decided it's all or nothing at this stage. I thought you were part of that plan?'

Brian, a man used to hanging on the ropes, took another jab to the ribs at the realisation that he may not have a job after all. Why hadn't Howard and Gary mentioned this to him? No wonder they couldn't outline his role when they'd met up again that afternoon. His face turned the colour of one of his meringue kisses. Why had he agreed to take this job? Was his salvation merely a mirage, another cruel twist of the knife? He looked so crestfallen Peggy's heart went out to him as she read the desolation on his face.

Struggling to soften the situation, all Peggy could muster was, 'Would you like to see the dessert menu?'

'I think I'll pass if that's OK, Peggy. Got to watch the waistline,' he added as if by rote.

'No you don't, Brian. You're in very good shape for a man of your age.'

Their eyes met. Nothing was said as each read the other's thoughts. Brian was once more cast into the pit of despond, and he knew that Peggy could see that too. Peggy just wanted to enfold Brian in her arms and tell him everything would be all right.

Finally, Brian broke first. 'Would you care to have a nightcap with me before you go to bed? I must say, you've been very kind to me.'

Peggy nodded her assent and cleared the table without saying another word.

Knowing Brian was staying at the Fountain Head that evening, Howard and Gary had taken the precaution of avoiding it and were ensconced in Howard's photographic studio. Howard knew they'd not handled the meeting with Brian at all well and was at a loss as to what to do next.

'We should have told him, Gary, we should. You could tell he was a bit confused.'

'What wer wi s'posed t'a told 'im? Wi did us best,' said Gary, as usual not quite able to see what the problem was.

'Brian Parkin expected a full breakdown of what we wanted him to do and we couldn't give it to him. We should have told him about Brandon Todd.'

'Wi dint bring Brandon-bloody-Todd in, did wi? 'E's not our responsibility.'

'But Brian Parkin is. We brought him in and we should have told him that our hand has been somewhat stayed since we signed him up.'

'That's up to Brandon Todd n' Backhouse. Serve 'em reet fer going over us 'eads. They can sort it now.'

'They may not want him. How terrible would that be?'

'Gettin' paid for doing nowt? Dunt sound terrible to me.'

Howard shook his head as he stared at the promotional panel behind the counter offering a free family portrait worth over £75. It was about time he updated that. Eventually he spoke, 'It would reflect badly on the BBA is what I mean; on us.'

'I dunt see 'ow.'

Howard, beginning to tire of Gary's inability to grasp much at all, pondered how he'd ended up running an organisation with just two active members. No wonder Simon Backhouse had decided to bring in a heavyweight. He and Gary were about as useful as a chocolate teapot when it came to saving Brim. Yes, they'd tried – well, at least he'd tried – but the sad truth is that they were out of their depth. The Parkin episode only went to underline that. They'd not even had the courage to tell Brian the truth today – they were still pretending to know what they were doing, acting like they were still in charge.

Howard knew the game was up. They were bloody amateurs. 'We're going to tell Brian tomorrow and we're going to put ourselves at the disposal of Simon Backhouse and Brandon Todd from this moment on. Time to march to a different beat, Gary. We've taken it as far as we can ourselves.'

As ever, Gary looked unsure but being unable to come up with a better plan simply shrugged in acquiescence to the greater need. Unity is strength.

The bar towels had been thrown over the beer pumps in the Fountain Head and the last of the staff departed for home as Peggy poured Brian a stiff whisky. A rare drinker herself, Peggy opted for a weak gin and tonic. Since their conversation earlier in the evening Peggy had been keeping a watchful eye on Brian. Once he'd gone back into the bar after dinner he'd been hail-fellow-well-met with the regulars, appearing to be well at ease. But Peggy knew that anguish had gained entry to the mansion of his mind to establish squatters' rights there. She guessed that this Brim contract was more than just another job; it was his only job.

'Are you all right, Brian?' she asked as she handed him his glass. 'You seemed a bit taken aback when I mentioned Brandon Todd earlier.'

Brian sat back in his chair and took a sip of his drink. 'You can see right through me, can't you? Is it that obvious?'

'You looked upset. I could tell that. I know you've had a tough time recently. It must have been hard for you.'

'Peggy. You don't know the half of it.' And with that he crumbled, his chin crushing into his chest, great blobs of salt tears dropping from his cheeks to mingle with his otherwise pristine fifteen-year-old single malt.

Peggy pulled the grieving gourmet towards her and tenderly massaged the back of his head. 'There, there, let it all out, you poor lamb. Let it all out.' And Brian did, in torrents, as if trying to weep the misery of the last three years out of his very bones. Peggy held on as wave after wave of brackish regret swept over him, a new swell rising every time it seemed he was slowing to a stop. For over five minutes she rocked him gently, waiting for the squall to subside.

Eventually, Brian gathered himself once more. 'I'm sorry. So sorry. I just couldn't help myself.'

'You've nothing to be sorry for, Brian. Especially to me. We've all had crosses to bear at some time. This is yours, and it will pass.'

'Will it, though? I think I've had it.'

'Don't be silly. Now don't talk like that.'

'Things have gone so wrong for me recently; I can't begin to tell you.'

'You take your time, Brian. I'm going nowhere.'

Brian took another sip of his whisky and sniffed. Over the next hour he told Peggy about the outrageous fortunes that had been visited upon him following his years in the sun as one of Britain's best loved TV chefs. He spoke for the first time, to anyone, of the false accusation against him, his unfaithful wife, his duplicitous agent and the car crash of his divorce. Even worse was the cruelty of the media who, having once courted him, were now so eager to trash and humiliate him.

Peggy sat quietly, taking in the tale of woe without speaking, holding and squeezing his hand to let him know he wasn't alone. Brian, for his part, didn't even question sharing these most intimate of emotions with a woman he had just met. He didn't know why – it felt natural. It felt right. It felt like a blessed relief.

When, at last, he seemed to have finished, Peggy poured him another whisky and attempted to reassure him that the worse was over. Of all the indignities visited upon the no longer galloping gourmet the one she could understand least of all was the treatment Brian had received at the hands of his ex-wife. She'd worked behind a bar long enough to know that when faced with exclamations of hurt and protestations of innocence from a slighted male there was normally something he wasn't telling. 'You poor thing. How could she have done all of that to you?'

'I've asked myself a thousand times, Peggy. Believe me, I never strayed and I never treated her badly. I wish I had in some ways and then I could have understood it more. I think she just thought I wasn't good enough for her.'

Peggy's heart cracked as she heard Brian's elementary

evaluation of his marriage. She had no doubt he was telling the truth – he'd been nothing more than a cash dispenser to a shrew of a woman who switched banks the moment her credit card was declined. 'She wasn't good enough for you, more like.' Peggy knew she had to rally him. 'You're better off out of it all, Brian, really you are. No one can do anything to you now.'

Dolefully, Brian placed his glass on the table and reached for his wallet. He extracted a grubby and frayed concertina of newsprint, which he handed to Peggy. As she read the ink – laced vitriol in her hand it was her turn to feel tears welling – was there no end to Brian's torments? She was shocked that such savagery could be so casually dressed up as journalism.

'The swine,' she exclaimed. 'Why would they write such vicious things about you? Or about anyone for that matter?'

'Because that's what they think their readers want. I'd met this guy too, a food critic called Gerard Lomax, and he was as nice as you like face-to-face. It's when people like him get back to the office they can't help themselves. They're just cowards.'

'You shouldn't carry it around with you, Brian. Throw it away. It's vile.'

'No. It gives me strength. It didn't when it came out, but it does now, and I need to keep strong.'

'You are strong, Brian. You'll get past this, you'll see.'

'Peggy, the reason I keep that piece of hate is to remind me I do have the will to survive. Only a few weeks ago that piece of paper nearly saw me off. I was so desperate, well, I couldn't see any future. At all.'

'You don't mean …?' said Peggy, shocked at Brian's intimation.

Brian stared at his feet. 'Yes. I contemplated doing the worse thing in the world to myself. In fact, I more than contemplated it – I was actually on the verge of doing it.'

'Thank God you saw sense,' Peggy said, now unable to resist her own tears.

'I didn't, really. It was a miracle. There was a knock on the door that forced me to stop.'

'Brian, you should never go down that road again.'

'The incredible thing is, it was my former agent's secretary who'd called. They'd had an enquiry from someone who didn't know they'd dropped me and she brought it round to me as an act of kindness. Peggy, it was the Brim job that stopped me killing myself. I thought it was a divine intervention, a sign that I'd hit the bottom and could start to come back up again.'

'And now you think they don't want you. Oh Brian, you poor thing.'

'I know they don't want me. I've been around enough to know Howard and Gary are a couple of balloons and there's no way Brandon Todd is going to touch me with a bargepole.'

'His loss if he doesn't but even if that happens, then so what? You're a talented man, you're a lovely man, and you deserve some happiness in your life. Forget about what you were before and think about what you're going to be next. You're on the way back up whether you do this Brim job or not.'

Brian stopped gazing at his feet to look Peggy in the eye. The difference between her and his ex-wife couldn't have been more pronounced. There was goodness in the world. 'I've been too self-absorbed about what's gone wrong in my life. You're right, Peggy – I need to pack it all away and look forward.' Brian felt a glow of warmth kindle in his very core and knew it was more than the whisky. 'Talking to you like this makes me feel so much better, Peggy. You a trained counsellor or something?'

'Just somebody who has had to move on in life as well.'

'Really? You seem so… so together. What happened to you?'

'That's for another occasion, Brian, really. Enough heartache for one night, I think. Listen, why don't you stay here at the Fountain for a few days while you wait to see what's happening on Brim? You'd be very welcome.'

Brian leapt at the idea. 'Do you know, I'd love that. I couldn't think of anywhere else I'd rather be – not that there is anywhere else I have to be. But I have one condition. You have to let me cook dinner for you tomorrow night to say thanks.'

'I'm not going to say no to that,' Peggy said. 'It's been a long time since somebody served up a decent meal under this roof, I can tell you.'

As Brian climbed the stairs to his room moments later he reflected that whatever happened now over the brewery contract, Brim might just have saved his life after all.

CHAPTER NINE

Simon Backhouse sat in his office strumming his acoustic guitar. *You Don't Miss Your Water 'Til The Well Runs Dry.* He was in contemplative mood following his recent meeting with Dave Rawson. The offer Colton's had made to buy Brimdale brewery was lying on his desk, threatening to burn a hole through the green leather, the wood and even the oak floorboards beneath.

How many offers had his family turned down for the brewery over the years? Dozens, probably. Simon knew, as the latest in a line of Backhouses in charge of the business, he had to uphold tradition but it was becoming increasingly difficult to do so. The world of brewing had changed so much in the last fifty years Brimdale was almost an anachronism in today's markets. Would one of his two young daughters ever take over in the family trade? It was doubtful. He and his wife, Regina, wouldn't want that to happen anyway.

Simon thought about his father, Matthew, who'd tutored him in his responsibilities to the family firm from an early age. It seemed a long time ago, and a huge responsibility to bestow on young shoulders. As the only boy in the Backhouse family his early life had been geared towards his future stewardship of the brewery. When he wasn't at boarding school in Shropshire, part of being 'toughened up' according to his father, he was set to work in various of the production stages at the brewery and would often accompany Matthew on visits to Brim's tied houses. Even his degree, a BSc in management at LSE, was selected to further prosper the business. Simon was born with a silver tankard in his hand whether he liked it or not.

As soon as he graduated Simon set about his real education, learning the ropes of the brewery business under his father. There was much to take in, from sales to relationships with tenants, from production to marketing, from accounts to dealing with the banks. Simon threw himself into his work and soon began to carve out a name for himself as an innovative and ambitious member of the board. He was the first to introduce a widget to their canned beer and the first to negotiate distribution deals with large supermarket chains. He also wanted to better understand the essential nature of Brim's magical qualities, which led him to a new apprenticeship of sorts under Tommy Whitelaw.

Brimdale brewery continued to hold its own as a successful independent brewer until Colton's of Leeds launched Brimmer – an outrageous and thinly disguised rip-off. It soon became apparent that Colton's, armed with the clown-sized pockets of its US parent company, was determined to argue for as long as it took. The family felt the strain, and in no small part the Leeds rival's manoeuvres may have contributed to the premature death of Simon's father who, shortly after the launch of

Brimmer, succumbed to a heart attack at the age of 57, leaving his son to step up to the plate.

Simon was not found wanting. Rather than shrinking from the challenge he threw himself wholeheartedly into his new responsibilities, continuing the legal fight against Brimmer and enlisting Defra's support. It was Defra who decided that the answer lay in applying to the EU to protect the brand forever. Simon had thought long and hard about that. Could they succeed? How long would it take? Could they endure such a battle? Now, after eight long years, they were nearing the end. But the end of what? The battle for geographical status, or the end of the road for Brim?

As Simon kept strumming he realised he was playing *Born Under a Bad Sign* – even he had to smile as he realised that was far from the truth. Still, he had his work cut out. Colton's offer had certainly shaken him. Could he ever sell the brewery? Surely, if he ever did decide to sell, Colton's would be the last suitor he'd consider. His thoughts returned to the campaign. He couldn't help but wonder why he'd persevered for so long with the hapless Howard and the gormless Gary at the BBA. They were hardly going to save the brewery. Had he left it too late to bring in Brandon Todd? What would Todd come up with anyway? Did any of it even matter? Getting a groundswell of public support was important but what if the application failed on technical grounds or simply because of EU prejudice and payback following the Brexit vote? Had he ever felt lower than the morning he'd woken up to the news of the referendum result?

No, he had to think of what he'd lined up for Brim,

where he'd been putting all his energies behind the scenes during the application process. A massive sales expansion in the UK and overseas for Brim and, even more excitingly, entry into the health and wellbeing markets at home and abroad with Brim mineral water and skin products.

He realised he'd kept quiet with Brandon over Martha Clamp – he knew all the white witch stuff sounded ridiculous and no doubt the PR *Meister* was going to send her the same way as Brian Parkin. But wacky as Martha was – and she was – it was she who'd opened his eyes to the wider possibilities of the Brimdale spring water.

Ever since he'd been a lad he'd been aware of the claimed restorative powers of Brim and understood that there *was* something in the water. He'd seen for himself the effect it could have on skin conditions and took it on trust that it worked. It was only when Martha Clamp approached him, to ask if he could provide her with spring water for her preparations, he began to take a closer look at salicin, *Salix Alba,* inspired by Martha's knowledge and endorsement. She it was who'd told him how the ancient Greeks, dating back to Hippocrates in 400BC, had used willow bark in their medicine for the treatment of pain, headaches and other ailments. She it was who introduced him to the knowledge that salicin was a natural and powerful anti-inflammatory with the power to relieve.

It hadn't taken Simon long to work out that he could launch a salicin based natural mineral water, face creams and natural pain relief tonics, all with some degree of authentication and exclusivity, and it was this dream that had sustained him over the years. If – when – they got a favourable EU ruling, the coast was clear to move on and develop these products for market. Brim beer sales could potentially be dwarfed by those for Brim bottled water and wellbeing treatments if they got it right. He was bursting with anticipation, which only made the long drawn-out bid all the more tortuous.

All this, plus the museum, the visitor centre and his plans for a Brim health spa ready and waiting to go live – and all depending on bloody Brussels.

Not long to go now. He switched to a more up-tempo, twelve-bar blues - *Shake Your Money Maker*. Yes, that was more like it.

Brian Parkin felt good. As he strode in the sunshine of the open air Brimdale market it seemed as if another enormous weight had been lifted from his shoulders. He'd had it all, then nothing. Then a reprieve that turned out to be a dud. But yesterday, with Peggy....

Brian's shopping bag was beginning to bulge with provender from the delicatessen, fish and meat stalls. He still had to get vegetables, decide what to prepare for dessert, and had to remember to call in at the off-licence for a good – no, their best – bottle of wine. He was busy; he was happy – cooking a special meal for Peggy tonight had given him renewed purpose. The shadows of the past few months had receded with Peggy's help. Could he now keep that gloom at bay?

Brian paused in front of the greengrocer's stall as his eye caught the mushrooms, heaped into a pyramid, dull and earthy in their ordinariness, vying for his attention. The last special meal he'd prepared, that had been so serendipitously interrupted, flashed into his mind. What had he been thinking of? He was going to commit suicide and the only person he'd have been cheating was himself. He urged himself not to get too carried away with Peggy's kindness but he couldn't help but feel a very special connection to her. Here he was, flushed with the prospect of a first date, like he was seventeen again. Doing his own version of a love-struck teenager's mixtape by offering to cook for her. *Barnsley Chop or smoothie-chops?* he chuckled to himself as he outlined his requirements to the stallholder. Tonight, for Peggy, he was going to prepare the best meal he'd ever made. Would a bunch of flowers be over the top? Maybe not as a table arrangement. Whatever happened in the future he knew he'd always have a soft spot for Brim – it certainly possessed restorative powers, in his case at least.

As Godfrey enjoyed his lunchtime tipple he noticed that Peggy was sporting a different demeanour today. She somehow looked younger and more animated than he'd seen her for some time, well, since she took over the pub 20 years before. 'Come on, Peggy, spill the beans. You just discovered chocolate isn't fattening?'

Peggy smiled. Today, not even Godfrey could annoy her. 'I think you'll find that I'm just being my normal, cheery self. What makes you think otherwise?'

'If I didn't know better, I'd say you were on a bit of a promise. You're not, are you?'

'I don't know what you mean, Godfrey. You're not getting jealous, are you?'

'As if.' Godfrey wasn't finished yet though. 'It's not that chef is it? You want to be careful there. Didn't you read about his "pancetta peccadillo" in the papers?'

'I don't concern myself with the gutter press, and nor should you, Godfrey.'

'So you are seeing him. Well, I never. I know you're keen on upping the food offer in here but that's a bit drastic, isn't it?'

'Well, if I am, and if I do, you'll be the last to know.'

Godfrey was a wily old goat in sussing out what was going on but she knew, deep down, he meant well. What was going on though? She was merely having a meal cooked for her by a new acquaintance. There was nothing wrong with that. It wasn't as if the banns had been read out at the local parish church. It was merely two people, who got on, sharing some time together. Did she really think that? No. To be truthful, she'd never felt like this about a man in her entire life. Being the single, female owner of a pub one would think Peggy wasn't short of marriage proposals, especially in Yorkshire, but romance had never really blossomed in her life. When she'd inherited the Fountain Head, following her parents' premature deaths, her life had been marked by a profound sense of loss that she found could only be offset through hard graft. While the pain of bereavement eased, the workload in the pub didn't and, before too long, Peggy was pigeonholed as a confirmed spinster, even if that had never been her intention. Now, for the first time, she felt unaccountably attracted to a man, this rough-hewn Epicurean who'd fetched up on her doorstep like a stray cat. Love, at last, was a possibility in her life. And why should she deny herself that opportunity?

Simon Backhouse was throwing a few darts in his office before setting off home when he received a call from

Richard Tasker. At the brewery the Defra official was nicknamed *Tisker Tasker* due to the unrelenting air of officiousness that accompanied his every move and utterance – Simon had met few people in his life who were quite so uptight and serious. Due to the EU application the two opposing personalities had nevertheless shared a considerable amount of time in each other's company over recent years. Even in jail, Simon joked, an inmate can ask for a move if a cellmate gets on his nerves. He had no such option.

Richard Tasker wasn't one for pleasantries. 'Brussels wants a new forensic reports on the aquifer and water,' he said. 'In my opinion they aren't necessary but the French delegate says it is so that's that.'

'What? Again?' Simon couldn't believe his ears. 'It will be the same as the last report and the time before that, except I'll have to shell out thousands of pounds to get it done.'

'Well, yes, you'll have to pick up the costs but this time they have insisted on a different company to conduct the analytical research. They've recommended the one that does the Evian and San Pellegrino accreditations. It will provide a "Triple A" endorsement in their view.'

'But they could take months to do a report. Surely they can see that?'

'It's down to you to organise it, so you'll have to check that they can do it within the established timeframe.'

'And if they can't?'

'I suppose we could apply to have someone else do it if the current deadline is being threatened. As long as the company is EU based and has an international reputation,

I think they'd go with that. The bottom line is; you need to get a new forensic report done.'

Simon groaned. 'Right. Leave it with me. Anything else?'

'Nothing really of note, which I take as good news. They have asked for more information on the level of local support for the application. Will you be able to add more detail on that in the economic impact study?'

'Yes. That won't be a problem at all,' said Simon. At least he'd anticipated that correctly, which is why Brandon Todd was now on board.

Tasker wound up the call in the same peremptory manner he'd commenced it. Realising Tasker had disappeared, Simon picked up the darts again and hurled them with violent force, embedding them deeply into the treble-free board. 'Jesus. Give me strength,' he said to no one in particular.

CHAPTER TEN

Brian hummed merrily as he familiarised himself with the small kitchen in the flat above the pub. Peggy had let him in an hour before so he could begin his preparations. They had already agreed on the 'house rules' for the evening – Brian was to be the king of the kitchen, and Peggy the queen of the dining room. They'd laughed and joked as they drew up their respective areas of responsibility.

As he cut, sliced and diced, Brian felt more nervous than he'd ever been for any of his primetime TV shows. He thought he'd done his last audition but realised how wrong he'd been. Checking his ingredients, Brian wondered if he'd bought enough butter and looked in the fridge to see if there was a supplementary supply to hand. Only margarine. Slipping off his kitchen apron – an old Christmas present to Peggy which featured a silhouette of James Bond and the legend 'Licence to Grill' – Brian went out into the hall and shouted to Peggy that he was popping to the downstairs kitchen for something he'd forgotten. Peggy, in her bedroom getting dressed for the evening, called back to let Brian know she'd be ready in five minutes.

Downstairs, as Brian exited the kitchen clutching a

half-pound of Yorkshire butter, he bumped into the pub's resident former county cricketer making his way to the gents. Godfrey, eying the back up grocery item in Brian's hand, couldn't resist. 'Last Tango in Brimdale, eh?'

'Godfrey, that's not very nice now, is it?'

'Too much dairy, bad for your health.'

'All things in moderation is what I think,' Brian said, a little tersely.

'Well, think on then. You don't want to be messing with Peggy if you're not serious.'

'I am serious. I mean, I'm not messing with her,' Brian protested. Why did he feel he had to reply to Godfrey's every comment?

'Last person who did got a forearm smash for his troubles.'

'Thanks, Godfrey, I'll bear that in mind.'

'Make sure you do,' advised Godfrey as he wandered off in the direction of his comfort break.

So much for a cosy tête-à-tête with Peggy – it seemed their evening was already big news. Brian hurried back upstairs – it had been a mistake to break cover. As he re-entered the flat Peggy came out of her bedroom. She looked stunning, radiant almost, in a classic, low-cut black dress that strained to contain her well-rounded form. She was wearing diamond earrings and the matching necklace that accompanied them drew his attention to her swelling breasts. The scarlet lipstick she'd chosen made his pulse quicken further.

'My, Peggy. You scrub up well.'

'I'll take that as a compliment, shall I?'

'Oh, yes. I meant it as a compliment, all right.'

'A pre-dinner drink, sir?' Peggy mock-curtseyed as she ushered him into the living room.

'I think chef could spare five minutes if Madam is insistent.' Thank goodness everything was set up in the kitchen.

As Peggy fussed over making him a Bloody Mary, Brian took in the room. It was uncluttered, tidy and tastefully, if sparsely, furnished. He noticed immediately the lack of photographs around the place except for a single portrait perched on top of the bookcase. The faded colour of the print dated it to the seventies he guessed. He went closer to inspect and saw an image, frozen in time, of a small girl and two adults standing outside the Fountain Head. Obviously, Peggy and her parents.

'Is that you?' he asked.

'I knew I should have moved that. Trust you to go straight to it.'

'It's lovely, Peggy. And outside the pub too. That must be your parents?'

'Yes. Dad was called Brian, too. Mam was Wendy.'

'You're very young in this picture. Do you have any others?' Brian couldn't help his inquisitiveness – he wanted to devour Peggy's background in huge chunks, to discover more about her, to find out what made her so special in his eyes.

'There's a box somewhere but to be honest I try not to dwell in the past.'

'Is that what you meant yesterday, when you said you'd had to move on in life too?'

'Something like that. Mam and Dad died in a car crash

when I was twenty-one. It took me a long time to adjust to them being gone.'

'I'm sorry. I didn't know. They can't have been much of an age when it happened,' Brian said.

'Forty-three and forty. Much too young – a complete waste.'

'What happened?'

'They were coming home from Halifax one night. It was snowing and they skidded into a lorry coming in the other direction at Causeway Foot. That was that. Snuffed out, gone, instantly.'

'You poor thing. And you took over the pub? You must have been fresh out of school?'

'Almost. But I knew I had to. And that's me. Been here since.'

Brian looked at his half-consumed aperitif and wondered if he should lighten the conversation in some way – talking about death wasn't normally the best badinage for a first date. As he gazed sympathetically in Peggy's direction his eye caught a second photograph, of a rather unusual nature, propped up on the table next to the settee. In this print he could see two leotard-clad women. One was laid flat out on the floor while the other stood above her, arms raised in triumph. As he looked further he could detect the ropes of a ring, what appeared to be a referee administering a count to the supine combatant, and rows of spectators disappearing out of focus in the background. An odd picture to have in a living room he thought, especially when there were so few others.

'I didn't know you were a wrestling fan, Peggy,' he said.

'I'm not.' Peggy replied. 'But that's the last photograph

of Mam, which is why I can't bring myself to get rid of it.'

Brian squinted yet again at the photograph. 'Really? Is that your mother? Which one?'

'The winner, thankfully. At least she went out on a winning note.'

Brian could have kicked himself for his stupid curiosity. 'Sorry – I'm asking you far too many questions.'

'It's all right. I never talk about my parents or the fact that Mam was a lady wrestler. But it was quite big back in its day and she was very successful at it. Dad managed her. What with that and the pub they did very well but you never know what's around the corner.'

Brian remembered wrestling had been very popular on TV when he'd been younger and had occasionally watched it with his father but he couldn't recall too many lady wrestlers. Now he knew what Godfrey had been alluding to when he'd said the last man to tangle with Peggy had received a forearm smash. That really wasn't funny at all.

'Did she have a stage name?' he asked.

'A ring name,' corrected Peggy. 'Yes. Don't laugh. She was called The Beast of Bishopsgate. That's the street out front. Now, are we having dinner or not? I'll tell you more about her some other time.'

Detecting Peggy's discomfiture talking about her mother, Brian looked at his watch. 'Sorry. I shouldn't probe. Right. Get yourself comfortable. A Parkin feast coming up.'

To further demonstrate how special this meal was going to be, Brian broke into the introductory theme of one of his old TV shows, *On Street Parkin*, where he'd explored the different foods sold by street vendors in various parts of the world.

Brian's taking to the streets
To find the well-loved treats
That make the world go round.

Peggy laughed. 'You silly goose. Get in that kitchen, now.'
Brian obeyed and soon a whirl of activity could be detected
from within the narrow confines of Peggy's galley as he
set about conjuring up his carefully planned repast. This
was more like it. He realised he'd not actually cooked a
proper meal for some months. Ironically, he'd been living
off ready-made meals, his love of food having temporarily
deserted him. Now he'd got his Mojo back and the scent
of service in his nostrils there was a gnawing appetite in
the pit of his stomach to be satisfied.

Meanwhile, Peggy was flicking through her meagre CD
collection to find an appropriate musical accompaniment
to their meal. She wasn't really a big music fan herself
but she'd noticed how Brian seemed to like humming
and breaking into song. Given how upset he'd been
the previous night, and the shocking revelations he'd
confided to her, she marvelled at his powers of recovery.
Maybe it was the Bloody Mary but she felt intoxicated and
light-headed. What would this evening bring into her life,
which had been empty for so many years? She'd even been
able to talk to Brian about Mam and Dad. Everybody in
Brimdale knew that subject had been off limits for years.
When she originally took over the pub, determined to
keep her parents' dream alive, some well-meaning friends
suggested she re-decorate it and adopt a wrestling theme
in her mother's honour and to make it stand out from
the competition. Peggy had been appalled at the idea and

had placed all of her mother's wrestling paraphernalia, including costumes, programmes, cuttings and numerous other items, into large containers that were now safely out of sight in the wardrobe in the spare bedroom. But she'd been able to talk about her parents, and even her mother's ridiculous Beast of Bishopsgate moniker, to Brian. How was that?

She'd shortlisted three CDs by now, opting first for a Classical Greats compilation. Surely that would provide a suitably gentle and unobtrusive background? Brian could always put on her Tom Jones collection later. She turned to her table decoration, bedecked with the very candleholders she'd been polishing when Brian arrived two weeks before. Was it really only that long? She'd only known him for, what, fourteen days, and already she felt that he was the man she'd been waiting for all her life.

Brian's head popped around the door. 'Are you ready?'

'I'm ravenous,' admitted Peggy, and indeed she was. 'Am I allowed to ask what we're having?'

'No,' Brian said. 'It's all got to be a wonderful surprise, unfolding before you.'

'It all sounds very mysterious.'

'What I will tell you is that I've themed the meal on Inn travel of yore. I thought it would be very appropriate given where we are.'

'Traditional with a twist,' they both exclaimed together, laughing heartily at their collective wit.

Brian brought forth the first dish, a dark brown oxtail and sherry soup with a hardboiled egg yolk floating in its midst. Peggy flashed a look at Brian so admiring and so affectionate that many a man would have succumbed to her charms there and then were it not for the fact that Brian was distracted by the need to add fresh parsley to his creation and thus missed her endearing gaze. In the background, the classical CD launched into Carl Orff's *Carmina Burana*, which, while not exactly the anodyne background Peggy had intended, nevertheless provided a far more appropriate mood setter for the pent-up pair.

Peggy began to sip the piquant potage, pausing only to gently dab her mouth from time to time with a slow seductive sweep of her napkin. She kept her eyes locked on her table partner as Brian next appeared with a platter bearing a lobster the same colour as the brickwork outside their window. Brian produced a sharp kitchen knife, turned the boiled crustacean belly side up, and expertly separated it into two neat halves before presenting a serving to Peggy together with a small cruet of tarragon butter. She followed Brian's lead as he used his hands to tear off a claw and crack the surrounding shell with the butt of his table knife. As Brian poured two glasses of Brim to accompany the seafood she marvelled at his choice and raised her glass in silent salute to his knowledge and playfulness. As she continued eating, the butter ran from the lobster's fractured pincer on to her bosom and once more she had need of her napkin, this time to restore her décolletage. Brian noisily sucked the succulent flesh from the lobster tail and made a gesture of throwing the shell over his shoulder in the manner of Good King Hal. Peggy could only groan a sigh of delight at the wondrous nature of their intimate banquet. Meanwhile, Ravel's *Bolero* was also boiling up to its orgasmic climax.

Brian's next course consisted of two whole, plump poussin residing on a dainty bed of lentils and wilted spinach, encircled with a barrier of small roasted beets and looking, in their bronzed perfection, like they'd spent the afternoon on a sun bed. Briefly pausing to pour two glasses of Brouilly, he then took the same knife he'd used to cut the Lobster and halved the poussin. Soon, both diners were slurping on the delicate drumsticks and ripping the flesh from the bones, pausing only to lick clean their juice-saturated fingers. Peggy fell on her food like a lion gnawing an unlucky Christian, with a pleading entreaty in her eyes to her dining companion to accept the sacrifice she was offering up. In return, Brian extracted the wishbone from one of the birds and offered it to Peggy who gained the advantage as it snapped in two. No wish passed her lips. Brian, who hitherto had been preoccupied with ensuring his dishes were *au point*, suddenly felt his defences, such as they were, overrun. As the *Choral* from Beethoven's Ninth thickened his sinews he felt unable to tear his gaze away from Peggy and a self-conscious simper suffused his face.

Brian, clearly a protein fan, hadn't been too sure about the next course but now instinctively felt he'd made the right choice as he brought in a platter of Whitby Oysters, already shucked in their shells and ready to be adorned with the lemon and Tabasco nestling in the accompanying ice. Peggy flirtatiously turned at a right angle to him, threw her head back, and upended the first of the salty molluscs into her mouth. Momentarily, it sat there protruding from her lips until, quick as a flash, it disappeared down her throat like a scorpion being swallowed by a stork. She almost leered at Brian as she reached for her glass of chilled champagne to help swig the bivalve down. Unerringly at this juncture, the CD player contributed a further allegro offering in the shape of Wagner's *Ride of the Valkyries* – as if their hearts could possibly race any faster.

Just as Peggy wondered if there was any more food to eat – surely not? – Brian brought to the table a bowl of fresh figs and pears. Simplicity itself. Taking a small silver clasp-knife from his pocket Brian cut the fruit into quarters and arranged it on a plate. Each gently nibbled and rolled the soft pulp between their teeth as they continued to regard the other with a new sense of recognition, understanding and desire. Their palates cleansed, and *La Rejouissance* from Handel's Music for the Royal Fireworks providing an additional – albeit totally unnecessary – hint, they both abruptly leapt to their feet and passionately embraced each other. Without a further, single word being uttered they made their way to the bedroom.

CHAPTER ELEVEN

Exactly three weeks after his first trip Brandon Todd was feeling a little uneasy as his train pulled into Leeds City Station. On his laptop he carried the presentation on how he proposed to win hearts and minds in the matter of the EU ruling, and to safeguard the future of Brim. Tomorrow he would share these proposals with Simon Backhouse and get the go-ahead to make them happen. But first, before he caught his local connection up to Brimdale, Brandon had another meeting to attend in the middle of Leeds. At Colton's Brewery. With Dave Rawson.

The invitation to discuss how he could assist Colton's with its PR had come out of the blue and, while he initially cited conflict of interest as he was working for a rival, Brandon finally conceded to Dave Rawson's observation that, as no contract had yet been signed with Brim, he was still at liberty to consider his options. Conflict of interest issues did of course happen from time to time in Brandon's business – ethically he wasn't allowed to work for two competitors in one field – but he could ruefully recall being shafted more than once by client promises that never materialised into fees while passing up offers that would have paid. So, ethics or not, he now tended to question the principle of 'a bird in the hand'. It was an insurance policy seeing Rawson, that's all. Maybe the Colton's contract would be bigger, and longer term – he owed it to himself to check it out at least. Still, he felt a slight pang of disloyalty to Simon as he took this unexpected detour on his journey up to Brimdale.

As Brandon applied his 'reception test' to Colton's premises the contrast with Brim's couldn't have been more marked. It was like checking in at a hotel or airport – impersonal, perfunctory and clinical. He was signed in and given an ID badge together with a note on what to do in the event of a fire. He perched uncomfortably on the modular seating, a series of fabric-covered pods arranged in a crescent shape in front of a huge TV monitor showing Sky News, until Rawson's secretary arrived to take him through.

Rawson didn't bother with too much small talk on being introduced. 'It looks like we might have saved you in the nick of time, Brandon. You don't want to be working for those jokers – stick with the big boys.'

Under these circumstances Brandon was keen to establish some ground rules. 'Well, we are at rather an advanced stage with Brim but I did want to hear you out before we finally sign. You do appreciate though that I am bound by confidentiality so can't discuss anything specifically to do with Brim.'

'I'm not interested in that rabble,' breezed the prospective client. 'I'm interested in what you can do for us.' Despite Dave Rawson's bravura it was fairly obvious he was bothered about 'that rabble', a suspicion hard to dispel when he continued to talk almost exclusively about the rival brewery. 'They've had it is my view. Won't win the EU ruling, and even if they do they don't have any money to capitalise on it – that means no PR budget for you. Would you really want to get into bed with such a bunch of losers, anyway? I hear their latest scoop is to sign up that has-been Barnsley Chop chef. I ask you. Hilarious.'

Brandon tried to bring the conversation back to his host's company. 'In terms of Colton's PR, what are your priorities? Is there a brief and a budget available? Would it be a competitive pitch?'

'You write it; you do it – that's the brief.'

'Well, that's an intriguing offer but normally we're given a bit of steer?'

'Here's the steer. We're going to blast Brim off the face of the earth, and Brimmer is going to go international and clean up. We've got plenty of money to put behind it – we're just waiting for the EU to see a bit of sense and then it's light the blue touch paper time. You stick with them, Brandon, and you'll go down with the ship. I'm giving you a lifeline.'

Brandon continued to hedge his bets. 'Well, of course, nothing is concrete at this stage in terms of agreements.'

'If you had a contract it wouldn't be worth sod all anyway. Let me tell you – in confidence, but I think you should know – we've just put in a bid for Brimdale Brewery so in all probability we'll own it before too long. I shouldn't really be telling you that, but there's no point in taking a job as first violin if the gig's going to be on the Titanic.'

Brandon absorbed this bombshell as he continued to listen to Rawson's rants for another half an hour before asking, 'So, how do you want to take this forward?'

'Simple. Just tell them you've had a better offer, kick them into touch, and we can get on with drawing up a contract with you. You can use my phone if you like.'

Brandon was in no such hurry. 'Well, that won't be necessary but you've certainly given me some food for thought. I'll call you later this week with my answer.'

As soon as Brandon was outside, walking the short distance back to the station, his mobile rang. Simon Backhouse was calling. Brandon felt like a schoolboy being caught red-handed with a porn mag.

'Hi Simon. Nearly at your place – just in Leeds at the moment.'

'I hope you don't mind, Brandon, but I've had rather an interesting proposition put to me this morning.' Proposition? Surely he didn't mean Rawson's offer? Simon continued. 'I don't know if you know but we have rather a famous author, Cora Songhurst, who hails from Brimdale. Guess what? She's just called to ask if we can help her with some research for a new book she's planning. Local angle apparently and wants to plunder our archives.'

'The historical writer? I didn't know she was from Brimdale. Maybe she could be of help?'

'Precisely my thoughts, Brandon, precisely. I hope you don't mind but I've invited her down the Fountain Head tonight to meet up. She doesn't know you're going to be there but "if we help her, she can help us" sort of thing.'

'One hand washing the other.'

'It should be a good evening anyway – it's the annual Ferret & Firkin Night.'

'Ferret & Firkin Night? Don't tell me – you'll spoil the surprise.'

'All I'll say is, I think you'll enjoy it.'

'I wish I'd have known – I'd have booked another hotel,' Brandon quipped. 'I've got a big presentation to make tomorrow, after all.'

As soon as he hung up Brandon's thoughts turned to the conundrum forming in his mind. Not the exact nature of a Ferret & Firkin Night but what to do about Colton's. Rawson was a Neanderthal, that much Brandon knew, and he clearly had an obsession with Brim. As for Rawson's 'write your own brief and cheque' offer, well, Brandon wasn't going to fall for that. Colton's didn't so much want Brandon working for them as not working for Brimdale Brewery. But why? Normally Brandon would have put the meeting down to experience and told Rawson later in the week that, after due consideration, he was staying with Brim. But Rawson's less than subtle bombshell that they'd put in a bid for Brim might make that an act of folly. If it was true – and short of asking Simon, how could he be sure? – he could end up with no new client at all. From a 'bird in the hand' to 'two in the bush'. This was going to require some serious thinking.

At Brim Over Hall Cora Songhurst was preparing herself for her first night out in Brimdale in quite a number of years. She couldn't quite believe how she'd agreed to meet Simon Backhouse in a pub of all places but it had seemed churlish to decline. After all, she was asking him for a favour and it would get her out of the house – and she was in dire need of a change of scenery. She sought out Alicia in the lounge where she lay stretched out on the settee. Radio Four was on in the background although Cora knew her mother wasn't really listening to it.

'Mummy, I'm popping out tonight for a couple of hours if that's all right?'

'Where to? You never go out.'

'You know you suggested that I speak to the brewery about their archives? Well, they've invited me to meet them this evening to discuss it.'

Alicia had pointed her daughter in the direction of the brewery when, despite Cora's initial misgivings, she'd convinced herself that a book on the Cluniac monks might be a winner after all. It was, in her mother's view, a stupid theme for a book but rather than talk her daughter out of it she'd quickly calculated that such an enterprise would help keep her daughter in Brimdale for quite some time. How clever she'd been to point out that the brewery would, in all probability, have more archive material on the Priory than any library in the area. Cora, fearing Alicia would deride her putative choice of subject for a new book, had felt a little shame-faced over her growing exasperation with her mother when she'd been so supportive and helpful on how to gather research.

'This evening? You should have arranged to meet them when Jean was here,' Alicia said, glad of the opportunity to not sound too considerate towards her daughter. 'Where is this meeting and who's "they"?'

'It's with the head of the brewery, Simon Backhouse, in the Fountain Head, Mummy.'

'The Fountain Head? What, have you joined a dating

agency or something? Who has a meeting in a pub with people they've never met?'

'It's not like that, Mummy. They're doing me a favour by meeting up at such short notice. If they can help, I may be on to something. If not, I'll have to shelve the idea.'

Alicia certainly didn't want Cora to jettison the project before it had begun. 'I suppose I'll have to look after myself, then.'

Cora, her furlough stamped, withdrew to her bedroom. She conceded her mother may have a valid point – it was a trifle odd to be going to the pub to meet a total stranger; but this was for work purposes, not some sort of romantic tryst.

Cora was convinced that she was on to something with the Cluniac idea and wanted to press ahead. At first she'd told herself that the world didn't need another *The Name of the Rose*, but the more she thought of it the more possibilities she conjured. The Cluniacs sounded rather exotic for a religious order and, there was no doubt about it, their monastic influence and power in the Middle Ages was extensive. And it was right here on her doorstep – her publicist would love that angle. More than that, the existence of Cluniac nuns played straight into Cora's literary *modus operandi* – she knew, instinctively, it would work. Was there enough research available around which to weave a compelling story? Mummy was absolutely right to suggest that the brewery should be the first port of call. Their whole business was predicated on what the monks had started and if anybody had data on the local order it would be the Victorian Backhouse forebears who'd established the Brimdale brewery back in the mid-1800s.

The meeting tonight would be significant in determining what Cora did next.

But before that, she had another quandary to solve. What *does* an award-winning writer wear to the local pub for a blind date?

Back in Leeds, Dave Rawson had just finished a short phone conversation with his wife. It always made him irritable to have domestic trivia thrust in the way of running a successful business empire and he didn't need reminding he had to pick his daughter up from Brownies later as his wife was going out.

The fact that he rarely saw his wife didn't seem to bother the man who considered his job to be his true bride. His partner of fifteen years, Jayne, had long ago given up on cosy companionship in their relationship and now placed more value on bringing their daughter up. In fact, life was a whole lot quieter when Dave wasn't around as he was always grumpy, and it was obvious he'd rather be anywhere else other than with his family. Dave justified his behaviour with the claim that he was working hard, providing a lifestyle that gave them the best of everything and leaving them wanting for nothing. By now, he was right, as his wife and daughter were past caring whether they had a husband and father in their lives. The most awkward part of their relationship occurred each summer when they were forced to take a family holiday together – husband and wife could barely restrain their relief on returning home, with another fifty weeks of respite until the next one. It never occurred to Rawson that Jayne was not, as she claimed, out with the girls tonight – she was spending the evening with her personal fitness trainer in a country hotel where she was looking forward to trying out some new exercises.

Rawson was edgy following his meeting with Brandon Todd. He'd intended to be a bit cooler with the PR maestro but once he'd got on to the subject of Brim he'd let his feelings get the better of him. Would Todd turn his back on them? You didn't normally get people like him having many scruples so he'd back the best horse in this race, and that would be Colton's, surely? Rawson knew he could put enough work Todd's way to justify his *volte-face* – money talks, after all. His confidential 'slip', that Colton's had made a bid for Brimdale brewery, had been intentional. That, if nothing else, should settle the manner.

Signing up Brandon Todd wasn't so much about stopping a definite goal-scoring opportunity for Brim as sapping their morale. Just as they thought they were raising their game they'd be hit by the grim reality they were a tiddler, a second-rate team with unrealistic ambitions. He wanted them softening up, and this would help. He wanted Backhouse to realise that resistance was futile and the Colton's bid was too attractive to turn down. The offer wouldn't be on the table forever.

But he still needed to be sure they would succumb, for them to recognise they had hit the end of the line. To achieve that, he had to keep the screw turned tight. He had to hit them harder. With that in mind, he picked up his phone and dialled Richard Tasker's number.

CHAPTER TWELVE

Peggy was putting the final touches to the arrangements for the evening's entertainment. The Ferret & Firkin banners were up, Simon's band equipment was in place, and Brian had been in the kitchen all afternoon preparing a selection of bar snacks to boost takings still further. Against her better judgement Peggy had agreed to let Godfrey be the master of ceremonies for the night – she knew she may live to regret it but he had promised to be 'one hundred and one percent professional'.

A big crowd was expected, and Brandon Todd was once again staying with them. At least he could have his usual room as Brian now had alternative sleeping arrangements after last orders. Peggy, however, was anxious – not about the evening as much as her decision to try to speak to Brandon about Brian's role in the Brim campaign. She'd not shared this planned intercession with her new companion but she was determined to help preserve his dignity by asking that he wasn't dropped from Brandon's plans. Anything would do – just as long as it wasn't an ignominious dismissal. Not that Brian looked like a man in need of favours as he laughed and joshed with her kitchen staff.

What a difference these few short weeks had made – for both of them. Peggy had given up hoping for love in her life a long time ago, while Brian had given up, full stop. Now they were like a couple of ditzy teenagers, particularly as they were still trying to pretend to everyone else that nothing was going on. That wasn't really washing with regulars and staff in the pub who could see the transformation happening right in front of their eyes. As Godfrey said to Brian over the first weekend, 'I see you've got your feet under the table.'

As Brandon Todd checked in that afternoon he was somewhat surprised to see Brian Parkin going back and forth as if he owned the place. Hadn't he taken the hint by now? The fallen star certainly didn't figure in the carefully worked out PR plan for Brim that he was to reveal to Simon the next day.

Because of the Ferret & Firkin night Brandon had arranged to meet up with Simon, and his esteemed local author guest, early doors. When he entered the lounge he found Simon already present, chatting to a woman he didn't recognise. Even though she was seated Brandon could see she was tall and athletic looking. Her lightly tanned bare legs and arms, protruding from a bright floral cotton print dress, added further to the impression of a healthy lifestyle. Her face, however, was not that of an athlete but more reminiscent of a Botticelli heroine with long, flowing, blonde hair, feline green eyes and a lustrous complexion totally devoid of make-up.

Brandon had somehow imagined that Cora Songhurst would be dowdy and scholarly in appearance, a Miss Marple in the making. Simon's guest was anything but.

This must be a friend or acquaintance of Simon's? No, introductions made, it was Cora Songhurst. Brandon's evening had just started to look up a little.

Simon brought the newcomer up to speed. 'Cora has just been telling me about a new book she's planning, set here in Brimdale, and I've already learned something I didn't know. You remember I told you it was Benedictines who had the Priory? Well, completely wrong. It was Cluniacs apparently. Altogether different kettle of fish.'

'Well that's one way of putting it,' Cora said in what could only be described as a 'posh Yorkshire' voice that sounded highly voluptuous to Brandon's ears.

'And you think the brewery may be able to help you with your research?' ventured the PR guru, his interest in monastic matters piqued for the first time in his life.

Before Cora had a chance to respond, Simon butted in. 'I think it may be the other way round, actually. We have hundreds of books and manuscripts in storage, some that have been there for over a hundred and fifty years. Cora would be doing us an immense favour knocking them into some sort of shape, especially with the museum in mind.'

All three looked pleased as the matter was settled. Cora could start, at her own convenience, delving deep into the Brimdale Brewery archives. Simon brought a round of drinks to seal the deal before excusing himself to re-string his guitar, leaving Cora and her vodka tonic in the capable hands of the UK's preeminent PR.

Brandon, never at a loss for chitchat, ensured their conversation didn't flag as he tackled his first pint of the night. 'I don't normally drink beer but duty calls and all that,' he confessed.

Cora, anticipating a quid pro quo request for her help on the Brim campaign at some point, ducked his comment altogether. 'Do you know what a Ferret & Firkin night consists of? I must say, it's a new one on me.'

'I was hoping to ask you,' Brandon said. 'I was depending on your local knowledge.'

'Ah. Been away too long in that case,' Cora conceded.

Brandon didn't know where the time went but, with Cora apparently not in a hurry to leave, the two continued to chat about publishing, PR, London, Yorkshire ways and care for the elderly as the evening advanced. To Brandon's mind, Cora was the most normal and likeable character he'd met since he'd ventured north on Brim business. While he was enjoying her company he wasn't entirely sure what her take on their conversation was – engaged, polite, enthusiastic or tolerant? She didn't seem too eager to leave but she was giving little away. Gamely, he batted on until nature called – he was on his third pint by now – and he was forced to excuse himself temporarily.

As he emerged from the gents, wondering if Cora would stay a little longer, he was cornered by Peggy who appeared to have been waiting outside in the corridor for him.

'Can I have a quick word, Brandon?'

Without any elaboration Peggy brought him up to speed on Brian's ailing career fortunes, the downturn in his personal life and the lifeline the Brim contract represented. In short, 'So you see, Brandon, if it's true what's being rumoured and he's to play no part in your plans, it will be another kick in the teeth for him.'

Despite the comforting mood created by Cora's

company and the moreish qualities of Brim, Brandon immediately felt under the cosh. He couldn't have external pressure applied to his plans like this, and since when had Peggy become Parkin's agent? 'I'm very sorry to hear all of that, Peggy, I really am, but business isn't run on sentiment. You must be able to see that?'

'I'll tell you what I see, Brandon. I see a man who a few weeks ago had reached the end of the line and had lost the will to live until the prospect of this job gave him hope.' Peggy knew she'd said too much, but couldn't help it. 'That's what I see, Brandon. Are you going to take that away from him? What then?'

Brandon returned to the lounge a little dazed, and not just from the effects of his alcoholic intake. He was being held to ransom. He couldn't succumb to that. As soon as he arrived back, Cora announced it was time she was going. As Brandon appealed to her to stay for one more drink the sound of Godfrey tapping on the microphone - 'Is this bloody thing on?' – filled the room. Show time. Definitely time for one more, if only to have their curiosity satisfied.

Godfrey, technical uncertainties resolved, commenced with his announcement. 'Good evening, Ladies and Gentlemen, and welcome to the Fountain Head's annual Ferret & Firkin night. As the name implies, we have ferrets and we have a firkin of Brim for the winner.' So that's what a firkin was, at least.

'Which of our plucky contestants will take home this nine-gallon cask of liquid refreshment? The one who can keep a ferret down his trouser legs for the longest duration.' A huge cheer went up around the room.

Brandon and Cora looked at each other in disbelief and started to laugh – surely not?

'First, a few house rules. Challengers may not have partaken of drugs before the contest. And that applies to the ferrets as well as the leggers. Secondly, all ferrets have been inspected to ensure that their teeth haven't been filed down or otherwise blunted. No sharp practices here, or maybe I mean the opposite.' A further eruption of sniggers and catcalls ensued but Godfrey had yet more regulations to underline and held up his hand to beseech silence.

'Thirdly, trousers must be tied securely at the ankle and at the waist to contain the ferret and fourthly, and this is most important, the wearing of undercrackers by contestants is strictly forbidden, on pain of disqualification.' More merriment swept the room at this disclosure.

'In the interests of fair play and sportsmanship I can confirm that I have undertaken the necessary inspections and can personally vouch for the eligibility of each entrant.' A *Good Old Days*-style 'whoo' sprang up among the crowd that now was standing room only.

'I can't believe anybody would do this just to win seventy-two pints of beer,' Brandon said to Cora. 'They must be stark raving mad.'

A fanfare blasted from the PA as four contestants, one last year's winner and introduced as the 'official world champion ferret legger', strode on to the stage. At the back of the line, much to Brandon's amusement, he recognised Gary Merriweather of the BBA.

'See that last contestant? I've met him,' he shouted to

Cora over the din. 'My money's on him. Where there's no sense, there's no feeling.' Brandon then spotted the other half of the BBA, Howard Amos, hovering next to the stage with a camera and flashgun – what a night this was turning out to be.

Godfrey strung it out for as long as he could before 'immersion' took place, describing in graphic detail how a ferret, once it had locked on to a bite, was virtually impossible to dislodge. A medical crew was on standby as a precaution and while the world record for ferret legging was five hours and thirty minutes tonight's contest would carry a guillotine of sixty minutes. As the ferrets were displayed, and their teeth exposed for the delectation of the spectators, few present thought that long would be necessary.

At the given signal, assistants handed a ferret apiece to the contestants who, much to Brandon and Cora's incredulity, each placed the ferret's head in their mouths for a few seconds before shovelling the carnivorous mammals into their trousers. Before the clock had ticked one minute one of the contestants, a young lad, raised his hand and screamed for his ferret to be removed. Catcalls of 'amateur' and 'chicken' ensued from the crowd. As the remaining contestants stood stock-still and stared into the middle distance their trousers bulged and shimmied, like schoolboys fighting under a blanket, from the movement within. After ten minutes, the second contestant conceded, leaving Gary Merriweather in a straight face-off with the world champion.

'I hope that ferret's well fed, Gary,' came a shout from the crowd. His countenance didn't alter one iota. Suddenly, a frantic thrashing in the world champion's crotch area presaged a discernible alteration to the world champion's facial expression. A small patch of blood appeared on his trouser front indicating that his ferret had found its supper. Not panicking, however, he took to flicking his fingers at the now stationary tumulus in an effort to dislodge it. Godfrey, commentating, assured the spectators that this manoeuvre was perfectly legal if not always altogether wise. Gary, in the meantime, looked like he was waiting for a bus, despite his ferret deciding to change trouser legs at this point. Sixteen minutes had elapsed when slowly, but surely, the world champion raised his hand in doleful submission. Gary had restored Brimdale's honour. As the assistants attended to extracting the persistent predator from the member of the fallen champion Gary punched the air in triumph, seventy-two pints of Brim to the good.

Such was the entertainment that Cora's earlier thoughts of leaving to go home to Alicia evaporated. She was having a good time and her mother would be asleep by now. Brandon returned to the bar, feeling almost superhuman as he ordered his fifth pint. Tommy had been right about Brim – you could drink it and drink it and you didn't feel drunk. Godfrey was still at the microphone, entreating guests to stay on for some live music and recounting how those bloody ferrets were more of a handful than Lillian Thompson, whoever she was. Peggy and Brian were behind the bar together, looking like they'd been there since the pub opened a century and a half back.

As soon as Brandon sat down next to Cora again, Howard and his lens arrived to capture the moment. 'Impressive performance by Gary, eh?' Howard said.

'Without doubt. I reckon I might take him on in next year's competition,' Brandon boasted.

Cora, clearly amused at Brandon's wit, nudged him playfully in the ribs. She'd not had as much fun in ages and it was clear that the evening was far from finished yet. Godfrey now ceded the stage to Simon and his band who, with a carefully selected set of up-tempo covers, were encouraging people to occupy the small dance square. After three or four numbers they hit the opening chords to *La Bamba* which saw Peggy and Brian dash out from behind the bar for three minutes of frenzied cavorting before retreating back to their positions behind the pumps, taking mock bows from the cheering crowd still thronging the lounge. It struck Brandon again that Peggy was surely over-egging it when she said that Parkin had reached the end of the line not so long ago? Surely she didn't mean...?

Brandon was now on his sixth pint of Brim and feeling in fine fettle. He and Cora – matching him drink for drink with her vodka tonics – carried on their conversation at almost shouting level in order to be heard over the volume of the music. Godfrey suddenly took to the stage again and whispered in Simon's ear. After a brief check with the other band members, Simon announced, 'By special request, Godfrey is going to sing us his favourite song.' Cue more good-natured banter from the crowd.

'God, what next?' laughed Brandon as Godfrey stood erect at the mic as the band struck up a jaunty drum and piano intro. Godfrey started singing – if that was the right word, as it was more of a recitation – about drinking medicinal compounds and its effect on a variety of characters.

'What's this?' Brandon asked Cora, 'one of Godfrey's own compositions?'

'I haven't a clue,' Cora replied. 'Ask the photographer'.

Brandon beckoned Howard who was swaying in tune next to their table and enquired, 'What's this song, Howard? It's mad.'

'You youngsters. It's *Lily the Pink*, from the sixties. No doubt a changing room favourite from his playing days. Very funny though.'

By now the whole room had caught on to the rather repetitive chorus and was belting it out with gusto. As if Godfrey's deadpan delivery wasn't enough entertainment, a clearly refreshed Gary now leapt on to the stage and proceeded to conduct a dervish like dance with the aid of a draft excluder down his pants in emulation of his earlier triumph. The bar was rocking as Brandon asked Cora if she fancied one final drink for the road.

'I really think I should be going, Brandon,' she giggled. 'I think I may have had one drink too many.'

'You should have tried the Brim,' he replied. 'I feel as sober as a judge.'

'Well, it's been a wonderful night, so thank you. And it's fantastic news on the archives. Maybe I'll see you in the brewery?'

'I'd like that,' confessed Brandon as he escorted her to the front door of the pub. As he watched Cora climb into a cab on the rank outside, he thought that he'd like that a lot.

Back inside the pub, Godfrey and Gary had now vacated the stage and Simon's band were playing out the evening with their standard blues set as the crowd began to disperse. Brandon decided one final pint would be in order to cap this wonderful night, and as a sort of good luck token for tomorrow's pitch. Taking his glass upstairs to his room, the chorus of *Lily the Pink* resounding in his head, he felt a surge of affection for the motley crew he had joined forces with. They were certainly odd, but tonight had only reinforced his earlier gut feeling that this was a fight that had to be won, and that he'd have to be on his mettle to help them over the line. Then there was Cora. How beguiling had she been? A very atypical Brimdalian in his brief experience. He'd certainly like to see her again.

Dave Rawson's offer from earlier in the day flashed into his mind – his bird in the hand versus two in the bush quandary. Well, it wasn't a predicament any longer for Brandon. He was sticking with Brim; Rawson could take a running jump. He couldn't give up on Brim now – he couldn't drop his new friends in it. Tonight had demonstrated that to him. That Rawson had even tried to lure him away from them showed he was worried. Good, that gave him heart. Brim was certainly fun – how many times could he say that about a client?

As he sipped his nightcap – his seventh pint of the evening – he flipped his laptop open and soon found himself Googling *Lily the Pink* instead. As he discovered the full history of the song and its inspiration, together with old video clips from 1968 of the track being performed by comedy and poet trio The Scaffold, his mind went into overdrive. He opened tomorrow's presentation and as he idly flicked through it he was gripped with the deflating realisation that maybe his recommendations were off the mark. Tonight he'd learned more about Brim than in all of his briefings over the past few weeks put together and, as he drained his pint and fell into bed, he realised that to achieve the brewery's aims he'd have to go a lot, lot further than his current presentation allowed. As ideas flashed though his mind, he fell into a deep, contented, beer-assisted sleep. Yes, Brim was most efficacious, in every case.

CHAPTER THIRTEEN

Cora Songhurst pushed the cornflakes around her cereal bowl and poured a third cup of tea. She knew she'd overdone it the night before but was determined not to let Alicia see her looking the worse for wear.

Of course, her mother was interrogating her. 'What time did you get in last night? I didn't hear you.'

'It wasn't late, Mummy. I was just quiet, that's all.'

'Well, was it worth it?'

'Very much so,' Cora said as brightly as she could manage. 'They've agreed to let me have access to all of their archives. I'm going to take a look at them later today to get started.' To placate her mother, she added, 'It really was a very clever idea of yours to ask them, Mummy.'

Alicia grunted, which Cora took for assent. Rather it was an expression of triumph that her daughter would now have a further reason to be chained to Brimdale for the foreseeable future. As Alicia buried her head in the Daily Telegraph, Cora let her thoughts return to the previous evening. She certainly wasn't going to tell Alicia about the ferret legging, or the time she'd spent with Brandon Todd. She knew what her mother's reaction would be. In any event, Alicia was proving coolly unconcerned about her night out now she knew she'd got permission to access the archives.

Brandon had been wonderfully warm and seemed genuinely interested in her career and background. Maybe he was just being professional – he was in PR after all – but she imagined that there had been more to their exchanges than merely passing the time.

Cora, in truth, wasn't the most experienced of women when it came to men. Being naturally shy, she hadn't enjoyed too many significant relationships – possibly the writing got in the way, but then she'd not always written. The renown she'd attracted as a successful author had made her well-known in literary circles but she was unlikely to be stopped on the Tube by admirers. Her natural diffidence extended to her professional projection where her publisher was instructed to keep interviews to a minimum and to let the work speak for itself. Now pushing forty, Cora was beginning to think that the prospect of a lasting relationship in her life was passing her by. Worse, she harboured an uncomfortable feeling she'd never be able to alter her natural passiveness to do anything about it. With Brandon though, she'd forgotten all about that. He certainly didn't lack confidence – maybe it was a Ying and Yang thing where they balanced each other out? She smiled at the very thought of it and then reprimanded herself for getting carried away. Still, it had been a wonderful night and she hoped to bump into Brandon again at the brewery. Maybe today in fact.

Her reverie was disturbed by Alicia. 'You look mighty pleased at the prospect at digging your nose into a load of dusty old books. No wonder you've never met a man who'd take you up.'

At the Fountain Head Brandon was nursing a mammoth hangover and cursing Tommy Whitelaw for his somewhat erroneous advice on the quaffing characteristics of the product on which he was shortly to make his recommendations. He'd woken up with a raging thirst at 5.30am and hadn't been able to get back to sleep. At breakfast Peggy kept on making jocular remarks about him needing a proper fry-up to soak up all that ale – his enthusiasm for imbibing his client's wares had not gone unnoticed, nor, for that matter, unappreciated. Still, he passed on the full English.

After breakfast, and despite his lack of sleep, Brandon returned to his room to get to grips with reviewing his presentation. He realised now that he'd been drunk – or *kaylied* to use the local vernacular – last night but nevertheless he couldn't shake off the realisation he'd taken to bed with him that his presentation was too pedestrian. Now he was forming new ideas and jotting down notes to radically alter what he was going to say. Under different circumstances he might have thought he was being unprofessional in making so many last-minute changes but he was genuinely excited at the new direction in which he was heading – now he felt truly inspired as to what Brim needed to do next. There was no time to capture all of these emerging thoughts in a computer presentation but that hardly mattered – it was what he had to say that was important.

Two hours later he was in the boardroom at

the brewery, ready to start. Simon, Howard, and representatives from both the local council and the trade association sat expectantly awaiting his words of wisdom.

Brandon began. 'On my laptop there's a presentation on how I planned to let the world know Brim is a truly unique beer.' He paused. 'But I've decided I'm not going to show you that.'

Howard and the rest of the panel looked confused. Was he not going to present anything to them?

He continued. 'Why? Because last night I realised that it doesn't go far enough in capturing the true essence of Brim.'

The panel exchanged further doubtful looks. Simon, however, reserved his judgment, calculating that this was some sort of stock opener for the PR maestro.

Brandon took up his thread again. 'Over the past few weeks I've learned a lot about Brim and I've put a lot of thought into how we can not only highlight the impending EU ruling but also put Brim on the map at the same time. I'd looked at a number of techniques and ideas to achieve this and, until yesterday, I was confident that they'd work. But last night, in the Fountain Head, I confess that I experienced somewhat of an epiphany, a turning point if you like. It made me realise that I was missing the true point about Brim and its importance to this town.'

By now the panel were all ears, craning forward to catch Brandon's every word.

'Brim isn't just a beer. It's far from ordinary. In short, it *does* perform miracles. It transforms, it reduces life's problems, it enriches people's existence.'

'But we can't say that,' said the representative from

the trade association in a blunt Yorkshire interruption. 'Claims like that can't be substantiated.'

'Very true, but I'm not intending to make a case for Brim scientifically. I intend to make people come to that conclusion themselves.'

'Well, it sounds like a pretty big leap of faith if you ask me,' said the local councillor, who preferred to deal in facts.

'Let me explain,' Brandon said. 'The town of Brimdale possesses some remarkable people who've overcome difficulties in their lives, who've achieved against the odds. We're going to tell their story, in a compelling way, and we'll be telling the story of Brim at the same time without any fear over scientific red tape.'

'People like who?' queried the trade association representative.

'You'll see. I haven't persuaded them yet.'

'Well, it all sounds a bit half-baked if you haven't even asked them yet,' grumbled the councillor, itching to get back to his office and do some proper work.

'The idea comes first, then the implementation. Believe me, they'll participate.'

'But why would they?' asked Howard. 'People round here can be very private.'

'Because they'll be part of a crusade, one of a team; because we're going to use humour to get the message across. Let me paint a fuller picture for you.'

Simon, who'd said nothing at this point, listened intently as Brandon went into detail over how his plan would unfold. It was decidedly different, it was definitely daring, and it was unlike anything Brim had ever attempted in the past.

Finally, the brewery chief spoke. 'I didn't know what you'd propose today, Brandon, but I certainly wasn't expecting that. But, you know what? I like it. I like it a lot. It could just well work. It's daft enough to work, that's for sure.'

'So that's a "yes", I take it?' Brandon asked.

'It is. Make it happen. Let's do it,' replied Simon.

The rest of the panel, unsure if this was a good idea or a bad idea, had nothing to add but were nevertheless grateful for Simon's decisiveness. Brim was going to go viral.

Brandon, feeling better now his hangover was subsiding and because of the green light his last minute punt had just received, knew exactly what he had to do next – sign up his first star. Five minutes after his presentation wrapped he was back in the Fountain Head and had ushered Brian and Peggy into the small office.

'Brian. I've just come from the brewery where we've been discussing the Brim campaign.' Peggy eyed Brandon fiercely, daring him to impart bad news. 'The fact is, your part in the campaign has just taken on a whole new level of importance, quite different, well radically different, to what Howard and Gary had in mind originally. I need to ask you to suspend any preconceptions and come along with me on this. You won't regret it.'

Brian couldn't believe his ears. He was in on the campaign after all. 'Fantastic, Brandon. Whatever you need, I'm there. Anything.'

'Well, you'd better let me explain what I have in mind before you say that,' smiled Brandon, knowing he still had a big sales job to do.

Five minutes later, Brian sat speechless as he absorbed the exact nature of the role he was to perform in the Brim campaign. It was left to Peggy to comment first, 'I'm not so sure. Isn't it going to make Brian look ridiculous?'

'It's going to make Brian look like the man, the personality, the winner he is,' Brandon replied.

Slowly, a big grin broke out over Brian's face. 'You know what, Brandon. Count me in. I'm up for it.'

Over the course of the next few hours Brandon had similar conversations with other targets for his viral vision. With all of them he met with initial reluctance and no little resistance, until all ultimately succumbed to his persuasive sales patter.

But there was still an essential element of the campaign execution he had to finalise and with that in mind he made his way back to the brewery and to the archives section where he hoped to find Brimdale's most famous author. Sure enough, Cora was still there, nose deep in the dusty documents having lost all track of time as she contemplated the cornucopia of calligraphy now open to her.

As Brandon suddenly appeared out of the gloom, Cora blushed, excited to see him again so soon after the previous evening.

'I was hoping I'd find you here,' Brandon said. 'You're just the person I wanted to see.' Before Cora could speculate why Brandon wanted to see her, he came straight out with it. 'I wondered if you might do some writing for me?'

Cora didn't know what he meant. Writing? What sort of writing? 'I don't quite follow…'

'I want you to write a song, Cora. Could you do that?'

'I think you may have mixed me up with somebody else, Brandon. I've never written anything like that in my life.'

'I guessed that, but that's partly why I want you to give it a go.'

In front of the huge shelves that contained the higgledy-piggledy stacks of random books and papers, Brandon explained what he was trying to achieve. Despite this, Cora was still hesitant. 'It's lovely of you to ask me but I'm not sure I could do it. Perhaps if you helped me I could try?'

'That's a deal. How about starting on it tonight?'

Cora was torn. 'The thing is, I have to look after Mummy. I don't think she'd be too happy if I was out for two nights running.'

'Maybe I could call on you at home? Would that work?'

Cora, petrified at what Alicia would think but unable to pour cold water on Brandon's enthusiasm, merely whispered, 'Yes, fine. About 8pm?'

Cora waited until around 7.45pm, when she was helping her mother to bed, to announce that she had a visitor calling round that evening.

Alicia immediately felt threatened. 'Who's coming round? You don't know anybody up here. Why do they have to come to the house?'

'The brewery has asked me to help on a small project in return for giving me access to the archives. I couldn't really say "no".'

'They didn't waste any time, did they? What's so pressing it has to be tonight? Is it that Simon Backhouse?'

'Brandon Todd, their PR adviser. I do believe it is rather urgent, otherwise I'm sure they'd have been able to wait.'

'Brandon Todd? That merchant of mendacity in my house? How could you, Cora?'

'Mummy, you're being ridiculous. Really.'

'Well, don't let me get in the way of you having a good time. I'll try not to pass away in the night and spoil your fun.'

Cora looked at the clock. Ten minutes more and she could close the bedroom door. 'Now, Mummy, settle down. You don't want to be getting agitated. I'm only downstairs if you need me.'

Alicia glowered her disapproval at this act of abandonment. Some daughter and carer Cora was turning out to be.

As Brandon stepped up to the entrance of Brim Over Hall the studded black door flew open – Cora had been hovering, intent on ensuring Alicia wouldn't be alerted to his arrival by a knock.

'I've just put Mummy to bed,' she whispered. 'We'll have to keep the noise down for a little while.' Brandon, touched by this consideration for an invalid mother, nodded and followed her into the kitchen at the back of the house.

Cora was a little on edge – she wasn't sure if this was from her mother's outburst, which she'd expected anyway, or from the presence of this male visitor into the sanctum of the family home.

'Can I get you a drink?' she asked Brandon. 'I'm afraid we don't have any Brim.'

'Thank goodness for that. I had quite enough yesterday so a cup of coffee would be lovely. We have work to do anyway.'

Before long, they were poring over her laptop as Brandon demonstrated the train of thought he'd embarked on since the previous evening. As Cora relaxed she could see how the sequence of thoughts had been triggered in Brandon's mind and marvelled at the machinations of his jackdaw mind. She laughed as he showed her the clips he had discovered, and finally they started to write, giggling like school children making up a song about the headmaster. It was a joint effort in every way as they swapped words, juggled ideas and gleefully edited their mini-opus. They took to singing out the verses *sotto voce* as they completed them to see how it all fitted together, sparking self-indulgent merriment at their own inventiveness and dottiness. Cora, for the second evening in succession, was having more fun than she could remember. Brandon was clearly in possession of a clever mind – he could obviously have written this song by himself. Had he enjoined her support for another reason?

At 10.30pm Brandon joyfully declared their task complete. As he turned to thank her for her efforts Cora couldn't contain herself any longer – without warning or any prior signal she bent her head towards his and hesitatingly kissed him on the lips. Brandon, who had been wondering how to engineer such an occurrence all evening, didn't waste any further time blessing his good fortune and immediately, and passionately, kissed her back. As the two locked into a fond embrace there came the sound of three dull thuds on the kitchen ceiling above. Alicia had decided that their meeting had gone on quite long enough.

CHAPTER FOURTEEN

Richard Tasker studied the reception area of Colton's. It was certainly different to the one in Brimdale he was more used to visiting. The call from Dave Rawson seeking his advice had come as rather a surprise. Rawson had explained that Colton's was planning a drive towards a greener energy policy and wanted to explore the implications for product consistency and quality – he'd been told that Tasker was the man to help. Satisfied that the request had nothing to do with the ongoing Brimmer legal case and flattered that the head of this international brewery had come directly to him on such a weighty matter, Tasker had agreed to a meeting. In any event he was keen to kick-start some new projects as the conclusion of the Brim application would soon leave a large gap in his portfolio of responsibilities.

Rawson had prepared well for the briefing – no sooner had Tasker sat down and been offered a coffee the brewery boss launched into a thirty-slide PowerPoint presentation on the brewery's future energy plans which concluded with a page headed 'The Big Three Questions'.

'I think that slide should read "The Big Five Questions",' Tasker volunteered. 'You've not adequately covered the role your suppliers can play in this, nor have you made enough of the sustainability issues.'

'You see, that's exactly why I wanted to get your input,' said an enthusiastic Dave Rawson. 'Tell me more.'

For the next hour Rawson made careful notes as the man from Defra outlined, in great detail, his thoughts and recommendations. As Tasker finally appeared to run out of steam Rawson attempted to draw a line under the subject saying, 'This is all going to be highly valuable to us. I can't thank you enough.'

'Well, that's what we're here for, after all.'

'Now, if I may be so bold, I have another question for you.'

Tasker looked at him suspiciously.

'I'm told that you're a bit of an expert on cycling. Is that true?'

A relieved Tasker confirmed the veracity of the grapevine rumour. 'Well, I'm a member of a cycling club, yes. It is rather a hobby of mine.'

'What a coincidence. Mine too. I'm a beginner to be honest. What do you ride?'

'An Eddie Merckx AMX2 Road Bike mainly, but I've also got a Bottechia 105. I should really sell the Bottechia but I've got a soft spot for it still.'

'How did you decide what to go for?'

'It's trial and error, really. You have to take different factors into account, especially the type of racing you're planning to do and the terrain.'

'I'm just about to make an investment in one – some of the prices are a bit eye-watering. I don't suppose you could spare another ten minutes to give me some pointers could you? It would really help.'

Normally, Tasker was disinclined towards idle chitchat during work hours, or even outside of it, but cycles were quite a different matter. 'I suppose I could. We cyclists should stick together, after all.'

'I tell you what; maybe we could continue this at the Wharf? It's such a lovely evening, I should at least buy you a drink for all of the advice you're giving me.'

Having committed himself so far, Tasker felt unable to decline.

Less than a mile away Simon Backhouse was meeting two Latvian scientists, Miks and Ingus, at the Queen's Hotel. Also in tow was Lauris, a post-graduate student from Leeds University who was acting as interpreter for their visit. Since Tasker had told him to produce a new forensic report on the well and the spring water he'd been struggling to find someone who met the EU's requirements who could do an acceptable report on time. Eventually, with the assistance of his UK analytical partners, he'd identified a small lab in Riga who could do the work. To his surprise the EU gave an immediate go-ahead, happy to spread their largesse to newer members of the European Union. Much to his annoyance Simon was picking up the bill for their flights and accommodation as well as the report but despite the expense he was more relaxed that he would now make the deadline.

Simon had offered to entertain his visitors that evening – he thought it was the least he could do to chaperone them on their first visit to Leeds. Introducing himself to

Miks and Ingus in the hotel bar after they'd checked in he found them already running up the extras column on the bill he'd be picking up. Looking at the two solid imposing figures, like models for old Soviet propaganda posters, Simon found it difficult to imagine that these two had contributed much in the way of melody during their country's Singing Revolution. He instinctively understood it wasn't going to be a quiet night.

'What would you like to do this evening?' Simon asked via Lauris.

After a short discussion, the interpreter laid out the visitors' preferred itinerary. 'Drink. Girls.'

'Eat first?' gestured Simon, pointing his fingers at his mouth.

'Eaten on plane,' confirmed Lauris after a brief conflab. 'Drink. Girls.'

Duly instructed, Simon nodded affirmatively towards his guests. He wasn't going to disappoint them.

Over at the Leodian bar on the Wharf, Dave Rawson persuaded Richard Tasker that a nice chilled bottle of Chablis would be a better choice than a beer on such a lovely evening. Unused to hospitality, Tasker felt a little uneasy as 'call me Dave' poured him a large measure. Rawson never let up in the conversation, interrogating and prompting his new friend on all aspects of club cycling, equipment, diet, apparel and fitness regimes. Eventually, as the bottom of the bottle was reached, Tasker made to bring the discussion to an end but Rawson was having none of it – he was finding this conversation so, so helpful, surely one more glass wouldn't do any harm?

As Rawson kept up his impression of a radio presenter with a fear of dead air the man from the civil service began to unwind as the steely Burgundy went to work on his inhibitions like a velvet-wrapped cosh. Sensing that Tasker's resistance was waning, Rawson changed the subject from bikes to the Defra Inspector's personal life. 'Do you have kids, Richard?'

'Yes, one. Ben. Five years old. I'm planning on getting him into the youth cycling class from next year.'

'Been married long, then?'

'Ten years. Debbie. We've known each other since school.'

'A childhood sweetheart? Sounds very romantic,' said Rawson as he caught the waiter's eye and signalled for another bottle without Tasker noticing.

'Something like that,' admitted the bashful suitor, his heart now swelling with love and pride for the most wonderful woman in the world.

'Does your job take you away from home much?'

'Not really. The odd trip to Brussels, but mainly West Yorkshire.'

'Still, it must be fascinating. Just keeping up with all the legislation must demand an awful lot of commitment.'

'Yes. That's not often appreciated. It really does.'

As Rawson topped Tasker's glass up again his new drinking buddy didn't even seem to notice they were on a new bottle. So far, so good.

In Whitelock's Ale House Simon was at least getting some sustenance into the Latvians as a buffer against the beer and vodka chasers they'd been knocking back relentlessly for the past three hours. They seemed to like the black pudding scotch eggs he'd ordered and asked for another plate with their next round. There was no doubt that Miks and Ingus were finding Leeds a wonderful place to visit.

Simon gamely asked some sensible questions regarding the scientists' homeland and line of work, but made little headway. He couldn't be sure if it was a case of Miks and Ingus not being interested, or whether Lauris was too frightened to interrupt their socialising with too many extraneous questions.

Simon noticed, too late, that their table was next to the approach to the ladies' toilet, which sparked some very unsubtle staring and nudging by Miks and Ingus every time a woman under the age of seventy made her way there and back. Sensing trouble, Simon resolved to move on after the current drink – that wasn't to be soon enough as it transpired.

On her second trip to the washroom one of the pub's female patrons, a hard-looking, forty-something blonde, decided that enough was enough. Casually picking up a half-consumed pint of bitter she launched the contents at the leering Latvians. Simon and Lauris froze as the arc of ale emerged from the glass and seemed to hang in the air before hitting Miks fully in the face.

"Ave a good gawp at that yer pair of gorillas,' came the accompanying advice as she placed the glass back on the table and strode back towards her friends at the bar.

Despite lacking the benefit of a translation from a cowed Lauris the two guests erupted into laughter at this peculiar local custom, banging each other on the shoulder in pantomime mirth.

As the landlord and two of the woman's male companions looked over menacingly at the sodden table Simon opted for a strategic, and rapid, withdrawal. Ushering his three charges out of the door while issuing plaintive apologies for the 'misunderstanding' to all those within earshot, he reached the sanctuary of the Turk's Head Yard before there was any further reaction. 'Girls, girls,' echoed Miks and Ingus, by now eschewing the need for a translator.

As Simon beckoned them to follow him down Briggate he allowed himself a brief recap on the evening to date: so far, so good.

Half a mile away, at the Aubergine Door gentleman's club in York Place, Dave Rawson tipped the waitress for the bucket of ice-cold champagne she had just brought to their table. Richard Tasker's eyes were spinning faster than a government media adviser on budget day as he tried to keep himself upright. He had never been so drunk in his life and had no desire to go home just yet – things were just starting to get interesting.

As Rawson had already figured, Tasker wasn't much of a drinker, and secondly, had never been in a lap dancing bar before. As two scantily clad girls slipped into the seats either side of them Tasker bellowed out 'a drink for the ladies,' drawing an exchange of knowing looks from the hopeful prospectors who had just hit pay dirt for the night.

As a statuesque Amazonian, hailing from Dewsbury, introduced herself to Tasker as 'Rihanna' he clumsily poured the two girls a drink, not pausing to wonder why there were four glasses on the tray in the first place. Similarly, he failed to notice that an introduction from the girls to Rawson was apparently deemed unnecessary. In an environment where the expression 'time is money' carried more meaning than it did to a Swiss watchmaker, barely two minutes elapsed before Rihanna pitched the inevitable invitation to Tasker – 'would you like a dance?'

Tasker nodded his assent and looked blankly at her awaiting further instruction. 'Why don't we go through to the VIP suite for a little more privacy?' Rihanna cooed as she took his hand and gently pulled him to a standing position.

'Whatever's more comfortable,' he said, not wishing to appear unworldly as he followed her through the curtains screening the far end of the room.

Rawson was content to sit and wait patiently, sipping Champagne and chatting idly to his non-dancing companion to whom he slipped a £20 note after every second record. After thirty minutes he went to check on his friend and not long after that he was requesting the assistance of the bouncers to help him get Tasker some fresh air – apparently the combined intoxicants of alcohol and Amazon had caused him to pass out. With practiced and effortless ease, the muscle-bound custodians hoisted the sorry punter up the spiral staircase to the street above. As Tasker was eased into a taxi, Rawson pressed £50 into the driver's hand and told him to take him home. As the cab headed off towards King Street, Rawson could reflect on a job well done. Although Tasker didn't yet know it, Colton's now had another ally in the fight against Brim.

Five doors down York Place from the Aubergine Door the night was still going strong for Simon and his guests at the Freedom Lap Dancing bar. Miks and Ingus had received dances from virtually every girl in the place and were about to start at the beginning again in their variation of a penalty shoot-out competition. After every dance, cashier for the night Simon dispensed £10 notes to the girls on behalf of the Latvians, an arrangement that didn't really meet with the dancers' approval as it reduced the possibility of tips. By now Simon had given up on rounds of drinks and had simply ordered a bottle of Vodka which Miks and Ingus continued to help themselves to with unceasing appetite. As sign language was a more than adequate form of communication in this scenario Lauris and his interpretation skills were largely redundant. Simon kept him there for the time being, just in case.

At a given signal from the DJ one of the girls stepped on to the raised dais in front of his booth and started to perform a series of gyrations on the pole that appeared to be holding the club ceiling up. Ingus, inspired by this display of athleticism, decided it was a good moment to throw a few shapes of his own. Stripping his shirt off with far greater dexterity and speed than any of the girls had hitherto displayed, he leaped on to the dais to join her. Primed to be on alert for such outward displays of emotion from customers, the girl made a nimble dismount from the pole and bolted for the dressing room. Now faced with an empty platform Ingus assumed the classic default position of the drunken stage crasher by leaping on to the vacant pole where he managed three complete rotations before two doormen interrupted his manoeuvres.

As they dragged him to the exit, Simon, a cheering Miks and a shell-shocked Lauris had no choice but to follow. Outside on the pavement, Simon instructed his young translator to tell the Latvians that it was now home time and that he'd be meeting them in reception at 9am. As they staggered the three hundred metres to their hotel Simon reflected on a highly satisfactory evening in his ongoing campaign for Brim's salvation.

CHAPTER FIFTEEN

Another morning, another hangover.

As he woke up most days with a hangover it would be inaccurate to say Godfrey was feeling the worse for wear. He was merely feeling like he felt most mornings. Godfrey sat at his kitchen table and tapped the top of his soft-boiled egg with a teaspoon. Two eggs with a round of white toast and a pot of strong tea would soon set him up for the day. Radio Four, the volume turned down, provided low background chatter as he turned to the sports pages of the Daily Telegraph to study the cricket scores. Opposite him stood the empty chair long vacated by his wife, Sadie, who had gone to the great pavilion in the sky some ten seasons before. Cricketing metaphors were never far away where Godfrey was concerned – he would still tell people that his wife of forty summers had been given out for sixty-three, caught behind by the grim reaper. He missed her terribly.

He wondered what she would have thought of his latest escapade, signing up for Brandon's Brim campaign? Godfrey always had plenty to say but rarely on behalf of a cause other than the liking of his own voice. Now he was going to pitch in to help put Brim on the map and influence a positive outcome from Brussels. As he started on his second egg – always at the small end, never the big end – he felt a pang of apprehension at agreeing to expose himself in this way; it could end in ridicule and ignominy after all. Deep down, Godfrey knew his compulsion to always get the first and last words into any conversation was a carefully constructed stratagem against this very outcome.

Brandon had asked him a very simple question – what would it mean to him if the brewery suffered the ultimate setback of losing its bid? He'd not really thought about it before but realised that not only would it affect the town it would very much hit his favourite watering hole, and if that was the case it would very much impact on him. Nobody had really talked about it in the pub before now, probably not wanting to tempt fate, but it was fairly clear that if Brim lost its cachet the coaches would stop coming in, the tourists would disappear – and Godfrey's daily sport would be severely affected. Everybody knew that Godfrey's cavils about tourists were fictitious. They were his audience, and he didn't want the curtain bringing down just yet. He regretted, not for the first time, voting Leave in the referendum. He'd not thought that through, had he?

And when Brandon told him what he had in mind for his contribution he couldn't help but feel a flush of pride – yes, that was very well thought through, give him credit for that. He looked at his watch and spoke to Bouncer, sitting patiently at his feet. 'Come on lad. Let's get down the cemetery and tell Sadie all about my starring role. Reckon we've time before the covers came off at the Fountain Head.'

Breakfast was the last thing on Richard Tasker's mind as he retched into the bowl his wife Debbie had thoughtfully left next to his bedside. That gesture, however, was the extent of her kindly ministrations as she now unmercifully berated him over the state he had got himself into the previous evening. When Richard failed to arrive home as expected she'd called and texted him a dozen times but had received no response until nearly nine o'clock when he sent her a text that said *havjecv drink. Wit clinet. Her soooon* When her husband did arrive home two hours later, helped to the front door by a less-than-impressed taxi driver, Debbie's earlier concerns turned to withering contempt at the sight of her husband's intemperance. Most of her invective simply passed him by given his sensory faculties were jammed due to inebriation – nevertheless, he gleaned that the general drift was not overly sympathetic. Under this onslaught, and desperate for the sanctuary of his bed, he had crawled up the stairs and flung himself, fully dressed, on top of the duvet. Debbie, disgusted, had turned the light off and slammed the door.

This morning he was faced with a difficult choice. Go to work in the state he was in, or remain at home for more tongue-lashing? In the end, his inability to get out of bed determined the outcome. Debbie was feeling no less charitable towards him than she had the night before and continued to terrorise him with a succession of enquiries – who had he been with, where, what had they been doing and why hadn't he called? It was a blessing, albeit a small one, that despite her ire she didn't accuse him of being with another woman.

Tasker, his mind still a whirl of confusion, took his punishment stoically. In the end, unmoved by his monotonous mantra – *I don't know what got into me and I'm really sorry* – Debbie left him to stew in his own juice. Alone in the bedroom he tried to assemble the thousand-piece jigsaw of the previous evening without the aid of the lid. He knew, instantaneously, that Rawson had played him for a fool. He'd set the whole thing up, and he had fallen for it. How could he have been so naive? Had he given away information on Brim? He tried desperately to remember what they'd talked about but all he could recall was cycles, gears and GPS performance analytics. He'd surely maintained a strict confidentiality over work-related issues? He had told Rawson that he couldn't talk about Brim in any case. Maybe he had mentioned that the bid was looking all over bar the shouting once the new forensics report was completed, but that was just stating a fact, not belying any great insider intelligence to Rawson. No, despite Rawson's insidious sleuthing, he'd maintained his professional standards.

But what about his personal standards? The image of Rihanna escorting him into the VIP suite at the club flashed in his brain and a cold sweat pricked his forehead. He couldn't remember anything after that point. Had anything happened? It was all a blur. How on earth could he have got himself into such a situation? One thing was for sure, he was never going to drink again, and he was going to make up for his beastly behaviour to Debbie and Ben. As for Rawson, he was going to give him what for. Tomorrow, when he'd recovered.

Two labourers who had made it into work were Miks and Ingus who were tucking into a plate of egg and bacon sandwiches thoughtfully provided by Simon before they set to their analytical endeavours. That they both looked in a shocking state after their night out in Leeds was of little surprise. Lauris had finally roused them from their beds in the Queen's Hotel at 9.30am, and it was 11am before they arrived at the brewery. Their flight back to Riga left at 4.30pm so they had a lot to do in the interim.

Fortified by their elevenses, Simon took them down to the aquifer where they could observe the water being drawn from source. Miks opened his metal case and started to pull out various test tubes, chemical strips, probes and scales which he spread out on the floor of the pump room. Through Lauris, Simon asked if they required any further help from his technical team only to be met with a sullen headshake from Ingus. As the two Latvians set to work, shuffling about filling test tubes, checking gauges and scribbling notes, Simon's chief engineer kept throwing astonished looks at his boss– they were certainly employing a different methodology to that of the usual technicians.

After two hours of the Latvians' to-ing and fro-ing, cavernous yawns, wiping of sweaty brows and incomprehensible grumbling, Simon sent Lauris across to ask Miks and Ingus if they wanted a brief break for lunch. The enquiry was met with an emphatically negative response, as both appeared to loudly chastise the unfortunate translator with a string of what Simon presumed to be Latvian profanities. The postgraduate, clearly flustered at this outburst, turned to Simon, a desperate appeal for further instructions etched on his face. Before Simon could intervene, and as Miks and Ingus appeared to crank up the barracking a further notch, the unfortunate Lauris suddenly stepped backwards, directly onto the rack of test tubes containing the day's samples that had been haphazardly placed on the floor. The crunch of broken glass stopped the scientists' diatribe in its tracks – Miks simply held his head in his hands while Ingus started to kick the huge holding tank in exasperation at their wasted efforts.

As Lauris bolted out of the door it was left to Simon to take control of the situation. Using sign language, he beckoned the two Latvians to follow him and escorted them to his office. As the two boffins engaged in frantic discussion he sent out a search party for Lauris. Ten minutes later, the petrified student having been lured back, they were able to collectively address the problem with which they were now confronted. For the first time during the visit, meaningful communication seemed to be taking place. In between an ongoing litany of insults directed at Lauris, Simon was able to ascertain that Miks and Ingus didn't have time to redo the work lost today and would need to return at another date, especially as they still had to inspect the aquifer itself. Simon explained that this was not acceptable as the report needed to be delivered to the EU commissioners. After much shoulder shrugging, Simon hit upon a solution – what if he were to provide them with the analytical data and photos collected during the last test, which was only done four months ago in any case? That way, they could complete their report, sample a beer at source and make their plane without rushing. After a brief exchange a relieved Lauris was able to confirm that this arrangement would be most satisfactory indeed to the Latvians as long as no one found out about it. Simon assured them that was the last thing that was going to happen.

'Looks like the fat lady's about to sing, then,' Mervyn said as he took in the news that Brimdale Brewery's application to the EU appeared to be heading towards a positive outcome – for their rivals.

'Well, that's what the Defra guy let slip last night,' confirmed Dave Rawson. 'All over bar the shouting in his view.'

'Kinda loose-lipped of him. Are you sure he wasn't spinning you a line?'

'No, pretty sure of that. He's the serious sort. I'm taking his comment at face value,' replied the Colton's boss, being particularly careful not to expand upon the circumstances of his intercourse with Richard Tasker.

'So where do we go from here?'

'Our offer is still on the table. You never know.'

'Pull the other one, Dave. Admit it, you've lost this one. You need to be working on our contingency plan right now.'

'Not necessarily. He thought they'd be home and dry once the latest forensics report was signed off. But, if there was something wrong with that report then the game would swing back in our favour.'

'Highly unlikely. You're clutching at straws. Dave, really, you gotta knock this one on the head. If Brimdale know that there's just a report standing between them and the EU ruling, they'll already know they've won. They'll tell you to stick your offer – in fact, I'm surprised they haven't already.'

'No news is good news – the fact they haven't turned us down means they're still considering it.'

'Listen, Dave, I admire your optimism, but it's time to let it go, believe me.' Mervyn was becoming a tad irritated at Dave's obsession with Brim, which appeared to be clouding his judgement. You can't win them all was Mervyn's experience – that's business, that's life. The cardinal sin was to keep wasting time and money on lost causes. 'Give it up for Chrissake and concentrate on what we do after the ruling. At least you've got a heads-up now.'

Rawson tried his best to cover the disappointment he felt as he bade farewell to his boss four thousand miles away. While there was no reason the latest forensic analysis should be different to the previous ten reports, any doubt, any doubt at all, could put back the timetable and place Brimdale under impossible pressure. That's where he had to place his focus.

As he ruminated on the dilemma his e-mail pinged and he glanced at his screen to see if it was important. It was from Simon Backhouse's solicitor:

Dear Mr Rawson

I have received instructions on behalf of my client, Simon Backhouse, to the effect that they wish to decline the indicative offer made on behalf of Monumental Breweries Inc./Colton's to acquire Brimdale Brewery. In addition, my client wishes to state, for the record, that Brimdale Brewery is not for sale and requests that you desist from making any further speculative offers of this nature in future.

Rawson slowly shook his head and cursed loudly. He knew what Mervyn would say if he forwarded this email to him. He hit the delete button.

At that exact moment, his mobile rang – it was Brandon Todd. Maybe he had better news for him?

'Brandon, good to hear from you. I hope you've had time to consider my proposition?'

'Well, that's why I'm calling, actually.'

Rawson held his breath. *Come on, give me some good news* he silently urged the caller on the other end of the line. 'Great. So have you given them backword, then?' Rawson made it a point of principle never to show weakness or resignation in any encounter.

'No, Dave, I'm afraid I haven't. I've decided to stick with the Brim campaign after all. Sorry – that's not what you wanted to hear.'

Rawson clenched his fists and just about managed to get his next sentence out without erupting. 'Is there any particular reason for your decision?'

'I have to say, Dave, it was a very close-run thing. I gave it a lot of thought, really weighed it up long and hard but in the end the Brim offer just edged yours by the thinnest of margins.'

Rawson didn't like disappointment in his life. 'I think you've just made one almighty big mistake. I hope you remember this when the wheels come off the bus,' he said tersely.

Brandon, enjoying himself in this unusual reversal of

roles for an agency man, neatly wound up the call with a conciliatory, 'Well, maybe sometime in the future? "Never say never" and all that?' God, Brandon had waited years to put a client on the receiving end of the standard agency 'gentle letdown'.

Rawson slammed the phone down and cursed loudly for the second time in two minutes. Had he lost? Should he give it up? Not bloody likely. Dave Rawson was no quitter. Not while there was still a chance over the forensic report. He was going to have to call on the services of his new best friend again.

CHAPTER SIXTEEN

Peggy was keen to keep Brian's mind off the Brim shoot. Following the first flush of enthusiasm a fortnight back, when Brian had said 'yes' to Brandon, Peggy had detected the occasional doubt over what he was letting himself in for. She'd talked it though with him twice now with Brian remaining adamant that it was the right thing to do, for him, for Brim, and therefore for Peggy – he wasn't going to pull out now. Hoping that he did know what he was doing, Peggy had decided that she wasn't going to mention it at all tonight – they were going to have a nice relaxing night off instead.

After they'd finished their evening meal – a delicate angel hair pasta with shrimp, chilli and tomato that Brian threw together in five minutes flat – he had a suggestion to pass the time. 'You know that you said that you'd tell me more about your Mam and Dad? Do you feel up to it now?'

Normally, the mere mention of her mother and father would have caused Peggy to bring the shutters down on any conversation but with Brian it was different. For the first time in her life she didn't have to shoulder, alone, the grief that had never consented to leave her – now she had a partner with whom to share her thoughts and her concerns. She had only known Brian for two months or so but the love she felt for him made it impossible to imagine being without him. Life had truly started the day he'd walked into the Fountain Head and told her how to polish her candelabra.

'I've not talked to anyone about Mam and Dad for years, you know that, don't you?'

'Yes. I know,' Brian said. 'I think it would be good for you to talk about them. Your mother in particular sounds a remarkable woman, and anyway I want to know what traits you've inherited from her. You're a remarkable woman too.'

'Do you really think flattery will work on me, Mr Parkin?'

'I'm counting on it.'

Peggy paused. 'Do you know, I am ready. Come on.' With that she stood up and gestured Brian to follow her into the spare bedroom.

Brian, about to make a wisecrack about what she had in mind, bit his lip. He knew that this was not the time for levity.

Peggy opened the wardrobe door to reveal two large storage boxes stacked in the bottom. 'Can you get those out?' she asked Brian. Colourful artefacts gleamed mysteriously within the two opaque plastic containers, like the treasures of Tutankhamen's tomb about to see the light of day after thousands of years.

Brian placed the boxes on the floor next to the bed and waited for Peggy to make the next move.

'It's almost twenty years since I last looked at these,' she said. 'I'm glad you're here with me.'

She lifted the lid of the first box and took the uppermost item, a large scrapbook, out. As they flicked through the stiff cardboard pages covered with Sellotape-edged newspaper cuttings, Brian realised that Peggy's mother's wrestling was no idle occupation – she had clearly been something of a celebrity in a sport that, back then, enjoyed popularity.

The yellowing and aged cuttings from both local and national newspapers caused them to chuckle at headlines like 'How wrestling brings out the beast in pub landlady,' and 'No holds barred when it comes to winning.'

'I see the papers haven't improved their headline writing skills over the years,' Brian noted.

Next, Peggy exhumed from the box a series of wrestling bills that depicted her mother's rise from undercard to headline status at such stout-hearted venues as Leeds Town Hall, Belle Vue King's Hall, Hanley Victoria Hall, Liverpool Stadium and Bridlington Spa Royal Hall. The posters, with their block lettering and solid black, red and blue colouring, had the appearance of Victorian Music Hall playlists where no concession to an unfamiliar layout could be allowed when as much information as possible needed to be conveyed to an eager public.

Peggy picked up an ancient copy of the TV Times that carried colour photographs of Wendy in the ring as well as in her everyday clothes behind the bar of the Fountain Head. 'She looks just like you in this one,' Brian said. 'She'd be proud of you and how you've managed without her, I'll bet,' he added.

At the bottom of the storage box was a handbill, with a

picture of the Beast of Bishopsgate drinking a pint of beer. Underneath was the legend: 'Brim is proud to support The Beast of Bishopsgate.'

'Look, early sponsorship,' Brian said excitedly. '"Proud to support" – it's not exactly sophisticated is it? She was a trailblazer in more ways than one getting that sort of support back then.'

'I never realised that Brim had given her any backing. Good on them,' replied Peggy. 'She must have been very persuasive.'

'She's passed that on too.'

Peggy took the lid off the second box, which contained mainly garments. 'Look at the embroidery on this,' she said as she unfurled a heavy black satin ring robe with an image of a she-wolf and 'The Beast of Bishopsgate' picked out in red and yellow silk on the back.

'You should use that as a dressing gown,' teased Brian, his wonder and admiration growing for this fighter of yesteryear.

'Just watch it, you,' Peggy warned.

Brian picked up a seven-inch record sleeve that had been secreted under the robe.

'What about this?' he said as he read the cover. '"Lady Wrestler" by Gags. She even had a record written about her. That's amazing.'

'I'd forgotten about that.'

'She really was famous wasn't she? How does it go?'

'I don't know, and I don't have a record player anymore.'

'We've got to find one,' Brian enthused. 'How brilliant.'

By now Peggy was rummaging in the bottom of the box and pulled out, judging by the numerous photographs they'd seen, her mother's standard wrestling costume of black leotard with a she-wolf emblem, black fishnet tights and white lace-up boots.

Brian's eyes lit up. 'Just look at that,' he said. 'She was hardly a beast dressed like that. She must have sent the punters wild.'

'I didn't know you were partial to sportswear.'

'That's not sportswear, Peggy. I reckon that's as sexy as any negligee or lingerie if you ask me.'

Peggy wasn't sure if Brian was being serious or not. 'Are you taking the Mickey, Brian?'

'No. Not at all. It's very fetching.' Then, 'I don't suppose…'

Catching his drift, she tittered. 'Brian! You naughty, naughty man.'

'You'd look fantastic in it, honestly. I'm getting all hot and bothered just thinking about it. In fact, I'm going out of the room, giving you five minutes and when I come back in I want you ring ready.' With that, and without entertaining any form of protest, Brian dashed out the door.

Peggy looked at her mother's costume. Could she? Was this some sort of desecration of her mother's memory or was she just being a spoilsport? Brian was clearly excited, and so was she if she was being truthful.

Exactly five minutes later the door flew open and Brian, swiftly stripped down to his boxer shorts and wearing a towelling robe from the bathroom, paraded in humming a fanfare on an imaginary trumpet. He stopped mid-note as he took in the sight of Peggy in her mother's costume.

'Ladies and Gentlemen…' he mock announced. Then, in his own voice, 'Do you want the red corner or the blue?' Without waiting for an answer he launched himself towards Peggy and pushed her playfully on to the bed. The element of surprise was always crucial in bouts of this nature.

Cora was spending the evening shuffling through a sheaf of handwritten notes on the desk in front of her – she liked to plan her writing by creating a series of pictograms and charts to sketch out plot, sub-plot, story arc and characters. Having spent a fortnight in the brewery archives her ideas were beginning to gel and an outline was forming. Cora's training at the British Museum was more than handy in tackling the heap of manuscripts and ledgers she found – it was evident nobody had looked at them for years, never mind organise them. She'd pinpointed an era around the building of the Priory in the fourteenth century for her first sweep. At this stage in her thinking she rather fancied that the central character for her new book should be a Brother Gilbert whose name made frequent appearances in the archives she'd unearthed so far, from young novice up to Prior over a thirty-five-year period. However, she was determined to keep her options open until she'd taken stock of all the years the Priory had functioned. Tomorrow, she'd earmarked for study a particularly dusty set of tomes she calculated were from the sixteenth century – she was in her element.

Her mind turned from Gilbert to Brandon. When

Alicia had conspired to so rudely interrupt their tender moment two weeks before, he'd taken it as a cue to make a hurried departure. Cora had gone upstairs to attend to Alicia barely able to suppress her anger at her mother's intercession, particularly as it was to complain that she couldn't sleep because of the noise of the wind. Cora was convinced that Brandon must somehow have welcomed this 'lucky escape' and her sense of embarrassment knew no bounds.

The next morning, however, Brandon had telephoned to say how disappointed he'd been not to be able to spend more time with her. Since then, he'd been in touch every day, initially about the song and the shoot but after a couple of days without any pretext. The warmth of his feelings for her was unmistakeable. Now he was due back in Brimdale for the shoot she was almost giddy with expectation.

Two bedrooms along she could hear Alicia snoring. At least she was asleep. In the three long months Cora had been back in Brimdale her mother's health had at least stabilised. While her coughing bouts and gasps for breath cut right through Cora, her mother could still manage the short walks outside of the house as long as her daughter pushed her wheel chair and the oxygen bottle was to hand for emergencies. Despite her frailty, Alicia insisted that Cora continue to undertake her book research and generally encouraged her to spend most of the day outside Brim Over Hall. It was as if she preferred Jean looking after her, maybe because it was more relaxing not to have her daughter constantly within her sights. Cora, instinctively understanding the effort it cost Alicia to deliver her cantankerous and shrill commentaries, didn't resist this indulgence.

Despite her genuine concern over her mother's health Cora was unable to stem the deep irritation she felt every time Alicia opened her mouth. It was as if the only thing that was keeping her mother going now was the opportunity to upbraid her daughter, or that's how if felt to her. Her illness hadn't diminished her ability to dish it out – the opposite in fact, as she seemed to thrive on it. Should she resent her mother in this way when she was so poorly and didn't have long left on this earth? Cora knew that, as merciful releases went, her own would rank in equal measure with Alicia's when the inevitable happened.

Dave Rawson had wondered how long it would take Richard Tasker to call him to fill in the missing details. Two days to be exact. Racked with guilt, Tasker was determined to set the record straight and draw a line under the excesses of the ill-fated evening he'd shared with the man from Colton's. He was concerned that news of his fall from grace should go no further than the man who had led him astray. As it turned out, Rawson was in no position to offer him instant absolution.

'Richard. I'm glad you've called. Coincidence, as I was just about to call you.'

'Yes, quite,' Tasker said, before launching into his carefully prepared *mea culpa*. 'Look, I'm afraid things got a little out of hand the other night. That was most untypical of me – I rarely drink. I can't imagine what came over me.' Rawson didn't respond, turning the screw by forcing Tasker to keep on talking in order to fill the silence. 'I mean, I wouldn't have even been out for a drink if you hadn't persuaded me.' Rawson knew Tasker didn't have the guts to accuse him outright of planning events so continued to grant him the floor. 'As you can imagine, it was very awkward when I got home. My wife was less than pleased.' Still not receiving a reply, Tasker felt compelled to carry on. 'I'd prefer it if we could just forget that the evening took place at all.' Hearing static from the other end of the line he added, 'Are you still there?'

Rawson decided he could now take a swipe at the ball. 'Look, Richard. What goes on tour stays on tour normally but, as it happens, we do have a slight problem.' Again, a long pause to crank up Tasker's anxiety. 'You remember that club we went to?'

Tasker, who hadn't mentioned the club in the hope that a lack of acknowledgement may somehow neutralise its existence, could remember it only too well. 'The one we were in briefly?'

'I don't know about briefly, but the Aubergine Door, yes. It appears that you may have let your guard down in there.'

'Let my guard down? How do you mean?'

'Well, I wasn't there when you went for a private dance, but the girl you were with, Rihanna, said you were a bit more forward than they're used to, which is saying quite a bit in there.'

'That's ridiculous,' protested Tasker, the panic in his voice rising. 'Nothing happened. I know it didn't.'

'You passed out, didn't you, so how can you be so sure?'

'I fell asleep; I didn't pass out.'

'Same difference, isn't it?'

'I most certainly didn't "drop my guard" as you say.'

'I've not got on to that yet. I know you dropped your guard because I've seen the evidence.'

'Evidence, what evidence?'

'You fell for the oldest trick in the book, Richard. When you passed out – sorry, fell asleep – she took some photos of you and her on her mobile phone. I've seen them – it doesn't look good.'

Tasker could barely breath. 'What's on the photos?' he asked meekly.

'You with your head buried in her chest. You can see the two of you, and the two of them, plain as day.'

'You've seen these photos?'

'Yes, I have. There are three of them. It's you all right.'

'She didn't have a mobile on her.' Richard could remember that much.

'I think you're clutching at straws there. She's done you up.'

'But why would she?'

'It's the girls' insurance policy against gropers, or drunks if they're too far-gone to notice. You were both apparently.'

As his world imploded Tasker tried desperately to piece the significance of these revelations together. 'What's she going to do with them?'

'I'd have thought that was rather obvious – take advantage of them.'

'But she doesn't know who I am.'

'She does. She'd have made sure she found out but

154

that wasn't necessary as you gave her your business card anyway.'

'Good God. What am I going to do?' He imagined his grand arraignment; Debbie, Ben, his parents, his colleagues at Defra and the captain of his cycling club all lined up in the jury box to pass judgement on his indiscretion.

'We're going to have to buy her off. It's a simple transaction. Find out what she wants and do a trade.'

'Money? How much money? I'm not a wealthy man.'

'Listen, Richard, leave this with me, and I'll see what I can manage. I feel a little bit responsible for taking you there, so it's the least I can do.'

'I'd be very grateful if you could help,' said Tasker, struggling for any form of life support to hand.

'The thing is, Richard, not to panic, and not to show fear. There's always a deal to be done.'

His spirit crushed and ground into a million tiny pieces, Tasker could only hope Rawson was right.

CHAPTER SEVENTEEN

Brandon Todd was in his element as the strands of the campaign drew together. He was running through preparations with Simon at the brewery – the countdown to the launch was ticking down. Simon's attire for today's important catch-up meeting included a plain white t-shirt with the slogan *Working Class Hero* spelled out in thick black capitals. The irony of the description tickled the PR adviser as he set about his update. Despite the perpetual dress-down garb favoured by his client Brandon had yet to abandon his own standard wardrobe principles, although it was no less ironic that Brandon considered his dress sense – smart suit, shirt and no-tie – to be relaxed, cool and casual.

Brandon ran through the list of names he'd recruited for the campaign to date. Simon was impressed at the PR's powers of persuasion but thought he'd spotted an omission. 'What about Martha Clamp? Have you approached her?'

'Martha. The witch? No, Simon, I don't want to go there.'

Looking slightly disappointed, Simon made one last bid. 'She's been ever so helpful and she's quirky, in a good sort of way. I thought she'd fit in really well.'

'I can see where you're coming from, Simon, but she's going to clash with the rest. Trust me.' Brandon couldn't resist joshing his client a little. 'You seem very keen on her – has she cast some sort of spell on you?'

'Very funny. I suppose I feel indebted to her, although she doesn't know it. Without her I'd never have got the idea for all the healthcare products I'm planning for Brim.'

'You want to be careful what you say, or she'll be after you for royalties.'

'I doubt that, but I'd like to do something for her if we get the chance to push on with the health side of things.'

Brandon pulled a face. 'Homeopathy is great, Simon, but effectively saying, "as recommended by witches" isn't going to make product fly off the shelf.'

'I know, I know,' Simon conceded.

'You've been inspired by her, not pinched her idea. It's not like Alexander Graham Bell and Elisha Gray fighting over who invented the telephone. You don't owe her anything.'

'I thought Alexander Graham Bell did invent the telephone?'

'Well, there you go then. Ideas are up for grabs; just make sure you hire the best lawyer when it comes to registering them.'

'But Martha's already selling bottled water and ointments made from Brim. Just locally of course.'

'How can she get the water to make them?'

Simon looked sheepish. 'I supply it to her. Have been doing for three or four years now.'

'You're giving her your main trade secret and inviting

her to make money off your back? I'd knock that on the head, Simon.'

'I was just being helpful. I thought it was a good idea at the time.'

'It's not now, though, is it? I'd stop that if I were you. Unless you're afraid she'll turn you into a toad?'

'I get the point,' Simon said, wearily.

In the Fountain Head, Gary and Howard were discussing the shoot. Gary had needed little persuasion to take part and was bursting to talk about it with other participants. Brandon, however, had placed everybody under a strict 'don't spoil the surprise' embargo in a bid to keep their powder dry for the campaign launch and Gary in particular was finding the furtiveness a strain.

'Gud job yer init, or ah wunt bi able t'mention it ter anyone wi' all this secrecy,' said Gary.

'I can see the point of the confidentiality,' Howard replied as he treated himself to a pineapple juice for a change.

'Yeah, me too, but it's killin' mi not tellin' folk.'

'Well it won't be long now.'

'I dunt even know 'oo's init besides me and thee.'

'I must confess, it was a surprise to be asked,' Howard said. 'You're in it on merit, Gary, of course, but I think I was an afterthought, probably in recognition of my work on the BBA.'

Godfrey, passing their table with Bouncer and picking up on the whispered conversation, slipped into the empty chair, a conspiratorial glint in his eye. 'You too?' he enquired.

'Mighta known you'd be init, Godfrey. No show without Punch,' Gary said.

Howard, a tad more polite, confirmed Godfrey's guess. 'Yes, both of us, although I must say we're not too sure what we're going to have to do.'

'Me neither,' Godfrey confessed. 'I just know when and where to meet both days, and Mr PR said we'd take it from there.'

'Is Bouncer init too?' asked Gary. 'Ah know you two dunt like to be parted.'

'No. He's been broken-hearted for days at the news,' Godfrey deadpanned.

'I'd git yur agent on t'hat if ah wur you,' Gary said.

'I am his agent,' Godfrey averred.

'Ah'd bet if that dog cud talk it've plenty of secrets to spill.' Gary was chancing his arm now.

'Possibly, but I doubt he'd share them with you,' was Godfrey's final word on this particular exchange.

'I'm sure they know what they're doing,' ventured Howard as he steered the conversation back to the wider aspects of the campaign. 'It seems a long way off from when Gary and me were at the helm. For the better, I mean,' before adding quickly, 'No offence, Gary.'

'Nun taken.' Gary's view of Brandon's talents had shifted somewhat since being entrusted with a key role in the campaign.

'Who else is in it? Do you know?' Godfrey asked.

'Havn't a clue. Wi know as much as you do,' Gary said.

Howard, recalling his ambassadorial choice for Brim had yet to feature in any marketing, asked, 'Do you think Brian Parkin will be in it?'

Gary just shrugged – his guess was as good as anyone else's.

Godfrey was no better informed. 'Whether he is, or whether he isn't, won't make much difference to him now he's moved in over the shop. He looks as well accommodated as the dairy cat these days. He'll cope whether he's in it or not, I'd say.'

Howard nodded sagely and left it to Gary to say what they were all thinking: 'Lucky bugger.'

The 'lucky bugger' in question had joined Brandon in Simon's office to discuss the press conference at which the TV chef and the brewery boss were to play major roles. As Brandon went through the questions to expect and the points to emphasise he could see that Brian was a natural performer – no wonder he'd been so successful on television. How cruel and unfair the treatment he'd received after being falsely accused and hung out to dry by the media. How viciously his ex-wife had reacted to his career meltdown. Now Brandon hoped he could help redress that balance.

Simon, too, impressed Brandon with his grasp of the sound bite as he practiced what he would be saying to journalists. It was all coming together – when this week's shoots were edited Brandon would set the media ball rolling.

As they wrapped up their meeting Brian suddenly noticed the record deck and LPs lined up behind the settee he'd been sitting on. 'Does that turntable work?' he asked Simon.

'Course it does. Couldn't manage without it,' Simon said.

'It's just that I've got a record I want to listen to and I don't know anybody who has a record player these days.'

'Well, you do now. Be my guest. Bring it round any time.'

'I don't need to do that,' Brian said. 'I have it with me here, now.'

'Stick it on, then,' Simon encouraged. 'Who is it by?'

Itching to hear it, but not wanting to disclose too much information about its origin, Brian dissembled somewhat. 'Oh, I just came across it by chance, and it was intriguing me.'

Brian changed the deck speed to 45 rpm and lifted the needle on to the run-in groove, sending a rumble through the speakers. As the song started up a heavy pounding beat and prominent stabbing piano could be heard before the singer came in:

I can't eat my dinner
I can't sleep at night
I go out in the evening
Looking for a fight
Because my baby
She just told me everything
She was a lady wrestler
'Til she got banned from the ring

'Somebody you know, Brian?' Simon laughed as he took in the opening lyrics.

'Shush,' Brandon hissed as the vocalist tilted straight into the second verse:

161

I know she ain't no beauty
I know she's overweight
But how was I to know
She was the beast from Bishopsgate?

'Bishopsgate? Bishopsgate in London?' Brandon queried.

'There's one here in Brimdale too,' Simon said.

Brian wondered if he should take the 45 off now but knew it was too late. Besides he wanted to hear the rest.

As the up-tempo beat continued its unrelenting pace Brandon said, 'Brian, this is absolutely hilarious. Where did you get it from?'

Brian was able to ignore this query as the singer thankfully continued the narrative:

You know last night when we were making love
She aroused my suspicion
She held me in a Boston Crab
And called for a submission

Now Brian couldn't wipe the smile off his face thinking back to his night of wrestling-inspired lovemaking with Peggy.

Much to Simon's approval, a guitar break now dominated for the next thirty seconds. 'Great playing. Sounds like Clapton. It's not is it?'

'Haven't a clue,' said Brian, who in any case couldn't tell a banjo from a bass guitar.

Finally, there was one more sentiment that the singer had to share:

You know I'm too scared to tell my baby
Our romance is through
You see I don't want no broken bones,
You'd be frightened too

As the chorus once more confirmed that indiscipline had concluded a promising career in the oldest form of combat sport, the three men clutched their sides with laughter.

'I've got to get a copy of that,' said Simon.

'You can copy it? That would be great,' said Brian. 'On to a cassette?'

'No, Brian. I'll create an MP3 file directly on to my computer. I can email it to you too if that's OK.'

'Me too, if you wouldn't mind. I've got to hear that again,' added Brandon. 'Come on though, Brian, what's the story? Where did you get it from?'

'I'm a dead man if I tell you.'

Brandon offered his customary reassurance to protestations of this nature. 'You can tell us, Brian. We're not going to tell anyone.'

'Yes, come on, Brian. It's a fantastic song. Tell us more,' added Simon.

Brian hesitated. Should he tell? He was in fact terribly proud of the record he'd just heard. How many people have songs written about them?

'You have to swear not to breathe a word. That song's about Peggy's mother. She was a female wrestler, a big celebrity back in the day. She died when Peggy was barely in her twenties and she's never really gotten over it.'

'She's kept that quiet,' Simon said.

'Yes. She doesn't like it to be mentioned but I think

we might be breaking that down now. We had a look at all of her mother's wrestling gear and cuttings the other night. It was like confronting a ghost for her. That's when I found the record. I was dying to hear it.'

'Peggy's kept all of her mother's memorabilia?' Brandon said.

'Yes – we even found a promo sheet with Brim on it – they used to sponsor her apparently.'

This was news to Simon, despite his command of the brewery's history. 'Really? When was that?'

'Well, she died twenty years back, so before then.'

'I wonder if she'd be interested in letting us use that in our museum?' Simon asked.

Brian didn't like the way the conversation was going. 'I don't think she'd be up for that, no, Simon.'

'But it's a great story,' said Brandon, now with his news editor's hat on.

'One that she doesn't want to go any further,' Brian reminded him.

'The last thing we would want to do is upset Peggy,' Simon said with some conviction.

Brandon said nothing, as his mind was already on to the next move.

CHAPTER EIGHTEEN

Richard Tasker stood facing the Aubergine Door – a door that was locked firmly in his face. Unable to concentrate at work he had decided to come down to the club to sort matters out once and for all. It was evident the club wasn't going to open for some while. He should have known that but he had to do something. Quite what he was going to do had the club been open he hadn't quite figured out but it felt like affirmative action, which had to be better than waiting around for Rawson to call. It had been a week since he'd learned the awful truth of his evening out and he'd barely eaten or slept since. All he could think about was how stupid he'd been to get himself embroiled in a situation like this and the disaster that exposure spelled for him. It was all Rawson's fault, and he couldn't be entirely sure he was being on the level with him. How he wished he could turn the clock back and never have set eyes on this place. He pulled out his mobile and called Rawson.

'I'm at the Aubergine Door. I couldn't wait any longer.'

Rawson sounded shocked. 'What are you doing down there? You could ruin everything.'

'I need to sort this problem out.'

'I understand that, but I told you not to panic. Have you seen anybody there?

'No. It's all locked up.'

'Right – walk up to Park Place and I'll meet you there in ten minutes. Believe me, we can sort this out. Keep calm.'

Tasker was once more in Rawson's hands.

Fifteen minutes later, Rawson sauntered nonchalantly into Park Square. He sat down on the bench next to the stressed and besieged Defra official.

'Listen, Richard, don't look so worried. I have it all in hand.'

'You do, do you? It doesn't look like it.'

'I think the problem can be fixed without her wanting anything – this can disappear as quickly as it arose.'

'But how? You said she was going to blackmail me.'

'She was, and she still may, unless the manager leans on her to forget all about it and delete the pictures.'

'But why would he do that?'

'I know the manager well – we supply him. Let's just say that if I were to do the club a favour over stock that wasn't invoiced, he'd be more than happy to call Rihanna off. She won't want to lose her job just to rook you.'

Tasker was far from sure. 'It all sounds very dodgy.'

'Well, yes, but unfortunately it was dodgy dealings that got us here in the first place.'

'But not invoicing for goods it's, well, it's fraud isn't it?'

'It's not exactly above board, no, but then again, with what she's got on you I don't think you can afford to be so moral all of a sudden. We'll stick it in the marketing and samples budget.'

Even when glimpsing an escape route, Tasker's mind still worked analytically. 'Why would you do this for me?'

'If I can help you, then you can help me. I scratch your back, you scratch mine.'

Tasker's heart sank yet again – he was being played, but what on earth could he give Rawson? 'I can't possibly help you in any way.'

'Well, that's not entirely true. You mentioned that Brim was having a forensic report done as part of its EU application?'

Tasker groaned as the truth of his indiscretion was confirmed.

'All I'm asking, Richard, is that you find a reason to query that report, a pretext to throw it back.'

'Absolutely not. I can't compromise myself at work. It's an outrageous suggestion.'

'Not as outrageous as you being humiliated at work and having to explain to your wife if these pictures go public.'

'No. I won't do it. I simply won't do it.'

'Listen, Richard. I'm helping you here. I'm not asking you to change the report – I just want you to query it. You'd probably do that anyway – it's the sort of thing your lot do all the time, isn't it, carrying out cross-checks?'

'But what possible advantage would my querying the report give you? It will still be proven to be *bona fide* after a cross-check.'

'Exactly, so what's the harm? Let's just say it gives me

a little more time for our contingency planning now it looks like Brim is going to get the EU nod.'

'I'm sure you've done that already,' Tasker replied.

'Be fair, Richard. I'll have to close Brimmer down once Brim wins its application – that's going to have an impact on my staff. They're the true victims in all of this.'

Tasker looked less than sympathetic for their plight. 'No. I'm beginning to believe you've engineered this entire situation. I'm going to wait until the club opens and go in and sort this out by myself.'

Rawson smiled. 'Richard. Think about this for a minute. If you go in there and show them how desperate you are, the price will go up. You'll turn this from a normal mug punter sting into a serious blackmail opportunity for them. You really don't want to do that, believe me.'

Tasker knew Rawson had a point. 'That may well be the case, but I simply cannot agree to your request to query that report.'

'I'll tell you what, Richard. I'm assuming that the report hasn't landed yet, so why don't you mull things over? Just take your time, and make the right decision. For Debbie and Ben's sake if nothing else.'

'You are contemptible, Rawson. Do you know that?'

'Richard, all I'm guilty of is caring too much. You'll see.'

As an indignant Tasker stormed off without saying goodbye Rawson leaned back on the bench and watched him head south out of the square. Any query over that report would make it impossible for the EU to rubber-stamp Brim's geographical status application this year. A delay would be as good as a 'no' vote; Brimdale wouldn't survive another year of uncertainty – he would make sure of that. Tasker wasn't going to put ruin ahead of a little white lie, surely?

In a laboratory on the outskirts of Riga, Toms Straume of Straume Laboratories was running over the forensic report his company had just completed on the Brimdale aquifer in the UK. Receiving this commission had been a tremendous boost for his company and Toms knew that it could potentially open up considerable new business opportunities throughout the EU for him and his team. He'd been pleasantly surprised to receive an enquiry to pitch for this work and had diligently drawn up a competitive quote while stressing how flexible they were when it came to meeting deadlines. The turnaround requirement on this particular job was a few short weeks – very tight in fact but as it represented a gateway to a whole raft of new business for his company Toms was intent on making the deadline. He had no doubt that their commitment to delivering the report before the due date was instrumental in them landing the job.

The shortage of time available to complete the report prevented Toms from personally overseeing the job – he and his wife were celebrating their twenty-fifth wedding anniversary slap bang in the middle of the project. In any event, he felt it was time his two senior team members, Miks and Ingus, assumed a bit more responsibility for a change. Since arriving back in Riga both had talked endlessly about their trip to Leeds and how stimulating the assignment was for them. They also reinforced their boss's appetite for the prospect of similar work that could come their way now they had a compelling case study firmly under their belts. Certainly, he'd never seen them so enthusiastic and keen to undertake similar commissions on behalf of their employer and he was proud of their commitment and positive 'can-do' attitude.

Nevertheless, Toms knew that Miks and Ingus could sometimes lack the essential attention to detail that he himself possessed so, as a safety net on such an important job, he decided to double-check the document before sending it off.

As he sipped his coffee he read the document with meticulous care and had to confess that he was impressed. Miks and Ingus had excelled themselves in respect of the detail, layout and conclusions contained in the report – maybe he'd been a little unfair in thinking they were incapable of being as thorough as he was. Then, as he surveyed the photographs embedded in the document, his eye was drawn to a small series of numbers, hardly visible to the naked eye, in the corner of a shot of the aquifer. As he peered more closely he realised it was a date. As the numbers came into focus he realised that it was a date from four months prior to when Miks and Ingus had visited. As he continued to stare at the photograph it slowly dawned on him the reason for the report's excellence – somebody else had done it, or parts of it at least. His pride in his primary workforce somewhat eroded, Toms paced the floor as he struggled to decide what to do. Get Miks and Ingus in and read them the riot act? Invent some pretext to re-do the report? Neither would solve the problem of ruining Straume Laboratories' largest-ever sales opening.

He returned to the report and went through it

again in fine detail. Satisfied at last that there was only the one single giveaway that betrayed the origins of the analysis, he accessed the report on the main server, went to the incriminating shot and cropped it so the date was eliminated. Now it was a work of substance and authority, ready to be placed before the EU panel. As for Miks and Ingus, he'd deal with them later.

'Ambrosia. Just wait 'til you get this down you.' Tony Gleeson, a former resident of the parish of Brimdale, was back in town for a business trip and keen to impress upon his two colleagues, Martin and Ged, the provenance of the ale that he'd been brought up on. As Peggy dispensed three pints of Brim in slow rotation, allowing each one to settle before topping it up, Tony regaled his colleagues with the minutiae of his personal history. 'My first pint was in here, at this very bar. I remember it as if it were yesterday. Nectar it was.' Martin and Ged waited patiently while their boss trotted out his usual 'everything is bigger and better in Yorkshire' spiel. It appeared to be a condition of employment that they had to put up with his endless one-upmanship – he was oblivious to the comments they made behind his back that if he loved Yorkshire so bloody much why had he lived in Stoke-on-Trent for the past fifteen years?

Still, a pint was a pint, and there was no denying that, as the landlady of the Fountain Head carefully and lovingly filled the three tall straight pint glasses with golden mellifluousness, there was an expectation among the visitors of something very special indeed – the pilgrimage didn't look like it would be in vain.

As she attended to the order, Tony further reinforced his local credentials by letting on to their server. 'I used to come in here all the time when I was a lad. Best pint ever.'

Peggy, who like most publicans had a good memory for faces, couldn't recall having ever seen him before. 'Did you, love? Well, it's nice that you've looked us up again.' Tony didn't notice his underlings sniggering at this less than effusive reception for a former pub stalwart.

Finally, they were ready. Tony raised his glass in salutation to his workmates and drank long and deep, as if he'd just finished a particularly arduous shift in a poorly ventilated steel works. Martin and Ged also took large draughts of the much-heralded brew, their eyes lighting up with pleasure as, for once, Tony's swaggering lived up to its promise.

Martin was the first to speak. 'You're right, Tony. That's some pint, that is. Superb.'

Ged was similarly impressed. 'Got to hand it to you, Tony. First rate.'

Tony, however, was now sniffing suspiciously at his pint and holding it up to the light, the better to inspect the contents.

'What's the matter, Tony?' asked Martin.

Tony looked at his pint again before confiding, 'There's something not quite right here. It's OK, but not as good as I remember it.'

'Well it tastes very all right to me,' Ged ventured.

'Well, you're from Birmingham so you wouldn't know a good ale from a pint of vinegar,' Tony shot back. 'No, I can't quite put my finger on it,' said the aficionado, his face contorting to denote his befuddlement.

As Peggy came back to their end of the bar, Tony had a question for her. 'Excuse me, love. I can't help but notice that this Brim doesn't taste quite like it used to. Have they changed the water or something?'

Peggy coolly eyed the visitor for a few seconds before replying. 'Well, if they have, you've done very well to notice seeing how nobody else has.'

Further down the bar, Godfrey whispered into Bouncer's ear and the Border Collie passed his own judgement on Tony's heresy by rolling over on his back and playing dead.

Martin and Ged simply tried to keep straight faces.

CHAPTER NINETEEN

At last, the day of the press conference had arrived. Simon Backhouse stood before the assembled hacks in the Brewery museum space ready to unveil Brim's vital message for the world. Behind him, in front of a wall of display panels bearing Brim's distinctive branding, sat Brandon Todd and Brian Parkin. The PR supremo had done an impressive job in attracting a strong media presence including two television news crews, national radio and national press. News conferences for Brim were usually only attended by the local press – now they were in the big league. Just what had Brandon told them to get them there?

Simon began by explaining the background to Brim's famous ale and the brewery's independent status before moving on to the ongoing geographical status application. 'Today we want to share with you our reminder to the EU, to the world in general, that Brim is not only an incomparable beer unique to this town but also a cherished brand that deserves to be safeguarded against imitators.' The general hush in the room didn't so much denote rapt attention from the media as much as their unspoken exhortation for Simon to get on with it.

'For centuries, Brim has been described as a miracle worker due to the naturally occurring presence of salicin in the water we use in the brewing process. Water that can only be found here in Brimdale. Nowadays, of course, we can't use terms such as "miracle" in our marketing, but believe me, Brim retains the ability to transform lives for the better.'

Brandon surveyed the room, spotting which hacks were paying attention, and which ones were fiddling with their mobile phones.

Simon continued. 'Of course, me just telling you this isn't enough. Which is why the people of Brimdale themselves have created their own message to highlight the importance of Brim to this town, and to demonstrate the life enhancing properties of our special ale.'

With that, the lights went down and a video clip flashed up on the monitors positioned down each side of the room. On the screens a line of people, all dressed in white suits, stood to attention. As four short xylophone beats led into a song that bore the unmistakeable melody of The Scaffold's *Lily the Pink*, the troupe started bobbing up and down as they sang:

Let's toast a toast a toast
To Backhouse's boast, his boast, his boast,
To make an ale so rarefied
With true devotion he brewed up a potion
Its miracle claims can't be denied

The camera cut to a close up of an old television set showing a clip from one of Brian Parkin's former TV programmes. Suddenly a large boot dropped from above and crushed the TV set:

The Barnsley chopper had cooked his last supper
When he got booted off TV
So they gave him a salicin shandy
Now he's doubled his programme fees

Cue Brian now stood triumphantly in front of a giant outdoor poster promoting a fictitious show: 'He's Back! Chop Sticks It to Critics. Wednesday 8pm.'

Next up was Godfrey, limbering up on the outfield at Headingley.

Fast bowler Godfrey, ran in from the boundary
But the umpires said he chucked
So they gave him a salicin shandy
Now the batsmen all get ducks

A triumphant Godfrey stood looking suitably vindicated as a succession of batsmen, all with duck masks on, paraded past him to the pavilion. Now it was Cora Songhurst's turn, with her staring blankly at a laptop and then pacing up and down the room in apparent frustration:

Author Cora, a dutiful daughter
Had a block and couldn't write
So they gave her a salicin shandy
Now she's won the Booker prize

A stroboscope of camera flashes signalled an awards ceremony. It was evident that production standards for the video reinforced the 'home-made' feel. Sometimes it cost a lot of money to achieve that look. The next cut was to Gary Merriweather on the stage at the Fountain Head:

> *Gary fed pellets to his big pet ferret*
> *And put it down his trouser leg*
> *So they gave him a salicin shandy*
> *To save his meat and his two veg*

Throughout the scene Gary could be seen mock fighting whatever was supposed to be down his trouser leg, drawing a laugh from the sardonic scribes. The chorus now cut in again, this time with the singers all apparently wrestling ferret sized shapes in their breeches in emulation of Gary. Back to the verses, this time with Simon sporting a pin stripe suit and a bored look on his face as he swivelled round in his office chair:

> *Businessman Simon worked with no tie on*
> *He dreamed of breaking free*
> *So they gave him a salicin shandy*
> *Now he's playing Glastonbury*

Cut to Simon kneeling astride his guitar and setting it alight, Jimi Hendrix style. Now we had Howard in his studio, taking photos on an old fashioned tripod mounted camera.

> *Snapper Howard shot film by the hour*
> *Until his shutter wouldn't click*

So they gave him a salicin shandy
Now he exposes double quick

A speeded up segment of film showed Howard, apparently naked, developing and hanging up prints in his dark room. Only one member of the troupe had yet to be featured. It was Peggy, ringing a large brass bell behind the bar of the Fountain Head and signalling no more drinks.

Landlady Peggy would serve no one afters
When the last order bell rang
So they gave her a salicin shandy
Now she doesn't give a hang

Cue a beaming Peggy pulling the bar towels off the pumps and throwing them over her shoulder. Finally, the tempo slowed as the entire ensemble drew the song to a conclusion:

To Brussels, they went with a summons
To keep the Brim name for their town
To stop violations, and pale imitations
Please, don't let us down

As the final chorus faded a smattering of applause greeted the video led, it must be said, by one of Brandon's assistants. As the lights came back up, Simon took to the microphone again.

'I hope you enjoyed our homespun adaptation of that classic old song which goes back to the late nineteenth century and a certain Miss Lydia Pinkham. You may well have heard the song *Lily the Pink* before but you may not have known that Lily did exist and that her vegetable preparation was sold as a women's tonic. Its success is probably entirely unrelated to the fact it was forty per cent proof. Variations of that song have been around for one hundred and fifty years. The thing about our version of the song is that it features some remarkable stories that are very much part of Brimdale's current landscape. Not the least of these is the story of Brian Parkin.'

Now it was time for Brian to take over the mic. The hacks went quiet as they waited for him to begin. This is really what they'd come for.

'Many of you will probably know me as the "ex-TV chef" or "former celebrity". You'll probably remember the lurid headlines that spelled the end of my TV career rather than the twelve years of programmes I actually made. I had everything one minute, and nothing the next. Not even my reputation.' There was some shuffling of feet among the media corps as they tried to look like such a misfortune had nothing to do with them.

'I'm not the first person to find themselves in such circumstances, and I won't be the last. How did I cope? It's a good question. I didn't is the answer.'

He produced his wallet from his back pocket and pulled out a scruffy dog-eared newspaper cutting. Brian knew he had the media's attention now. 'And just when I thought things couldn't get any worse there was another kick in the teeth to remind me that I was not only finished, but also worthless and an object of derision. Let me share with you what it feels like to reach that point.' As Brian read the 'Who's Smiling Now?' piece by Gerard Lomax, each excruciating paragraph, every trenchant word of it, one could almost hear the brewery cockroaches scurrying beneath the barrels.

Finally, he finished reading. 'Not very nice, is it? Some people may have shrugged off such a hatchet job – it's only a piece of newsprint after all, a bit of fun that no one will remember the day after tomorrow. But do you know what I decided to do about it?' The audience held its breath waiting for Brian to answer his own question.

'I decided to kill myself.'

As Brandon had calculated, the short gasp from the audience signalled that the media was now discerning the true story of today's conference.

'And when I say I decided to kill myself, I was literally seconds away from doing it. But as you can see, I didn't. And why? Because a miracle happened, that's why. Call it divine intervention, or whatever you like, but the truth is I was minutes – no, seconds – away from taking my own life when I was interrupted. What stopped me drawing my last breath? A knock on my door and the news that Brim wanted me to help them with their campaign.'

Some hacks tried to fire questions at him about exactly how he had planned to take his own life but Brian ignored them and carried on.

'Here was a lifeline. I was wanted. I could do some good. I could remind myself that the blackness can be avoided if you don't rush to meet it. For me, at least, Brim was a saviour.'

More questions erupted from the floor. 'How do you feel now, Brian?'

'I can tell you exactly how I feel now. I've never been

happier in my life. I have found a new purpose and moved on. Brimdale is very much part of my world now and this is where I plan to stay. I have a job to do in helping the town in this important campaign but as you've just seen, serious issues don't always have to be dealt with in a serious manner to get the message across.'

From the floor: 'And what is your message, Brian?'

'It's this. Miracles can happen. Never give up hope.'

Brandon announced it was time to wrap things up. 'Thank you, everyone. Brian and the rest of the Brimdale residents in the film clip are available for interviews but first we'll move to the courtyard where our performers can satisfy your photo needs.'

Two hours later, Brandon sat down with his team of local heroes for a debrief. Spirits were high as the choristers joked about the final edit which none of them had seen until the moment it was shown to the press.

The architect of the launch was pleased. 'So far, so good. Well done, everybody. A big thanks to Brian for baring his soul out there. That can't have been easy, Brian, and we're grateful.'

'Yes, well done, Brian. Mighty brave of you,' said Godfrey who few could remember being quite so respectful. Gary and Howard patted Brian on the back to signify their solidarity and approval.

'There's no doubt that the media will lead on the Brian angle,' Brandon said. 'That's fine, that's what we want. This way, the video we've done will get seen by more people who'll arrive at it through Brian's story than if we'd just stuck the film online. The video tells Brian's story, but it also tells yours, and it tells Brim's. You've all got stories to tell the media and we're setting those up now – I want people to associate your life-changing experiences with Brim and Brimdale.'

Gary interjected, 'Ah've already bin asked to do a ninterview wi t'local telly.'

'It will be the first of many, Gary, believe me,' Brandon said. 'The campaign website is now up and running and rather than just being informative we're asking the public to back our campaign and send a message to Brussels. It's fun – to register support for the bid you have to hit a cartoon ferret on the head with a mallet.'

'Ah'm not so sure ah condone cru'lty t'animals, like,' quipped Gary.

'And I thought you in particular would approve,' Brandon said. 'The video is up on YouTube, and we'll be able to monitor the number of hits alongside the number of public likes. Every time momentum starts to flag, we'll spice it up with a new story or angle. We're on our way, everybody.'

CHAPTER TWENTY

Brian and Peggy were watching the six o'clock television news. The national BBC news. Today's press conference was story number five. 'Got to hand it to Brandon,' said Brian. 'He's put Brim on the map all right.'

'And you,' Peggy replied.

'It's both, isn't it? Look at how they're using the song and explaining what Brim wanted me for in the first place. It's working like magic.'

'A miracle, no less,' echoed Peggy as she gave him a big hug.

'Not as big a miracle as you appearing in it though.'

'It's a good job I let you off for blabbing about Mam to Simon and Brandon. See how you've mellowed me?'

'But you're glad you did now, aren't you?'

Peggy looked at the photos of her mother and father now adorning the living room and said, 'Yes. I'm glad. I should never have bottled up all that grief. I should have been celebrating Mam and Dad, not burying them in the bottom of the wardrobe.'

The loved-up couple stayed tuned in for the local television news where they made story number two. The top of the programme featured a vidclip of Brian's dramatic 'I decided to kill myself' soundbite with the voiceover announcing, 'Coming up; find out why a famous TV chef owes his life to a local beer.'

'What are they like?' said Brian, knowing only too well what 'they' were like.

Following Brandon's instructions, Brian hadn't answered any calls on his mobile. The PR's rationale was that he was going to aim for an exclusive interview instead of making his prize asset available to everybody. Nevertheless, Brian could see plenty of people were now trying to get in touch with him, mainly from numbers he didn't recognise but many from people he'd not heard from in quite a while.

As Brian turned the TV off he knew that the reporter was right. He did owe his life, and Peggy, to a miracle beer. He knew that if the news coverage went according to plan he could well find himself fielding fresh job offers and opportunities from the people who had ignored him for so long. Brandon had probed him on that topic and he acknowledged the possibility. Deep down though, he knew he didn't want that life again. That wasn't why he was doing this now. This was his way of saying thanks.

Dave Rawson was also taking in the news. Not just the television news, but radio, online and Twitter. Brian Parkin and Brim were now trending. He knew Brandon had played a blinder and wondered how he had persuaded that has-been Parkin to spill his guts to the nation. Had Brandon made it all up in any case? Last-second intervention? Saved by a miracle? Brim's magical qualities? All poppycock.

As for the video, how twee and unoriginal was that? Record an old song with new lyrics and stick any Tom, Dick and Harriet in there 'making it their own'. The media was so gullible. Every time a group showed a bit of leg for a cause it was the new 'Calendar Girls' or 'The Full Monty'. Brim was getting more media coverage than if it had been announced Moses was to receive some new commandments on top of the Cow and Calf rocks at Ilkley Moor. How Rawson hated the pathetic tabloid standards of today's media.

He knew this development was serious for Colton's. Brimdale was upping the stakes. He logged on to the video on YouTube. Already over thirty thousand views. He clicked on the thumbs down button to register a dislike and then moved on to Brim's new *miraclescanhappen* website. Already five thousand ferrets hit on the head – five thousand cretins telling the EU it backed Brim's bid.

The EU wouldn't care a fig over any of this quaint, parochial eccentricity. It wouldn't alter the judgement they would reach over Brim's geographical protection status – that would have to be based purely on the facts. Particularly the forensic report. He'd left Tasker to hang – sometimes the silent treatment was far more effective – but he knew it wouldn't be long before the report arrived on his desk and then Tasker would be forced to make a decision.

The Colton's chief knew he had to keep a grip on his emotions. It was a good day for Brim but it could all be forgotten by tomorrow. Plus, it didn't alter the fact that if the EU decision was delayed, Backhouse would surely have to relent and cash in on the Colton's offer while he still could? The judgement was due in a month. They were cutting it fine. There were still grounds for hope.

Yes, that's how he would apprise Mervyn of the latest developments.

Cora bit the bullet and decided to tell Alicia of her involvement with the Brim campaign before Jean mentioned it. 'Can we watch the local TV news tonight, Mummy?'

'I'm not wasting my time on that rubbish. Cats stuck up trees and record number of potholes on local roads.'

'It's just that I'm on it tonight.'

'You are? You kept that quiet. What for?'

'You know I'm researching my new book at the brewery archive?'

'I thought it was customary to promote books after you'd finished them, not before you start them?'

'It's not about the book, Mummy. It's about the Save Brim campaign. They asked me to help them and I said "yes".'

'You always were a martyr to lost causes. How can you possibly help?'

Cora decided that it would be more prudent to let the TV report satisfy Alicia's curiosity from this point. 'Just wait and see, Mummy. It will all be clear when you've seen it.'

Twenty minutes later it was clearer for Alicia if not entirely welcome. 'Do you know what I think, Cora? I think you've just ruined your career. How could you lower yourself to take part in that circus?'

As Cora felt the familiar sting of her mother's tongue

she began to flounder. 'They asked for my help, Mummy. What was I supposed to do? If the brewery closes the whole town will be in trouble.'

'You'll never see this town again once I'm gone. Why are you so bothered?'

'It's where I come from, where I grew up. Can't you see that?'

'Sentimental claptrap. You've made a fool of yourself, Cora, that's what you've done. Who can take you seriously as a writer after that? Booker Prize? I don't think you'll be seeing one of them any time soon with displays like that.'

'It's supposed to be humorous. Can't you see that?'

'I can see the irony in you being described as a "dutiful daughter". Off making pop records and ruining your career when you're supposed to be here looking after me.'

Cora couldn't take any more. She ran to her bedroom with tears streaming down her face. She had only agreed to take part in the shoot at the last minute after Brandon had written a verse especially for her and told her that Peggy was also going to be in the video. She knew Alicia was never going to like it or approve, but for goodness sake, she was a grown woman capable of making her own decisions. No, what really hurt was the accusation that she wasn't a dutiful daughter. Was Alicia right? It was her mother after all who encouraged her to go out during the day – they both knew too much time together wasn't particularly healthy for them. But there wasn't much time left. Had Cora been selfish? Had she been carried away by Brandon's persuasion? Should she abandon this book to spend more time with Mummy while she could? She threw herself on the bed and allowed the tears to continue flowing.

Simon Backhouse was in his office taking stock of a busy day. The media interest had exceeded his expectations, of course it had, and he knew he'd been right to recruit Brandon Todd to assist. The town had rallied magnificently too – it had been touching to see how characters like Godfrey, Howard and Gary had mucked in, and even more impressive that Peggy had been strong-armed into jumping into the ring. Cora, too. A few weeks ago she wouldn't have said boo to a goose and there she was carousing on the video with all of the others. She'd even written half of the song – remarkable.

But was it going to be enough? Had it all come too late? Simon didn't need to look at his calendar to know that decision day was looming. Brandon could boost public awareness and generate support for their application and that would send a powerful message to the faceless bureaucrats of Brussels who would determine their fate. That's what Tasker had said – demonstrate the level and feeling of local support for the application. Well, they were doing that now, but that was nothing compared to the importance of the forensic report. Home and dry, subject to the forensic report, according to Tasker. Why had they had to ask for a new one?

He picked up his guitar and began to strum abstractedly – Robert Johnson's *Hellhound On My Trail*. At least they wouldn't have to wait long to find out now. Tasker had told him they were expecting to hear from Brussels on the report 'in due course' – exactly how long was that? Still, get the OK, and they'd make it over the line – just. Anything other than that and the game would be up – they wouldn't be able to survive financially into next year.

Should he have torn up Colton's offer? Yes. He knew he couldn't sell, and in any event the thought of giving Rawson any satisfaction was inconceivable. God forbid he should ever sell to that lot but if the news from Brussels turned out to be bad Simon knew his problems of the past few years would pale into insignificance compared to what would follow.

Richard Tasker sat watching the local news roundup at 10.30pm. Debbie had gone to bed in a huff following an argument. For some weeks now she had suspected something was wrong with Richard and had tried to get him to open up over what was on his mind. He'd told her, none too convincingly, there was nothing wrong – he was just feeling a little tired, that's all. Debbie's doubts over his wellbeing were very much rooted in the evening he'd arrived home absolutely paralytic – he'd still not really explained what he'd been up to when he went AWOL.

Tonight's exchange of words erupted as they watched the early evening news. Debbie had been excited to see Brimdale Brewery's campaign featured as, after all, some of this media glory rubbed off on her husband. When he coldly dismissed the video and Brian Parkin's outpourings as a 'trivial and inconsequential masquerade,' Debbie had flown off the handle and accused him of being miserable and impossible to live with. Now, as Tasker watched an edited version of the story, he reflected that Debbie was right.

Since the night at the Aubergine Door his life was falling apart. He was irritable, anxious and full of foreboding. What made it worse was that Rawson hadn't been in touch with him since they'd met in Park Square so he had no way of knowing if there was any chance of him relenting on his demands. Two or three times he'd been on the verge of calling Rawson but always chickened out. One evening the previous week an agitated Tasker, finding all of the suspense too much, set off for Leeds to have it out with Rihanna. He got as far as parking his car in the City Centre before turning around. He'd ruefully remembered Rawson's words about not showing weakness. If she knew how desperate he was, he may never get free.

All along, he reasoned that Rawson might not be telling him the truth about the photos. He'd not seen the incriminating evidence after all – not that he wanted to. But if he upset Rawson or turned up at the club he could make a bad situation worse. And now Brim was banging the drum in public with bleeding hearts, talk of miracles and a daft video. The walls were closing in on him.

Rawson wasn't going to go away and he didn't doubt he'd follow through on his veiled threats. The thought of abusing his position and authority at Defra by querying the forensic report caused him enormous self-disgust but, at the same time, he could wipe the slate clean and begin again if he just exercised this simple get-out clause. Waiting and stewing was bad enough but one of the reasons he was feeling especially stressed today was that he had received an email from Brussels that afternoon – the EU was forwarding the new forensic report to him the following day and it would be with him before 12.30pm tomorrow. Then he would have to make his mind up. What would his world look like in twenty-four hours?

CHAPTER TWENTY-ONE

Cora was still upset as she set about the next section of the archives at the brewery. Alicia had been quiet at breakfast and not much had been said about the *contretemps* the previous evening. Still, Cora couldn't forget the wounding accusation from her mother that she was hardly a 'dutiful daughter'. She stared at the books, undisturbed for over a century in some cases, and wondered again if Alicia's charge hurt so much because it was actually true? What was she doing among these musty, decaying folios when Alicia was soon to be similarly lifeless?

Her appetite for research somewhat dimmed, she stretched to reach a large heavy tome at the back of the top shelf. As she strained to grab it she accidentally knocked it over causing it to fall with a large thud against the side panelling. Looking up, Cora could see that the impact had dislodged the panel, revealing a small opening. She grabbed a chair and clambered up to investigate. Behind the dislodged panel she spotted what looked like a rolled up manuscript protruding from the darkness. Climbing still higher, her feet now planted on the lower shelf, Cora pushed her face to the opening to discern a tumble of rolled up papers tucked away within a small compartment hidden from sight for goodness knows how long. She carefully extracted the rolls from the space and took them over to the large table to have a better look at them.

Cora had successfully deciphered most of the documents she'd read in the archive so far, but these were different. She calculated they were from the fourteenth century. As well as containing considerable Latin text she could also see that the scrolls appeared to include a number of drawings, diagrams and a map. It was quite unlike anything she'd found in the archives to date. Over the next hour she studied them, trying to interpret their content and import. Suddenly her hand sprang to her mouth to suppress a gasp of realisation. Was she misinterpreting what she was reading? Surely this couldn't be true? Had she unravelled the papers incorrectly to come up with a ludicrous explanation? Because if she was right, then a terrible trick had been played.

Rolling up the manuscripts and placing them carefully in her bag, she knew but one person who would be able to offer a definitive explanation. Two minutes later she was on her way back home to Alicia.

Simon was agitated as he led Richard Tasker into his office. Tasker had insisted on seeing him in person to discuss the forensic report that had arrived at Defra that lunchtime. Simon had pleaded with Tasker on the phone to tell him straight – what was the outcome, a 'yes' or a 'no'? The government official insisted that he would only discuss the report face-to-face so Simon had been forced to endure an agonising two-hour wait while Tasker made his way over.

Simon observed the usual etiquette of offering his

guest a drink and enquiring after his general health, apparently in no hurry to start the meeting proper. Such nonchalance was deceptive as inside he was as taut as the top E string of the guitar leaning against his desk.

Finally, he casually opened up the subject that had dominated his thoughts for so many weeks. 'So, you've got the report then?'

'Yes, it arrived by email this morning.'

Simon, suppressing his annoyance that Tasker was being unnecessarily obtuse over the findings, prompted him further. 'And?'

'And? Well, I'm afraid that there's a bit of a problem.'

This simple announcement struck Simon with the same visceral force as an encore at a Who gig. Richard Tasker's arcing windmill severing not only the top E but the other five strings on his guitar as well. In slow motion amps were being thrown to the floor, the drum kit violently kicked over and cherry bombs detonating before the final ritualistic splintering of the guitar among wailing feedback and smoke. The brewery had had it. They were buggered.

Simon blinked to clear this image of Armageddon from his mind before meekly enquiring, 'We failed?'

'No. You passed. You were given the all-clear on the forensic report.'

Briefly tangling with the conundrum of how to perform an encore with no instruments, Simon rewound the last comment. 'We didn't fail? But you said there was a problem. Did we pass or did we fail?'

'You passed. The report was fine, and the EU committee has accepted it. That isn't the problem.'

Simon, now wondering where the after-gig party would be held, was determined to let nothing interfere with his elation. 'If the report's been accepted, we don't have any problem. At all. This is fantastic news.'

'No. We do. I'm afraid I have a problem with it.'

'What do you mean?'

'I've read the report and I'm of the opinion that the data contained in it is insufficient on which to base an assured judgement.'

'You can't be serious. It's the same data as we've always had. I mean, it's the same procedure that's always been followed, surely?'

'Yes, I believe it is, and maybe it's something I should have spotted before, but I think it would be prudent to commission further in-depth analysis before signing the report off.'

'You're telling me that the EU has approved a report that confirms what we've always known in any case, but now, at the last minute, you want to ignore all of that and do more research which will scupper our chances of getting approval next month?'

'It's just a safeguard. It's my job to make sure,' said Tasker, by now looking at the table edge rather than at Simon.

'Despite the fact that everything we've worked on together all of these years will have been in vain. You can't do this.'

'Strictly speaking…'

'No. The EU has approved the report. Why go against it? This is crazy. I'm not going to let you do it.'

Tasker was finding it difficult to maintain his

argument. It *was* crazy. And what if Simon was right? Could Defra override the EU and call for another report? What would his bosses say? Had he thought this through enough? Struggling, he imagined Rawson brandishing the photo of him and Rihanna to his wife and the shock and dismay on her face. 'I understand that it may not be welcome news, but...'

'No. Listen. I'm *not* going to let you do it,' repeated Simon, a murderous look in his eye.

'I appreciate that ...' Tasker was mumbling now.

'Here's the thing. We've worked on this for eight years. It's been tough. You've put as much time into this as us. The one factor that looked like it might derail us, the report, isn't a problem – we've passed. And yet you're prepared to come up with some trivial "concern" that will screw up the whole application and, if I'm being honest, throw the brewery on the scrapheap.'

'I think you may be overstating the position somewhat...'

'I've never been closer to the truth. Are you prepared to throw our workforce on the streets? Decimate the town by having the brewery closed? Be known as the man who shafted Brimdale when you've just spent years supposedly working on our behalf?'

Tasker stared out of the window, unable to reply. He should have known he wouldn't be able to carry off this simple act of duplicity.

'Well?' asked Simon. 'Can you live with that?'

'I can't live with that, no,' confessed Tasker. He looked at Simon directly this time, his face a picture of dejection and hopelessness. 'And I can't live with the alternative either. I'm afraid I've done something very, very, stupid.'

Alicia was surprised, and not a little pleased, to see Cora return home before lunch. She knew she'd been sharper than normal the previous evening and guessed Cora wanted to talk things through. Alicia felt she should eat a bit of humble pie for once and recant some of her more acerbic observations. Her daughter, however, appeared to have another priority on her mind.

'Mummy, I need your help,'

Unaccustomed to such admissions of need from Cora, Alicia couldn't decide whether to be pleased or concerned. Instinctively, she chose the latter option. 'Really? It's not often you ask me for help.'

'I know, Mummy,' Cora said, secretly pleased that this predicament had thrown her in Alicia's direction. 'But wait until you see this.'

Cora sat down next to Alicia and carefully unrolled the three documents she had found in the archive that morning. 'I've not been able to transcribe all of it as it's in a different style to the rest of the archives but looking at the diagrams I'm beginning to piece together what I think it's all about. But what I'm guessing at is inconceivable.'

Alicia pulled on her reading glasses to study the documents. 'Hmmm. Paper. Romanesque. Fourteenth-century I'd say. Look at how the lettering is so varied – these were not for public reading, that's for sure.' She continued to study the folios, switching from one to the other, all without saying a word. Cora sat patiently watching her mother peruse the documents, recognising the look of studied application she'd not seen from her for so many years.

Finally, Alicia looked up and turned to Cora. 'I deduce that you reached the same conclusion as I?'

'I think so,' said Cora.

'Well, spell it out, Cora, spell it out.' The clock had been reversed some two decades or so – Alicia was back at the university dealing with a hesitant student.

'Well, if I'm right, and the charts appear to support this supposition...' Cora began uncertainly.

'Yes, if you're right, then...?'

'There was a spring at the Brim Over Priory, but it didn't rise there.'

'Correct. Because...?'

'Because the monks built an underground waterway to channel the water to Priory.'

'Correct again. You can see that the spring rises in Keldmire, twelve miles away on this map.'

'But why?'

'Ah. Good question. In both Pagan and early Christian lore water sources were considered sacred – you've heard of holy well? This is one such. The Cluniacs moved here to these parts in the early fourteenth century, yes?'

Cora nodded.

'The Priory at Keldmire was destroyed in a fire around the same time – quite common as the building would have been constructed mainly of wood at that time. I hadn't linked the two events before but it's obvious that they decided to rebuild here instead of Keldmire, probably because of population shift or access to stone. This area evidently offered more than Keldmire had, except for one thing.'

'A spring.'

'Precisely. The Cluniacs didn't want to leave behind their most important asset – the spring. How ingenious. Normally it would be relics that would define a holy house, but not, it seems, in their case.'

'They didn't move the actual spring – they diverted it.'

'Yes – that's more accurate. It must have been a considerable engineering feat to achieve that – the spring disappears in Keldmire and pops up in Brim Over – you can see it on the Priory map here.'

'But there's no spring there now,' Cora said. 'Anyway, after all these years that waterway couldn't be functioning now?'

Alicia peered at the map again. 'You're right, Cora. You found these manuscripts at the brewery though – what if they diverted it again?'

Cora's eyes widened as the penny dropped. 'To the brewery,' she exclaimed. 'The aquifer is at the brewery now, or rather, it purports to be there. It has to be the same one.'

'The magic ingredient of their beer, no less.'

Another realisation struck Cora. 'But we've been campaigning to protect the brewery because of the uniqueness of the water that's used in the beer.'

'I see what you mean. Well, strictly speaking, the beer is unique if it's using water from the original well.'

'Yes, but it's not from Brimdale; just everybody thinks it is.'

'I can see how that may be an issue. Most curious.'

Cora was excited too, not only at the discovery but also at the teamwork displayed by the Songhurst scholars in solving this puzzle. But had they solved it?

'Mummy, I have to tell Brandon about this – do you mind? He needs to know.'

Alicia, now fully caught up in the ramifications of Cora's discovery, totally forgot about any earlier prejudices. 'Not at all, Cora. I have to admit; this is all very intriguing. Very intriguing indeed.'

CHAPTER TWENTY-TWO

Brandon rushed from Brimdale to Brim Over Hall as fast as he could. It wasn't that Cora had told him why she needed to see him so urgently; he was simply glad of the opportunity to see her at all. He wasn't expecting to bump into Alicia though, so was a little taken aback when he was led through to the kitchen to be introduced to her. She wasn't at all what he expected. In his conversations with Cora about her mother he had formed a distinct impression of a frail old woman at death's door. He was also aware of the strained relationship the two shared. Now, on meeting Alicia for the first time, he was confused. She seemed quite animated and if she disapproved of Brandon she was keeping it well hidden.

After Jean had been summonsed to produce tea and scones, Alicia took charge. 'Now, Brandon, there is something that you should know.'

Cora sat placidly, yielding the floor to her mother.

'Cora has managed to make a simply wonderful historical discovery in the brewery's archives, which has massive significance for the town.'

Brandon was impressed, especially at Alicia's obvious pride in her daughter's academic prowess. 'Really?' he said. 'Well, that sounds like good news for the campaign – is it something we can use?'

Cora, at last, contributed to the exchange. 'I think that's highly unlikely.'

Without undue elaboration Alicia and Cora outlined their theory and presented the evidence to hand concerning the Brimdale spring that wasn't. Brandon's induction into Cluniac chicanery brought with it the thunderbolt that everything he'd been promoting was a fraud if the Songhursts were right in their interpretation of the documents.

'I hear what you're implying,' said Brandon, 'but let's not jump to conclusions. Is it possible that the spring *allegedly* diverted to Brim Over has simply dried up, and that the aquifer at the brewery is actually a different one?'

'Well, we considered that,' Alicia replied, 'but the odds are stacked against it. In any event, the Cluniacs wouldn't have gone to the trouble of diverting the spring at Keldmire to Brim Over if there had been one in Brimdale. They'd have simply built the Priory there.'

Brandon was still looking for get-outs. 'Could the drawings be a figment of somebody's imagination? I mean, surely such a thing couldn't have been built back then?'

'These are not idle jottings, I can assure you.' Alicia was into her stride, and now it was Cora's turn to sit back and feel a tinge of family pride. 'You see, Cora had a little difficulty in deciphering the Latin at first because it's not ecclesiastical – it's classical. I suspect that an expert brought over from France, or even Rome, conceived these drawings. Also, the sophistication of the actual watercourse plan with its cisterns, siphons and waterwheels is most impressive. They built this, I have no doubt.'

'Wouldn't it have taken years to build it though? And what about the cost?' asked Brandon.

'Oh, they wouldn't have worried about that,' Alicia said. 'They were in no hurry; they rarely were. If it took over a hundred years to erect a cathedral back then, this would have been the equivalent of sticking up a garden wall. As for cost, they'll have paid with plenary indulgences in the main, that is, given the labourers blessings. Not that the peasants would have had much choice. All very economical.'

Brandon no longer doubted that they built it but was struggling to link the spring in Keldmire to what was now bubbling up under the brewery and going into its 'Salicin Shandy'.

However, that wasn't Alicia's department. 'Well, that's enough excitement for one day. I'm going for a lie-down now. Lovely to meet you, Brandon,' Alicia said as she reversed her wheelchair from the table.

Cora couldn't believe what had got into Alicia but knew she preferred this seldom seen version of her mother to the one she was used to dealing with. It was bemusing to be left alone with Brandon in such a stage-managed way, like a couple of seventeen-year-olds trusted to behave if they were treated like adults. Romance was the last thing on Brandon's mind though as he grappled with the implications of what he'd just learned.

'What I can't work out, Cora, is where the spring at the brewery rises. It's inconceivable it's the one that was at Keldmire, or here in Brim Over. It doesn't make sense.'

'Mummy has a point though, that if there had been a spring where the brewery is now, the Cluniacs would have built the Priory next to it and not needed to do this massive engineering project.'

Brandon had run out of reasons to doubt the news and his spirits sank as he weighed up the implications. 'We're going to have to confront Simon with this. We've just launched a campaign to preserve and protect Brim's geographical status and now we think its unique ingredient may be from ten miles away. It's fraud – well, it's fraud if Simon knows about it. Either way, we're all going to look fools if it's true.'

Suddenly, Cora didn't feel so clever having made her amazing discovery after all.

Unaware of how far the pint he was now drinking may have travelled to meet him, Godfrey was enjoying an early evening snifter in the Fountain Head. The buzz over the launch had stimulated trade and the pub was half full with visitors, many of whom had never set foot in the place before.

Gary was busy telling Godfrey and Howard about the US news crew who had spent the afternoon with him shooting a piece on ferret legging. 'Silly buggers believed everythin' ah told 'em,' boasted the current Ferret & Firkin champion. 'Got t'presenter to try it too but 'e dint tek to it. Five seconds 'e managed, t'big jessie.'

'I hope you managed to mention Brim?' said Howard conscientiously.

'Too right, I did. Told 'em it wer mi secret ingredient, and t'ferret's as well. Wi wer both drinking it. 'Ad to mek sure wi did a few takes, mindst.'

Godfrey wasn't to be outdone. 'Well, they want me to be a guest on the television next week when Yorkshire are playing. Said I would add exactly the right sort of colour they're looking for, whatever that is.'

'You'll have to be on your best behaviour for that, Godfrey,' advised Howard. 'They don't have a delay on that, I believe.'

'A delay? What's that when it's at home?' asked the latest addition to the coterie of cake-consuming cricket cognoscenti.

'It just means, well, just make sure you don't swear or say anything that's inappropriate because you'll be going out live,' said Howard helpfully.

'As if I would,' protested Godfrey. 'Why, I'll be as quiet as a container load of illegal immigrants at Dover docks.'

Howard rolled his eyes and decided to change the subject. 'Well, Godfrey, can we count on you and your new found fame to help out at the Beer Festival?'

'When is it?'

'I'll give you a guess. Same day it's been for the past fifty years. We're reckoning it will be the biggest one we've ever done, what with all of this publicity.'

'Ah'll do mi ferret legging if yer want,' Gary chipped in.

'Good, because I've already written that into the programme,' said Howard. 'I guessed you might be up for that.'

Not to be outdone, Godfrey signalled his support. 'Well, I wouldn't like to disappoint my fans, so count me in.'

'Don't worry, Godfrey, we will. Your usual party piece?'

'Too right. What about him?'

Brian Parkin had just appeared carrying a plate of devils on horseback to place on the bar. Howard beckoned him over to their table. 'Brian, the very man. We were wondering if you'd be up for helping us out at this year's beer festival?'

'I am helping as far as I know. Peggy's doing the bar and food and I've been commandeered already.'

'That's good of course, but we want to cash in on the video as well, with everybody that was in it,' Howard explained. 'I was wondering if you and Peggy…'

'Can I stop you there, Howard? I'm not going to ask Peggy to get into that wrestling kit for the beer festival, and I'd suggest you don't ask her either unless you're looking for a fat lip.'

Howard quickly modified his tentative enquiry, 'Just to feature you on the posters and such like, nothing more?'

'Yes, no problem,' Brian agreed. 'Just keep off the cossies and we'll be all right. What are you going to do anyway, Howard?'

'Take the photographs of course.'

Godfrey had a question to ask. 'Is the festival before or after they get the decision from Brussels? It can't be long now?'

'We've asked Simon, but he doesn't know yet,' Howard replied. 'It would certainly sour proceedings if they said "no" before the festival.'

'As opposed to after?' asked Gary, not quite sure what the difference was.

Brandon and Cora sat side by side on one of Simon's office sofas. The normally laid-back brewery head looked a little more tense than normal – and they'd not even started on their discovery yet. Surely he couldn't have guessed what they were here for? It appeared that Simon was expecting an impromptu update on the campaign coverage but Brandon didn't dwell on getting to the main point on his agenda.

'Simon. Have you seen these before?' he asked as he pushed the three pieces of parchment over to him.

Simon studied the documents carefully for a minute. 'No, never. What are they?'

'They're from your archives,' Cora replied.

'Never seen them before – what's the significance?'

Cora and Brandon exchanged glances. Was Simon being entirely truthful, or did he really not know?

Brandon brought Simon up to speed. 'Basically, these documents indicate that the Cluniac monks diverted a spring at Keldmire to Brim Over in the fourteenth century. Twelve miles. There was no spring marked here in Brimdale which begs the question as to where the aquifer here at the brewery actually rises.'

Simon looked at the papers again. 'You found these in our archives?' he asked.

'Yes,' said Cora. 'They were hidden in a compartment in one of the shelves.'

'Strictly speaking then, these are brewery property.'

Brandon steered Simon back to the case in point. 'Who owns the papers isn't the issue here. What *is* the issue is where does the Brim aquifer rise, because if it wasn't here in the fourteenth century how has it miraculously appeared here now?'

'It must be possible for a new well to appear, surely?' ventured Simon.

'Possible, but unlikely I would have thought. Simon, is there anything you can tell us to cast light on this puzzle?'

'I'm not sure what puzzle you mean.'

'The puzzle that for over one hundred and fifty years you've been promoting a beer whose core constituent is water from the spring in this brewery, in this town. Water that contains salicin. Water that's unique to this location. Water that's the basis of your application to the EU for geographical status. And these documents suggest that there is no spring rising here. That's a big enough puzzle, surely?'

Simon sat weighing up Brandon's summary before replying. 'It's all conjecture though, isn't it?'

'It may well be, Simon, but it would be relatively easy to investigate if you knew what to look for. Plus, if it's true the aquifer doesn't rise here then we've all been taking part in a fraud. I know ethics aren't normally associated with my profession but even I would have to draw the line at being party to a deception on this scale.'

Cora looked admiringly at Brandon as he honourably cited the importance of standards in the realm of PR. This day was providing one revelation after another.

Simon suddenly stood up and went to the old cast iron safe in the corner of the room. Brandon had imagined the ornately decorated strongbox to be of a purely decorative nature the first time he'd seen it but as Simon turned the dial first this way and then that, he realised it still performed its primary function. After rummaging around he pulled out an old black leather satchel and rejoined Cora and Brandon on the settees.

'Let me say, first of all,' said Simon, 'that I've never seen the documents you've found.' He looked them both in the eye and they could see his will to keep up the pretence had evaporated. 'You're right though in what you've guessed – the spring here in the brewery doesn't rise here; it rises in Keldmire.'

Brandon took in this not quite unexpected news: 'I think you'd better explain what's been going on, Simon.'

'Back in the 1850s when the town was just starting to be developed the Backhouse family knew there had been a spring up at the old Priory and decided it would be ideal for their brewing plans if they could open it up again. All they had to do was divert it down here to the town – not a very big job in actuality.'

'So they thought the spring rose at Brim Over?' Cora said.

'They thought that originally, yes, but on excavating the area they discovered it wasn't the real source. They were nothing if not thorough and eventually traced it to Keldmire. The documents you've discovered, Cora, must have been central in that discovery.'

'But the old water channels surely weren't working by then?' Cora said.

'No, of course not,' Simon replied. 'They'd have collapsed centuries before because the original pipes would have been made mainly of wood and lead. What they did was replace the original pipeline with an entirely new watercourse between Keldmire and here and built the brewery on top of it.'

Brandon was finding it hard to believe such an engineering achievement could have been carried off so easily. 'Twelve miles? And nobody noticed?'

'Well, it's just over ten actually, as we're nearer to Keldmire here than Brim Over, but yes, they replaced the entire pipeline. Nobody would have questioned it in those days and in any event they also installed the initial water supply infrastructure for the fledgling town at the same time. Victorian benevolence in action.'

'But the pipeline can't have lasted all this time. How do you maintain it?' Brandon challenged.

'We're talking Victorian engineering here – most towns today are still dependent on Victorian era sewerage and drainage; it was built to last. The clever thing the family did was to buy up most of the land in the corridor between here and Keldmire – it's remained relatively undisturbed and we can still access the pipeline if we need to.'

'What's at Keldmire now?' Cora asked.

'You mean the spring? It's in the basement of Grange Manor, one of the properties built by the family. That's where I live.'

Brandon could hardly believe his ears. 'I've never heard anything as mad in all my life. How on earth have you managed to keep this smokescreen up?'

'We've had to keep it up, that's the thing. That's why we've never sold the business.'

'But why apply for EU geographical status for goodness sake? That's just asking for trouble.'

'We had no choice. When Colton's launched Brimmer we knew we were looking at the end of the brewery unless we could get them to stop. It was actually Defra's idea to apply to Brussels. I knew the risks, but we were screwed either way. The only hope now is getting the nod on the application or we have to close down the brewery, full stop.'

'And continue with this deception?' Brandon said.

'What's the alternative? This town was built on the back of the brewery and it will decline if the brewery closes. That's not a very hard choice to me.'

'How come nobody has discovered your secret in this day and age?' Cora said. 'They must be all over you with Food Standards and tests.'

'Our friends from Defra, yes. Well, we've had to use our imagination over recent years. An arm's length company my grandfather set up does the forensic reports – that's how we get round that problem. We had a nasty scare last month when the EU insisted on an independent report.'

'So they're on to you?'

'No, as it happens. Obviously the water is going to test OK as it does contain salicin but the threat was they would inspect and discover that there wasn't actually a natural aquifer here. I managed to distract the scientists sufficiently to ensure they used my data, not theirs, and didn't have time to inspect the actual source.'

Brandon couldn't quite believe how resourceful the unassuming Simon had proved to be. 'And you got away with it?'

'Apparently, yes. I've just been told that the report has received the OK from the EU. But, if you'll pardon my composure over that and you discovering the secret of the spring, we have a much bigger problem altogether to deal with now.'

'I find that hard to imagine,' said Brandon.

'It turns out that our Defra inspector is being blackmailed to question the report, which would cause a delay, and mean we wouldn't get the ruling this year. If that happens, we'd have to close the brewery – we're running on fumes as it is.'

'That little Tasker guy?' Brandon correctly identified the victim. 'Who's blackmailing him? How?'

'Dave Rawson at Colton's has set him up. He's got compromising photos of Tasker in a lap-dancing bar. Rawson put an offer on the table to buy us some weeks ago. He knows if we get the EU ruling we'll win on the Brimmer passing off case as well, so it's a smart move on his behalf.'

The mention of Rawson's name and antics didn't exactly surprise Brandon who'd seen enough of him to form a deep dislike. He thought better of confiding in Simon that Rawson had told him about his bid for Brimdale brewery, saying only, 'It's ironic that he's getting Tasker to question the forensic report – if only he knew.'

'It's a lucky punt. We're not for sale, because we're unsaleable, but he doesn't know that, either,' Simon said. 'But we can carry on if we get this ruling and the only thing stopping us now is Tasker.'

'And Tasker is going to do as Rawson says?' asked Cora.

'Rawson isn't going to let him off the hook. I'm not even sure he's got any photos but Tasker is a quivering wreck who's convinced himself giving Rawson what he wants is the only thing that will save his skin.'

'How do you know all of this?' asked Brandon.

'Because Tasker came here this morning to tell me. He

somehow thought it was the decent thing to inform me he was going to query the report, and then couldn't keep up the act. He's a broken man.'

'So you can't expose Rawson because you compromise Tasker anyway?' Brandon said.

'Correct. What I've told Tasker to do is to pretend that he's not had the actual report yet, to buy time. So you see, while you finding out about the aquifer is unwelcome news, it still doesn't displace my bigger problem.'

'I can see where you're coming from with that,' agreed Brandon.

'I have to ask, Brandon, and you too, Cora, what do you intend to do with all of this information about the spring? Is it handcuffs time?'

Cora looked to Brandon for his guidance on this moral dilemma. The PR man didn't flinch. 'Where do I stand? I think if it's good enough for the Cluniacs to practice a little deception to promote their cause, and if it's good enough for the Victorian Backhouses to indulge in some prestidigitation to establish the town, then I'm not going to cry foul. I'm not going to be responsible for closing the brewery, especially when Rawson is trying to shaft you.'

Cora threw her arms around Brandon and gave him a warm kiss of approval.

Simon looked relieved. 'Thanks, both of you. Now, what are we going to do about the problem we *do* have?'

CHAPTER TWENTY-THREE

'What message, Brian, do you have for the media following your experience at their hands?' Brandon's gamble on securing a high-profile exclusive had paid dividends – he'd landed a half-hour television special for Brian with chat show darling Tabitha Toft and she was now dancing around the topic of Sausagegate. The chef was well briefed.

Brian looked to camera: 'My message to the media is, quite simply, think before you strike that blow. What is the human cost of your action? Forget what your solicitor says you can get away with legally and ask yourself the question, how you would *feel* if you were the victim? Then decide what to write.'

'So you think we need stricter press regulation to prevent the sort of attacks you were subjected to?' cooed Tabitha.

'No, that wouldn't work. We simply need some good old-fashioned decorum in the newsroom, and fewer journalists who hide behind their keyboards. Would you say it to my face? If so, fine. If not, then don't print it.'

Tabitha wanted to show off her hard journalistic chops. 'Isn't that a little disingenuous in this day and age,

Brian? Isn't it the case that journalists are simply giving the public what it wants?'

'There may be a germ of truth in that, Tabitha, but I don't recall any journalistic code that says it's all right to make things up and print them as fact, as happened in my case.'

Tabitha nodded sagely as she let the audience know that Brian's point was one she could possibly agree with. She moved the discussion on. 'What do you say to the hate campaign that's sprung up on Twitter and Facebook against Gerard Lomax in light of the piece he wrote about you?'

'I have to say it must be very distressing for him. I feel for him, I really do. His story pushed me over the edge – I nearly took my own life because of it. I hope, whatever is being thrown at him now, he doesn't reach that same level of desperation.'

Tabitha pounced. 'Can you share with us, Brian, what went through your mind as you reached that point of hopelessness?'

'I can tell you exactly. Nothing. Once I'd decided to do it, then it was a job on my to-do list. I just needed to get it done. Crazy to think that now, but my main mission was to somehow teach people a lesson, and to make them feel partly culpable.'

'And then there was what you call the "intervention"?'

'A miracle more like. I was in the last chance saloon but luckily for me they served Brim in there.' Tabitha wore her best compassionate face as Brian ran through his account of the timely arrival of his lifeline. 'The miracles don't stop there either, do they, Brian? I believe you're now in a new relationship as a result of your work in Brimdale?'

Brian was off again, with further copious references to Brim, its restorative powers matched only by Peggy, and his new purpose in life. As the media regulator was counting up the number of Brim mentions Tabitha signalled the end of the interview by asking Brian if he had one final message for the audience in the studio and at home. Brian gazed mournfully into camera one and, with all the dignity he could muster, intoned, 'No matter how bleak things look, no matter how irretrievable your situation, don't succumb. Remember, miracles do happen. A miracle happened to me; it can happen to you, too.' Cue lights fade, end titles and a super of the phone number viewers who were experiencing similar suicidal tendencies could call.

The next morning, Brandon took stock of the campaign coverage to date. Virtually every national had featured Brian's primetime TV interview while simultaneously highlighting his involvement in the Brim campaign. As a bonus, the debate about media morality had been re-heated to the point where poor old Gerard Lomax had taken temporary leave to avoid the bile now being directed his way, the general consensus being that he was a pathetic, insidious, talentless, bullying creep. Much to Brandon's amusement, Lomax's editor initially tried to defend his writer but as that had only generated more opprobrium the Sunday Splash was now reviewing its editorial guidelines.

Media opportunities were pouring in for Brian,

from TV guest spots to radio interviews, from photo features to at-homes. Now the TV exclusive was out of the way Brandon planned to spread Brian wide, not least because the chef was a media natural who knew how to push the Brim message. It wasn't only Brian the media was interested in though – demand was high for Peggy too, particularly in conjunction with Brian, the Richard Burton and Liz Taylor *de nos jours*. Add in requests for Gary and his ferrets and Sir Godfrey and his homespun philosophising, Brandon calculated the campaign still had plenty of legs to carry them all the way up to decision day. Of his performing troupe only Cora was proving media shy and in a way Brandon was glad that he didn't have to share her with the world.

These traditional media channels were only the tip of the iceberg for Brandon. It was online where he believed the real results would ensue. As each news piece appeared the number of hits on YouTube for the *Salicin Shandy* video soared – it now had over one million views. On the Brim campaign website over four hundred and fifty thousand people had now whacked ferrets to show their support. Brim's dedicated Facebook page had now garnered over half a million 'likes' and a new Twitter hashtag, #salicinshandymiracles, was trending with contributors submitting their own 'miracle' verses for the song. Even Brandon couldn't believe the impact that had been created but this was nothing to what the video had inspired.

A new dance craze meme, dubbed the 'Mad Ferret', had swept YouTube with contributors shooting and posting clips of themselves doing Gary's ferret dance in the most unlikely of places, sometimes solo, more often in unison. Most were filmed using stuffed toys in the mini-productions but there was a hardcore of purists for whom the use of small furry animals (not always ferrets) down their trousers remained *de rigueur*. Before long, the 'Mad Ferret' channel had overtaken the *Salicin Shandy* video in terms of hits and likes and had gone fully international.

It was probably the most successful campaign Brandon had ever done, which made it all the more ironic knowing what he did about the aquifer and Rawson's scheme to scupper their chance of success.

Brandon's next stop was to Brim Over Hall where he'd been invited for lunch. Alicia had insisted that Cora bring her new friend around for a more leisurely get-together than the first time they'd met. Cora was finding it hard to understand the change that had overtaken her mother since she'd got involved in the mystery of the manuscripts – it was as if she'd been given a personality transplant. Still, Cora wasn't going to argue about that.

Alicia was full of praise for Brandon's endeavours as they dined on cold beef salad prepared by the trusty Jean. 'I have to confess, Brandon, that I didn't really hold with the black arts of PR before I met you, but you do seem to be making a real difference.'

'Thank you, Mrs Songhurst. So you've been following the coverage?'

'Oh, do call me Alicia, Brandon, please. Yes, the coverage is quite fascinating, particularly the way in which it's gone viral so effectively.'

Cora wasn't aware her mother had been taking a crash

course in social networking and online marketing and continued to dumbly chew her radish, in awe at this latest development in Alicia's makeover.

'Ah, I see you're well up on it, Alicia. Very good,' Brandon replied. 'The thing is, these days it's the media reporting on the media so to speak, so we now have to work on a number of fronts – not just traditional media like television and newspapers.'

'Quite. I'm also impressed at how you superimposed the Brim campaign message onto the story of Brian Parkin. The use of humour contrasted against the latent tragedy of the chef's downfall. Ingenious.'

'Thank you, Alicia,' said Brandon, rapidly warming to this switched-on, retired historian. 'It's a fine balancing act but it's working, I'd say.'

Before Alicia went on to further critique Brandon's strategy she deemed some refreshment other than water might be in order. 'Cora, be a good girl would you and open a bottle of red? We are being neglectful hosts to our guest, aren't we? I think I may take a glass too.'

Cora swallowed the cherry tomato in her mouth with a gulp, and scurried off to the kitchen to find some wine. Her mother hadn't taken a drink since Cora had returned home – could she even have one?

On her return to the dining room, and as Brandon manfully attended to corkscrew duties, she whispered to Alicia, 'Mummy, are you sure you can drink?'

'Oh, Cora, one glass of wine never hurt anybody. Now, Brandon, to the matter in hand.'

Both Brandon's and Cora's expression betrayed that, unlike Alicia, they weren't too aware of any matter in hand.

Without waiting for either of them to ask for clarification, the elder Songhurst proceeded. 'The media campaign is going brilliantly. Good. Given the length of time invested into the EU application we can assume, on balance, that it will be granted. So much the better. The brewery will be saved and further prosperity will rain down on the town, etcetera. Excellent. So that leaves the small issue of what to do about the fact that the Brimdale spring is, in fact, the Keldmire spring? This wine is very nice, by the way.'

Brandon recognised how Alicia had forged an unrivalled reputation as an academic back in the day. Cora began to suspect her mother might have been drinking before Brandon arrived – it would be one possible explanation for this unaccustomed brio.

It was left to Brandon to go first in the game of scruples that Alicia had just initiated. 'That is the key question, of course.' And, in time honoured PR tradition, he threw the question back at Alicia. 'Tell me, Alicia, what do you think we should do about it? I'm very interested in your take on this.'

Alicia's online crash courses hadn't extended to media interview techniques yet, so she obliged. 'What would I do? My first thought was that, if it's a lie, it should be unmasked. Should such dissimulation prosper?' She paused. 'But when I heard from Cora about the extent of the Victorian Backhouses', shall we say, enterprise, I became rather persuaded to the view that what's been achieved is quite marvellous.'

Brandon was relieved. Alicia wasn't going to blow the gaff. 'My thoughts entirely,' he confirmed.

'You see,' continued Alicia, 'there is an enormous

parallel here to some of the greatest deceptions in history. Sometimes it's justifiable to bend the truth. We don't condemn Churchill's legerdemain in the Second World War, do we? We still find the story of the Trojan Horse compelling. And isn't it the case that all organised religion is based on deception anyway?'

Cora made a mental note to check the contents of her mother's medicine cabinet before retiring that evening. What had got into her? It was like she was back at university, sparring with fellow tutors on some academic theory or other. 'Mummy, do you think you should rest now?' she asked.

'Do you know; I think I might do just that. I do believe that wine has gone straight to my head,' her mother giggled.

As soon as Alicia retired for a lie-down Brandon asked Cora if they could take a closer look at the Old Priory. As the two strolled towards the ruined pile of stones Cora shyly slipped her hand into his.

'Mummy was outrageous today,' she said. 'I've not seen her as animated as that in years.'

'She just needed to feel involved, I guess. It must be terrible to reach old age and think you don't count anymore. She's certainly sharp.'

'Usually in the wrong way, if you see what I mean. She was a very eminent historian in her day, you know.'

'I see where you get it from then, Cora. You should be proud of her.'

Being proud of her mother wasn't a thought that had visited Cora for a long while. She'd stayed away for years, hiding down in London when she should have spent more time with her family. That her mother was cantankerous while Cora was timorous didn't mean she should be frightened of her – she only wanted the best for Cora and that was her way of showing it. Was she proud of Alicia? She was today, that was for certain. She thought back to her childhood and how she aspired to be as brilliant as Alicia in the world of academia. They were different, but maybe Alicia was proud of her too? She regretted the years they'd drifted apart – what a waste. But there was still time, albeit not much, to reconnect.

'What about your parents, Brandon? Do you see them a lot?'

'Not as often as I should. Too busy rushing around. I know I should make more of an effort.'

'You get on with them, though?'

'Oh, yes. They've very down-to-earth and supportive.'

Cora seldom categorised Alicia as down-to-earth or supportive but the simplicity of Brandon's relationship with his parents raised the thought that, maybe in her case, the state of the mother and daughter relationship lay with her as much as Alicia.

Brandon let go of Cora's hand and jumped up on a pile of stones that had once formed the outer perimeter of the Priory. 'Where do you think the spring was?' he shouted as took in the full extent of the site.

'I haven't a clue. We should have taken more notice of the Backhouse documents. It will have been outside the central buildings though – they'd have built around the well I guess.'

Brandon climbed down from the wall. 'Come on, let's

go exploring,' he said as he took hold of Cora's hand again. For half an hour they criss-crossed the weed-choked plot, trying to imagine the life that had pulsed within these fractured partitions all those centuries ago. Cora pointed out to Brandon what she believed to be the cloister, the chapter house and the dormitory but it was only when she identified the kitchen that they began earnestly looking for any evidence of a well. It was Brandon who spotted it first, a flat semi circle of stones that had once formed part of the well surround. He jumped up and down on the soil within the semi-circle causing Cora to cry out in concern. He laughed at her anxiety, knowing that there was only solid earth under his feet after all these years. She joined him in the middle of the arc and they sat down, illuminated by a shaft of light that penetrated the derelict chapel standing between them and the sun.

Cora broke the stillness. 'If feels so strange sitting here, at the heart of all of the commotion. The eye of the storm. The monks could never have known their subterfuge would have endured for centuries.'

'Alicia was intriguing in what she said though, wasn't she? Religion and much of our history is based on deception – that's quite an observation. The bigger the lie the more people will believe it.'

'That's rich coming from a PR man,' teased Cora.

'Why, thank you. I wouldn't class myself in the same league as the Third Reich or the Council of Nicea but I'm working on it.'

'What are you going to do about the blackmail over the report? Everything hinges on that now.'

'What would the Cluniacs have done?' asked Brandon.

'Something clever, that's for sure.'

'Maybe if we sit here long enough, inspiration will strike.'

'And what should we do in the meantime?'

Brandon smiled and pushed her gently backwards on to the soft earth. 'I'm sure we can think of something,' he said.

CHAPTER TWENTY-FOUR

Brian and Peggy had spent the best part of two weeks conducting interviews and photoshoots, banging the Brim drum for all they were worth. At last they had a morning to themselves.

'I should really go down and get the place cleared up,' Peggy said.

Brian was in no hurry to lose her to cleaning duties in the bar. 'There's no mad rush. Anyway, I've something I want to talk to you about.'

As the two finished a breakfast of Eggs Benedict rustled up by Peggy – Brian's culinary influence was now rubbing off on the landlady although she had used ready-made hollandaise sauce – he at last opened up on a subject that had been occupying him for the past few days. 'We get on well, don't we, Peggy?'

Peggy hardly needed to confirm that they did, but nodded anyway.

Brian continued. 'I know we've only known each other for a few short months but being with you makes me happier than I've ever been.'

Peggy blushed. She reached over the table and held his hand. 'Me too, Brian. You know that.'

His confidence boosted, Brian pressed on. 'You know I don't want to go back to television and all of that malarkey?'

'If you're sure, Brian, yes.'

'So it struck me what I'd really like to do is to, well, make a go of it here. With you.' Peggy held her breath.

'I'd like to get a proper restaurant up and running here at the Fountain Head. Just think, Peggy, with me and you at the helm, we can't go wrong.'

Peggy, on the verge of thinking perhaps another kind of proposal was in the offing, simply said, 'Oh?' while dropping his hand in disappointment.

Brian waited for a few seconds. 'And, yes – I almost forgot.' He clumsily went down on one knee. 'I was rather hoping that you'd marry me as well.'

Peggy screamed in delight and threw her arms around his neck. 'You silly bugger, Brian. You had me going there.' Then, putting on a solemn face, 'Actually, the restaurant sounds a good idea although I'm not so sure about putting the chef on a lifetime contract.'

Now it was Brian's turn to look worried. She let him sweat for a few seconds before putting him out of his misery. 'Go on then. Your first job can be our reception.'

Alicia buttered her third piece of toast and helped herself to more marmalade. 'I must say, I do feel much brighter this morning,' she confessed.

Cora, who had decided to give the archives a miss for the time being, was still marvelling at her mother's apparent powers of recuperation. 'Well, that's good, Mummy. Perhaps you're strong enough for a short stroll?'

'That would be exciting. Can you take me down to the Priory? I'd like to have a closer look after all this talk.'

'I think it may be difficult to get the wheelchair all the way there but I can take you down the lane at least.'

Fifteen minutes later, Alicia and Cora surveyed the ruined edifice from the nearest vantage point the lane afforded them. 'Have you been in there recently, Cora? Alicia asked. 'Do you know where the spring is?'

'I think so,' Cora said, reluctant to admit that she and Brandon had become more than acquainted with its exact location. 'But we can't get the wheelchair over there.'

'Then we'll have to go on foot,' said Alicia. 'Pass me my stick.'

As her mother struggled to rise from the wheelchair, Cora objected. 'Mummy, no. We can't leave the oxygen here. It's too risky.'

Alicia wasn't in the mood for such trifling considerations when there was exploring to be done. 'It's quite all right, Cora. I think I can manage for ten minutes, don't you? Don't be such a fusspot.'

Cora linked arms with Alicia and escorted her slowly over the flat green pasture towards the Priory walls. Once there, Alicia was determined to be helped through the gap in order to take a proper look around. Cora kept looking back at the wheelchair parked on the lane as if fearing it might fly away of its own accord. Was this madness, or was this unexpected excursion actually good for Alicia?

As her mother began to point out the various buildings on the site while providing a running commentary Cora couldn't help but acknowledge that it put her own role as a historical guide to Brandon firmly in the shade.

Eventually, Cora steered her mother – who was showing few signs of fatigue – to the spot where she believed the spring to have been. At last Alicia asked for a brief rest and sat down within the same semi-circle that had embraced her daughter and Brandon a few hours previously.

'Yes, Cora. This would be it. Well done. Can you imagine all the fuss this little spot has created?' she said as she stretched out her legs as if preparing to enjoy a picnic.

'It's what happens next that's the big issue.'

'I'm sure Brandon will know what to do. He seems perfectly resourceful and capable, I'd say.' Not receiving a response from her daughter, she continued, 'If I'm not mistaken, you and he seem to get on very well, Cora. Do I detect signs of romance?'

Cora looked down at the ring of earth that, if it could talk, would be able to tell Alicia of more than the machinations of the Cluniacs. She felt her colour rising as she said, 'I like him very much, Mummy, yes.'

'I'm glad, Cora. Good for you.'

Her mother's unexpected blessing made Cora suspect some form of trap was in the offing. Was Alicia trying to determine if Brandon was more important to her than her mother? She tried to remove any lingering doubts in her mother's mind. 'I like him a lot Mummy, but I know this isn't the best time to become involved. You're my most important priority.'

'That's very nice of you to say so, Cora, but don't lose this chance of happiness just because of a frail old lady.'

'I think "frail" may be understating your condition, Mummy. I think we all know the true state of your health.'

Now it was Alicia's turn to look down, as if trying to

penetrate the earth below to detect the long disappeared spa. 'We're all going to pass on at some stage,' she said.

At that, Cora burst into tears. 'Mummy, I'm so sorry I've not been a better daughter to you,' she said as threw her arms around her mother's neck.

Alicia held her daughter, comforting her distress and telling her it would all be all right. 'I'm sorry too, Cora. It's not you who should be apologising.'

'I can't bear to think of what it will be like when you're not here, Mummy.'

Alicia pulled away from her daughter to look her square in the face. 'Cora, there's something I should tell you.'

Cora pulled herself together, stopped her sniffles and returned her mother's gaze. What terrible news had she been keeping back about the true extent of her illness?

'As we said yesterday, sometimes it's justifiable to bend the truth?' said Alicia. 'Well, I may not have been entirely honest with you over my diagnosis.'

The look of incomprehension on Cora's face forced Alicia to expand on her last sentence. 'The thing is, Cora, I'm ill, yes, but not as ill as perhaps I led you to believe. I just wanted you back, you see. I've been very selfish.'

Cora stared at Alicia, the realisation that her mother had lured her back to Brimdale by pretending to be terminally ill slowly sinking in. 'You're not dying?'

'We're all dying, Cora, but in my case possibly not as quickly as I led you to believe.'

'But why lie about it?'

A shame-faced Alicia could only bow her head in silent self-reproach. Then she pulled herself up on her walking stick. 'Come on, Cora. Let's go home, and I'll try to explain.'

As the morning sun continued to climb clear of the Priory's ruined remains a dazed Cora meekly followed her mother through the gap in the wall and back towards the wheelchair.

In the Grote Markt in the middle of Brussels Gary was going through his by now well-practised routine. The photographers clicked away as he enacted the 'Mad Ferret' for the cameras. Gary didn't know the difference between a Fleming and a Walloon but that was the furthest thing from his mind – he had been entrusted by Brandon to carry the Brimdale campaign message to the very seat of the decision makers and he was giving it everything he'd got. Alongside him were four male models Gary had been rehearsing with for the past two days. It was evident that they'd been picked more for their looks than their terpsichorean tendencies yet as they enthusiastically rammed their phallic looking ferrets down their tight leggings the watching crowd cheered wildly, despite their utter incomprehension as to what was going on.

Brandon had been unsure whether to set up this 'away day' for the campaign, especially in light of the Brexit vote, but when he ran the idea past the local press and broadcast stations they clamoured to cover it. In fact, the local media were having great fun with the Brim campaign and couldn't get enough of it – this being silly season, after all. Brandon persuaded Simon to fund the cost of the flights in and out of Brussels, including those for the 'embedded' journalists, and another coverage spike was assured.

After the 'Mad Ferret', Gary and the boys set about handing out samples of Brim to passing lunchtime workers and tourists enjoying the sun. The TV and radio crews collected vox pops from bemused Belgians, Germans, French and Americans on their reactions to the ale and the campaign, and threw in some Brits for good measure including a visiting Bradfordian who just happened to be passing. Typically, he dominated the local coverage that evening as he gave thanks for this unexpected manna from heaven: 'They reckon Belgium is good for beer but it goes right through you – you've only got to look at the statue of that little lad peeing to tell you that. This is the best pint I've had since I got here.' Unfortunately for his friends and relatives, whom he tipped off to record that evening's news bulletin, the footage of him dancing the 'Mad Ferret' didn't make the broadcast.

The beer samples exhausted, Gary and the models were next ushered up Rue Wiertz in the direction of the European Parliament Building so they could hand in a Brim petition. The fact that the Parliament wasn't sitting was immaterial (if it had been sitting Brandon would have vetoed the entire trip) but a clear last-gasp message was being sent to the vacationing bureaucrats of the EU that Brim's geographical exclusivity was not to be denied. Whether they ever got to know about the visit, or saw the image of Gary and his four mallet-wielding assistants clubbing a giant cuddly toy ferret, was doubtful; as Brandon knew, this press trip wasn't for their benefit.

CHAPTER TWENTY-FIVE

Richard Tasker was out of breath and sweating heavily as he wheeled his bicycle – the Bottechia not the Merckx – into his front garden. Since his confession to Simon Backhouse about the 'predicament' he was in his tension levels had risen higher still – if that was medically possible. This morning he'd risen at 5.30am to do a twenty-five mile ride through the country lanes in the hope that the exertion would temporarily ease the persistent anguish dulling his every waking moment. He'd enjoyed over an hour's respite as the hedgerows and sky had merged into a blur but now he'd hit the brakes, so too did his short-lived reprieve. He had forty-five minutes to shower, dress and have breakfast before setting off for work.

As he closed the gate behind him he noticed a small brown paper parcel on the front step. Too early for the postman to have called, he picked it up to read the typewritten label on the front: 'Private. Richard Tasker'. A wave of nausea rose in his stomach and he almost dropped the parcel back on to the porch. This was it. Somehow, with this innocent looking package, Rawson, or Rihanna, or the two of them together, were calling in their debt. Trembling from both the exhaustion of the bike ride and the fear of what he was about to discover, he sneaked down to the bottom of the garden where he couldn't be seen from the house. Plucking up his courage he tore away the outer covering to see what new horror had been dreamed up to humiliate him.

Inside, much to his confusion, was a can of Brimmer Ale and a neatly typed note that read:

Warning. This can of Brimmer is laced with a lethal dose of rat poison. Ask David Rawson at Colton's what he intends to do about it. No police, or people die.

What on earth was this?

He looked around, as if the person who had left the parcel was somehow still in the vicinity waiting to gauge his reaction. What had this to do with his night at the Aubergine Door? Nothing as far as he could discern. He squatted down on the ground with his back against the wooden gazebo as he struggled to unravel this new mystery. What did it mean? Who had sent it? What did it have to do with Rihanna? Slowly, it dawned on him. It had nothing to do with the drunken and lascivious Richard Tasker who had disgraced himself that fateful night but it did have something to do with Richard Tasker of Defra – somebody was trying to hold Colton's to ransom. Now he had a contamination threat to deal with Rawson over, whether he wanted to or not. Slowly he picked his way back to the house to start the day ahead. A day that had just got considerably worse, if that was at all possible.

Too busy for breakfast, Dave Rawson was opening an anonymous looking cardboard package in his Leeds brewery office. In it he found a can of Brimmer and a note that read:

> *This can contains rat poison. There are ten others in stores across West Yorkshire. To find out where will cost £50,000. No police or ten people die.*

Rawson continued reading, to be informed when he would be contacted and told how to pay the money. Shaking his head and tutting, he screwed the neatly typed note into a tight ball and lobbed it with the can and its wrapping into the bin. *Jesus,* he thought. *Not another one.*

He clicked on his computer and scrolled down his bookmarks. First stop, the Brim YouTube page. He let out a low sigh of exasperation as he noted the current number of views: 3, 286,305. Next, the Brim web page: 1,090,268 ferrets whacked on the head. Irritated, he quit the page with a vicious stab of his finger – how on earth had they managed to pull this off? Still, one word from Tasker and it would all come crashing down for Brim. It was a week since he'd last heard from the Defra inspector – surely he must have the report by now? He looked at his watch. 8.30 am. He wasn't going to wait any longer – it was time to tighten the screw on Tasker and make sure he didn't bottle it.

As he picked up his mobile, it started to ring. In a quirk of supernatural timing, the screen display announced Tasker was actually calling him.

Rawson answered. 'I was just about to phone you. Well, has it arrived?'

Tasker, flustered at the gruffness of this welcome, and not quite sure if Rawson was referring to the can of Brimmer he'd received or the forensic report from Brussels, struggled to sound assertive. 'If you're alluding to the report, it's still not here, but that's not why I've called.'

Rawson was at a loss to imagine any other topic that might occupy a loftier ranking in Tasker's current list of priorities. 'Are you serious?' he queried.

Encouraged, Tasker assumed an officious air. 'I have reason to believe that you may be the victim of a contamination threat. Has there been any suspicious activity or demands at your end?'

Rawson eyed the contents of his waste paper bin. How the hell did Tasker know about that? 'No. What are you on about?'

'I have been sent a can of Brimmer with a note that says it contains rat poison. I need to ascertain that the public isn't at risk.'

Rawson sat up straighter in his luxuriously appointed high back executive chair. 'Look, Tasker. This sort of rubbish happens all the time. Nutters and creeps pick up stunts like that from TV and pop a ransom note in my in-tray at least once a month. It's a hoax, that's all.'

'So you have received a threat?'

'If you can call it that. I've chucked it in the bin where it belongs. No Brimmer has been adulterated in any way, believe me.'

'You don't know that until it's tested. There are very strict rules in situations like this. The product has to be analysed immediately.'

'Give me strength. Listen, it's a wind-up. As simple as that.'

'I'm afraid it's not that simple, Mr Rawson. As I know

about the threat I have no option but to advise the police while we conduct the appropriate tests.'

The crisis manual in Rawson's head flicked through the pages headed product recall, rebuilding consumer confidence and sales dip. He'd also have to tell Mervyn. 'Richard, we don't need to involve the police. Think about it, it would be a waste of their time, and it would get out to the press. The fact that it's a hoax wouldn't matter – the effect on the public would be the same as if there *were* contaminated products out there.'

'So, you'd rather wait for the blackmailer to tell the media what he's done while you sit there with your head buried in the sand?'

'It's a try-on, that's all. We must contain this at all costs.'

'And risk people dying? I think not. I'll be in my office in 15 minutes and will be sending the sample I have for immediate analysis. Then, if the product is clear, perhaps we can stand down the usual protocols. But the police still need to know of the threat.'

Rawson couldn't allow that to happen. 'Perhaps you could come here first before doing anything? I'm sure we can sort something out.'

Warily, Tasker agreed. It was about time they had a talk anyway.

The Brim Beer festival had taken place each year for as long as anyone could remember. While, in the past, it had been a highlight in the calendar for many local families, in recent years it had rather lost its way, failing to keep up with the times. Now, with Brandon's input, Howard was envisaging the best festival in living memory. To cash in on their new online fame the Festival was getting its own film trailer featuring two new local figureheads, Godfrey and Gary. As the final preparations for the shoot were being attended to, the two stars sat in the taproom of the Fountain Head having a calming pint – they felt this would prevent them from fluffing their lines.

As the pair was contemplating a second drink Howard came rushing into the bar. 'You're not going to believe this,' he exclaimed. 'Guess what?'

'If my auntie had bollocks, she'd be me uncle?' offered Godfrey.

Howard ignored him. 'We've just heard the date of D-Day from Brussels. It's only the day of the bloody festival. How about that?'

'Well,' joked Godfrey, 'that could spoil a really good party. Can you take out insurance for that going wrong as well as it raining?'

'Don't be so negative, Godfrey,' Howard protested. 'Just think. It will be the pinnacle of the day, a cause for celebration, a triumph.'

'If you say so. Or like finding out your wife's left you for the next-door neighbour. I suppose we'll have to change what I have to say on this film now as well?'

'Already done, Godfrey. Brandon's just done you some new lines.'

Gary, having chewed over the significance of Howard's news, spoke up at last. 'Dust'at mean, after t'Festival, all this is over? No more campaigning?' The Ferret & Firkin champion, rising TV star and intrepid overseas emissary had become accustomed to his new life in the limelight and didn't want to lose it.

'All good things must come to an end, Gary,' said Howard. 'What we've got to do is go out with a bang, and get the right result of course.'

'Maybe we should get a bookie on the day to take bets on the outcome – that could raise a few more quid.' Godfrey was back to being helpful again.

'I don't think we should trivialise the importance of the ruling, Godfrey. If it's a "no" from Brussels this could well turn out to be the last ever Brim Beer Festival.'

To Gary, any such thought was defeatist in the extreme. 'We carnt lose after all this, surely? Wi mus' be nailed on.'

Howard was less than sure. 'It's not a foregone conclusion. We can't take anything for granted. What we must do is do our best and wait.' Reluctant to continue with such a debate he drew a line under the discussion. 'Godfrey, can you just try these new lines?'

The cricketing legend stood to address the imaginary camera and intoned the words on the piece of paper Howard had just thrust into his hands. 'It's decision day at the EU – will Brim win its bid for geographical exclusivity? Come to the annual Brim Beer Festival to hear the ruling live and judge for yourself if miracles really can happen.' He turned the paper over and found it to be blank. 'Is that it? "Will it be a lock-in or a lock-out?" would have done just as well, I reckon.'

Not to be outdone, Gary was keen to take advantage of this last-minute rehearsal. 'Can I do mine an'all, Howard? One more fer luck?' Receiving no objections, Gary drew himself up to his full five feet and six inches. 'And don't forget yer can 'elp mek 'istory by tekking part in t'biggest ever mass ferret legging record attempt,' he boomed as he inserted his official stuffed ferret mascot down his track suit bottoms and theatrically wriggled it to and fro. 'I'm mad ferret. Are you mad ferret too?'

Howard looked satisfied with his fellow BBA committee colleague's effort. 'Very good, Gary. The same again to camera will do just fine.'

'After all,' added Godfrey, 'how can you improve on perfection?'

CHAPTER TWENTY-SIX

Simon Backhouse was idly strumming *Stop Breakin'*
Down by Robert Johnson. While mightily relieved that
Brandon and Cora had pledged to safeguard the secret of
the well the brewery owner was still praying that Richard
Tasker wouldn't succumb to Rawson's blackmail attempt.
Time was pressing on.

He had watched in wonder as the Brim campaign
gathered momentum – Brandon had proved to be an
inspired appointment. Brim was now a worldwide viral
phenomenon, they had enjoyed extensive national
headlines and they were rarely absent from the local media.
Salicin Shandy had made the Top 40 music chart and they
even had a TV production company wanting to talk to
them about turning their story into a TV series. However,
as the number of hits and likes continued to climb and as
each new piece of favourable coverage appeared, Simon
could only fear that while he was winning the battle he
could well lose the war.

He had received a further call from Tasker who
wanted to pop in and 'give him an update' following a
meeting he'd had with Rawson. What had transpired at
that showdown? He would soon know.

Tasker's demeanour when he did arrive offered few grounds for optimism – he was like a jury foreman who refused to look the accused in the eye before delivering a 'guilty' verdict. Simon sat him down and pressed him as to where they currently stood on the forensic report and Rawson's chicanery.

'It's very complicated,' replied Tasker, 'and there's been another development that has a bearing.'

'Just tell me,' urged Simon.

'I did as you said and pretended that the report hadn't arrived,' Tasker began to explain. 'Rawson didn't soften on his demand for me to query the report but at least he backed off for a few days. Then, this morning, I received news that Colton's was at the centre of a contamination threat.' He produced from his brief case exhibits A and B in the form of the can of Brimmer and the ransom note he'd received that morning which he'd now placed inside two sandwich bags to preserve any incriminating fingerprints. 'I called Rawson and went to see him about it but he dismissed it all as a clumsy hoax and didn't want to do anything about it. But of course, I can't ignore it.'

Simon, who had run crisis exercises on receiving blackmail demands in the past, recognised instantly the trouble that going through the police and the authorities would create for his rival, even on a bogus claim. He was also quick to spot the opportunity this development offered. 'But, this is fantastic,' said Simon. 'You're staring the solution in the face.'

Before he could continue there was a knock on the door and Brandon Todd strolled into the office. 'Sorry, Simon. Didn't realise you had company.'

Tasker looked terrified that he'd been caught doing, well, he didn't quite know what, but the presence of a third party, particularly the PR supremo, only added to his discomfiture.

Simon, however, beckoned Brandon into the room. 'Actually, your timing couldn't be better. We may need your help on a small matter.'

Reassuring Tasker that Brandon was in the loop and he was in safe hands, Simon recapped to the point where he'd stumbled upon a possible get-out.

'At first I thought this contamination threat was a further complication,' Tasker picked up the thread, 'but, as you just said, when I was driving over to Leeds it struck me – if he gave me back the photos and took his chance on the forensic report, I could omit to mention I'd received the parcel and he'd have no trouble.'

'And did he bite?' queried Brandon.

'I didn't get that far. He actually accused me of setting up the hoax and threatened to point the finger at me if it ever got made public. I think he would too – he's a nasty piece of work.'

'You didn't set it up, did you?' asked Simon, incredulously.

'Don't be absurd. Of course not,' Tasker replied. 'But it appears we continue to have somewhat of an impasse.'

Simon was weighing up the evidence so far. 'How do you? You've got him over a barrel – no pun intended. If you report the contamination threat he has big problems – I know that. If you do nothing about it, you get him off your back – the photos are a small price for him to pay.

And, as far as he knows, we may still fail to get the EU's backing on the application anyway.'

Tasker shook his head. 'You're forgetting one small thing,' he said. 'What if it's not a hoax? People could die. If I've not reported it and that happens I'm going to have a lot more to worry about than those photos. I should have reported it hours ago in any event – I just can't take the risk.'

'And if you get it analysed to make sure it's a hoax, then the police have to be informed anyway, so Rawson will shaft you in revenge.' Simon said.

'Yes – exactly. What can I do?

Brandon, who had been listening to the exchange, chipped in at this point. 'But if you knew that the cans didn't contain poison, that it was a hoax, then a relieved Rawson would give you back those pictures in return for you gently forgetting about it?'

'But I can't prove it's a hoax until it's analysed, and if I analyse it I have to tell the police. And if you're going to suggest you get it analysed here then I'm afraid that won't do either. It has to be done at our facilities,' Tasker protested, still not prepared to bend the rules.

'Is this the can?' asked Brandon.

'Please, don't pick that up, Mr Todd, it's evidence. I must be getting back to the office and reporting this. I've tried, but I'm sorry.'

Brandon ignored Tasker's entreaty and drew the can from its protective sandwich bag. 'Looks like a normal can to me,' he said. Then, as both Tasker and Simon looked on in horror, he yanked the ring pull, upended the can and took a long, satisfying draught of the contents. Wiping his mouth with the back of his hand he said, 'So, that's Brimmer? Not a patch on Brim. I really think you've got nothing to worry about on the poison front, Mr Tasker.'

Simon and Tasker continued to stare at him, waiting for him to collapse and writhe in agony. Brandon, looking as smug as an investment banker on bonus day, continued his tease by proffering the open can towards them and inviting them to take a swig. Then, having made his point, he said to Tasker, 'I think you've got some photos to collect now?'

'How about "The Feast of Bishopsgate"?' Brian was coming up with a new name for the restaurant as he worked on his menus.

'Are you still harking on about that wrestling theme?' Peggy said. 'I tell you, it's not going to happen.'

Brian laughed. He knew it wasn't going to happen either but couldn't resist the temptation to wind Peggy up. Following their decision to pair up, in every sense, the two had been busy drawing their plans together for the new restaurant and their wedding. Brian had initially resurrected the idea of using Peggy's mother's wrestling memorabilia to decorate the new restaurant but had been forced to concur with Peggy's view that it didn't sit well with the offering. 'It's not sophisticated enough,' she'd said and while Brian wasn't used to having his cooking called sophisticated he knew that Peggy had a point.

Brian had thrown himself into the planning of the new restaurant venture. It was classic, no-nonsense Parkin with a twist. Designed for the location and aimed at getting people in, not scaring them away. Peggy was in awe of the way Brian came alive when dealing with the details of the new eaterie. 'You forget, Peggy, I started off doing this,' he told her as he planned the transformation of the dreary restaurant space in the Fountain Head, hitherto known only for its pedestrian fayre. Brian was aiming at simple classicism with new white linen tablecloths, traditional white porcelain crockery, new glassware and cutlery. 'The food is the hero here,' he preached. He'd pared the menu down to a handful of choices on starters, mains and desserts and was planning to tackle the wine list next. Peggy loved the way Brian was sharing all of his plans with the kitchen and waiting staff, explaining his approach and teaching them that without attention to detail on service the best food and setting in the world was of no avail.

Still, the last word on the name of the new catering establishment was left to Peggy who decided that they should retain the Fountain Head moniker. 'Everybody will know it's new without changing the name, Brian,' she said. 'They'll know it's you.' And he agreed, because he knew she was right. They made a good team.

The wedding arrangements were very much in Peggy's hands as Brian busied himself on the restaurant. The theme wasn't to be too dissimilar to the restaurant – classy and simple. Brian had declined to add more than four or five names to the guest list – this was his life now and he didn't want to drag the past along with him as he crossed a new frontier. Peggy had applied for a licence to conduct weddings in the pub, not least because she thought it would come in handy when they came to sell functions in future. They'd be the first. On the question of the big date, Peggy had initially suggested the day of the annual Beer

Festival but Brian felt that the day after would be better as the day of the festival would be mad busy; also they were hoping to make it a double celebration if good news came from Brussels. If the EU rained on Brim's parade at least the wedding would cheer people up. Peggy had to agree that Brian was right – their thinking complemented each other's.

Dave Rawson knew immediately that the broken, pathetic Richard Tasker of recent weeks had disappeared. As he breezed into his office for the second time that day, the man from Defra looked different – Frank Spencer had turned into Vinnie Jones. Now the boot was on the other foot.

Tasker took charge. 'You'll be pleased to note that I haven't reported the hoax yet, or processed the forensic analysis of the sample.'

Rawson relaxed momentarily. Perhaps he wasn't going to blow the whole thing after all.

'But now I've had time to consider it, I thought it only fair to advise you that that is exactly what I am going to do,' Tasker continued.

Rawson knew he'd overplayed his hand but nevertheless still tried to keep up the bluff. 'So you'd rather be humiliated and risk your marriage and your career because of your misplaced Boy Scout honour? You know what will happen if those pictures get out.'

'You know, and I know, that there are no pictures, Rawson. You've been taking me for a fool.'

Rawson said nothing.

'I've nothing to fear, Rawson. You can do your worse. I'm past caring if I'm being honest.'

Rawson realised that the tables had been turned. Tasker was going to drag Colton's into commercial and legal hell. 'Listen, Richard, it's nothing personal. We can sort this out. I don't want you to report the contamination threat because it's a hoax. You don't want those pictures to see the light of day. It's a simple trade.'

'Except if that can does contain poison people could be killed and both you and I will be complicit in that act.'

'For Christ's sake, it's a bloody hoax. How many more times? We get them all of the time. Let me analyse it here if you're so worried about it.'

'No, that won't do at all. I'm afraid I've wasted enough time here already,' Tasker said as he stood up. 'I'm going.'

'No, don't,' urged Rawson who knew his stratagem had failed. 'Look. I've got the photos here. If I delete them, do we have a deal?'

Tasker wasn't going to be taken in a second time. 'There are no photos. Stop trying to insist there are. It's pathetic.'

Rawson took out his mobile and, opening the photo library, thrust the phone in Tasker's face. 'What are those, then?'

Tasker's lost night, captured in 8-megapixel, swam before his eyes. There *were* photos after all. He could hardly focus as Rawson scrolled through three sickening images. In the first picture the majestically sculpted Rihanna was propping him up as he sat next to her in a booth. She sported a beautiful smile in stark contrast to his slack comatose expression. As Rawson skipped to the second picture Tasker's eyes nearly popped out of his head – while he remained slumped in the identical position to picture one, Rihanna had dispensed with her bra and was demonstrating exactly why she was in demand at the establishment known as the Aubergine Door. Rawson swiped again – it got worse – now Tasker's head was wedged firmly in between Rihanna's welcoming and curvaceous bare bosom.

Resisting his natural inclination to flight rather than fight he dug in, telling himself the existence of the photos didn't change anything. 'So they exist, OK. That doesn't alter what I have to do. I can't risk people dying, and neither can you.'

Rawson, panicking at the prospect of Colton's being involved in a contamination scare and all that it entailed, played his last, desperate, card. 'Look, Richard, look. Stay right there.' And with careful deliberation he held up the phone in front of Tasker's face once more and slowly, theatrically, deleted the three offending images. 'Gone. End of problem. Slate wiped clean. I've done my bit; you can do yours now and forget this stupid hoax?"

'How do I know you haven't copied them? And what about Rihanna? She could still have them.'

'No, no, they're the originals. *I* took them on my phone, and paid her to pose. She thought it was just a lark to wind you up the next day. That's it, they've gone. They don't exist anymore.'

Tasker, shocked and relieved at the same time that the photos had existed and now possibly didn't, had to be sure.

'It still doesn't solve the major problem that what you call a hoax may be anything but. Unless…'

'Unless, what? Just say it,' said Rawson.

'Taste the can now, and prove it isn't poisoned.'

'What? Are you joking?'

'I can assure you I'm not joking. If you're so convinced it's a hoax, and you want to prove that to me, then one sip is all it will take. You're off the hook, and so am I, and we'll both know that there will be no comebacks. Drink it.'

Rawson looked at the can Tasker had relieved him of that morning and which was now being proffered towards him. He looked back at Tasker. He was serious – he meant it. The thought struck him – what if it wasn't a hoax? No. It had to be. He wasn't going to be shafted by this little worm. He pulled the ring on the can, stared at the opening for a good ten seconds, closed his eyes tight shut and raised it quickly to his lips. He swallowed a mouthful and banged the can back on the flat surface of his desk. 'There. Happy now?'

Tasker took in the sight of the defeated brewery boss and considered that, yes, he was happy now. It had been a shock to see the incriminating photos but at least their brief existence had given him the most unexpected bonus of all – he'd forced Rawson to grovel and humiliate himself. Rather an unexpected revenge. Yes, Richard Tasker was very happy indeed.

CHAPTER TWENTY-SEVEN

'She's been pretending all this time to be worse than she is. I can't quite believe it.' Cora had finally plucked up the courage to tell Brandon about Alicia's deception. The two were whispering in the kitchen, as the chastened Mrs Songhurst had taken to her bed for the evening, no doubt tired out from the exertion of confession. 'I thought she was dying,' Cora added to underline the scale of the falsehood practiced by her mother.

'Well,' said Brandon, 'it's not as if she's some spring chicken with her best years ahead.'

'Yes, but she's overegged the pudding, wouldn't you agree?'

'She was lonely, that's all. She was missing you, and that's the only way she could think to make you pay attention to her.'

'So it's my fault for neglecting her, is that what you think?'

'Nobody is blaming you, Cora, but look at it from Alicia's point of view. After your father died she feels marooned, isolated, alone. You're down in London, and that distance is exaggerated when you're the only family she has left.'

'I suppose I could have made more of an effort but she was always so combative. The last thing I thought she wanted was more of my company – I always thought she considered me a nuisance.'

'Until you thought she was dying, and you came,' said Brandon.

'I'd have come if she'd have asked me to. She didn't have to lie.'

'Didn't she? I suspect Alicia thought otherwise.'

'That's what she said when we spoke about it. I still feel that it was a rotten trick to play.'

'It was a little white lie, that's all. Which had a beneficial outcome, didn't it? You and Alicia have reconnected now; you've given her a new lease of life coming up here and you've discovered you have a mother to be proud of. Just look at her over the past week – she's brilliant if you ask me – just like you.'

'She's brilliant all right – I never thought she'd be capable of such trickery.'

'And you're forgetting the most important thing here. If it wasn't for Alicia bending the truth a little, we'd never have met. What's to complain about?'

Put like that, Cora couldn't find much to disagree with in Brandon's summation. 'What should I do now, though? Stay here in Brim Over, or go back to London and come up every weekend or something?'

Brandon understood that she was asking about her relationship with him as well as his advice on her mother. 'I don't think you need to be chained to Alicia every day of the week, not now you understand each other a little better. I'd like to see you in London, but I like it here too now so why don't you spend half of your time here, and half in London for the next few months and see how it goes? You've a book to write, anyway.'

'Yes, but perhaps not the one I thought I was going to write.'

'So tell her. Let her know you're not going to disappear again. Enjoy your time together.'

'Yes. You're right. I will.'

'And while you're at it, tell her that she'll be seeing a lot more of me, too.'

'Do you mean that?'

'Yes, of course. I've developed quite a liking for a pint of Brim over the past few months…'

Cora laughed. Had life ever been as perfect as this?

Rawson steeled himself as he called Mervyn's mobile. He had much to update him on, and needed to get the tone right. He'd left it until ten o'clock in the evening to call him in the hope that his boss may be in a better humour than he seemed to be whenever he called him in the morning.

As soon as Mervyn answered the phone, he knew this calculation had been misplaced. 'Rawson? Can you make it quick? I'm kind of tied up here.' He'd caught Mervyn on the golf course.

'Right, of course,' Rawson replied, and decided that, rather like pulling a plaster off, a quick tug would be preferable to a slow and excruciating exposure of the wounds that had been inflicted on his ill-conceived plans. 'Well, it's not good news, Mervyn.' His boss, lining up his next tee shot, said nothing. 'Brimdale brewery knocked back our offer. No deal. And I understand that the EU is about to grant Brim's application, barring a last minute miracle.'

'Well, you're right about one thing, Dave. It's not good news,' replied Mervyn, silently gesturing to his companion to go before him. 'But it's hardly unexpected news, is it? I told you this would be the likely outcome but you wouldn't let up with your wishful thinking that somehow it would all turn out in our favour.'

'I had grounds to believe that it might,' said Rawson, none too forcibly.

'A little fairy tell you, or what? I warned you, Dave, you had as much chance of winning as a one-legged man in an ass-kicking competition. Contingency plan is what I said, so what is your plan? What's our damage limitation?'

Rawson tried to sound on top of things. 'Of course, I'm on with it now. A full report by Monday morning.'

'Last Monday morning would have been better. Or the Monday morning before that,' said Mervyn, sternly. 'Jeez, it's not like I didn't ask.'

'Absolutely, Mervyn. I hear you,' Rawson twined.

'Do you? You seem to have got a bit hard of hearing recently if you catch my drift.'

'No, all understood. Leave it to me, Mervyn.'

Mervyn's partner, having teed off, was now waiting for his companion to take his shot. Mervyn had a shot of a different kind for Rawson. 'You and I are going to need a talk soon, OK?' With that he closed the call, took his 3-wood, lined up his drive and promptly hit his ball into the bunker on the left of the fairway.

'Goddamn useless, dumb piece of junk.'

He wasn't referring to his club.

'Well, I guess this is it. Not long to wait now.' Simon was having a meeting with Brandon to discuss the festival and the announcement of the EU's decision.

Brandon was in confident mood. 'This time next week, all being well, Brim will be looking at a whole new future.'

'We're not there yet,' Simon said. 'Still time for it to go wrong.'

Brandon wasn't having any of that. He'd been making plans to carry the announcement from Brussels live at the beer festival but the bureaucrats had not been prepared to play ball. 'This isn't the Olympic Games,' had been their tart response. Simon had fretted, that in appearing presumptuous, they could still turn a potentially positive outcome into a negative one. In the end, Brandon had decided that the announcement could come in a live link from the Defra offices where the news would be received first. 'It's just to add a little extra drama,' he'd assured Simon, who considered he'd had quite enough drama over the past few months already.

Simon wasn't convinced that the news would be positive in any event. Life had a habit of kicking you in the teeth, especially if you were a fan of the Delta blues, so he was reluctant to hope too much. Brandon was right though, there were more grounds for optimism than against, and he remembered Tasker's comment that if all the committee could do at these late stages was to ask for a new forensic report, then perhaps everything else must have been accepted. Yet, you could never predict how these politicians would act and he wasn't going to start counting chickens at this stage. Dealing with the bid would have been enough stress and strain for anyone, never mind Cora and Brandon confronting him over the secret of the spring and the underhand and desperate tactics employed by Rawson in his attempt to railroad the brewery. As it was, he felt drained.

Brandon continued trying to cheer him up. 'You realise, Simon, that Brim, and Brimdale, is famous now? You're firmly on the map and ready to kick on with all of those plans you've worked up. You must be chuffed?'

'Yes. Of course,' replied Simon. 'This is where the hard work starts and all that.'

'Come on,' Brandon joshed. 'The festival will be fantastic. The media will be all over it, what with the record-breaking ferret legging attempt, the mass *Salicin Shandy* recital and the announcement itself.'

'It will certainly be livelier than previous festivals, that's for sure.'

'By the way,' Simon said, 'you'll never guess – Rawson did have photos of Tasker on his phone. He showed them to him. He wasn't bluffing after all.'

'A bit gruesome for Tasker.'

'I can imagine. But they've been deleted now. Tasker got his revenge though.'

How?'

'He only forced Rawson to drink the can of so-called contaminated Brimmer to demonstrate it was a hoax. He was so petrified of the police screwing up the business for months, he did. Totally unnecessary, but Tasker wanted revenge.'

'The worm turns – I wouldn't get on the wrong side of him if I were you, Simon.'

'Rawson deserved it. Tisker Tasker certainly thought

so. I'd love to have seen Rawson's face when he drank it though.'

Brandon had a confession to make. 'Look, I never mentioned this, but if it's any consolation, Rawson tried to stop me working for you – offered me double to drop you in it.'

'And you turned him down? Why?'

'Because he's a snake in the grass. It's not often we PRs find someone we can look down on so I gave him the brush off.'

Simon realised how close Rawson had come to undermining them. 'If you'd jumped ship we would have had it.'

'Nice of you to say so. But I didn't, so no need to fret about it. You should thank Cora as much as me. Once you'd introduced me to her I wasn't going anywhere else.'

'Yes, so I see. It's wonderful the relationship you've struck up. Her mother hasn't got too long left though, has she?'

'Thereby hangs another tale. Suffice to say the undertakers have been called off for the immediate future. She was pretending to be terminal to get Cora back to Brimdale. It worked, anyway.'

As Simon took in this news a look of indignation spread across his face. 'She pretended to be dying to get her daughter to spend more time with her? That's outrageous.'

Brandon could only laugh at his client's umbrage. 'What's that expression about the pot calling the kettle black, Simon?'

'Well, here's the thing, Brandon. I didn't start our

deception – it's my lot to maintain it and I can tell you there are days when I wish I didn't have to keep pretending. You could drop me in it for a start.'

'I can see it's a burden. But it's not as if you're maintaining the secret exclusively for your own personal gain. Others depend on it whether they realise it or not. We're not going to tell anyone.'

'Some days I almost wish it had been discovered. Or I think that if the ruling is negative it wouldn't be so bad - I could just quietly close the whole thing down and disappear.'

Brandon recognised how heavily the weight of the one hundred and fifty year old secret was lying on Simon's shoulders but now was not the time for client introspection. 'I've seen these signs before, Simon. Pre-match nerves; hedging your bets on the result. Come on, we've got a beer festival to finalise and we want everything to be perfect, particularly as Alicia is turning out too.'

'Cora's mother?'

'Yes. Amazing isn't it? It's another miracle.'

Simon raised his eyebrows in wry amusement at Brandon's last comment, and rustled in his desk drawer for a second before passing a manila envelope to his PR champion. 'A present for you,' he said.

Brandon, somewhat bemused, opened it to reveal a photograph of a beaming couple, looking blissfully happy together. 'Me and Cora! Why, this must have been taken the first night we met. It's a great pic.'

'Yes, on Ferret & Firkin night, no less. I got it from Howard. You looked so loved-up together I thought you'd like it.'

'That's possibly because we both had quite a bit to drink. That night was a turning point in more ways than one.'

'Well, I hope you'll treasure it always,' the brewer laughed.

'I will, Simon. I will.'

CHAPTER TWENTY-EIGHT

Brimdale Stray had never been as full for the annual beer festival. The high profile of Brim following its campaign helped, as did the multiple attractions on offer. Best of all though was the glorious weather that had decided to bless this most propitious of days. Howard Amos had taken the precaution of doubling the scale of previous events with more marquees, bars, catering and rides to justify the billing of 'Brim's biggest, best and most important beer festival ever'.

Loudspeakers mounted on the main stage blared out rock music as Gary Merriweather prepared to lead a thousand volunteers in the mass 'Mad Ferret' dance. Many more spectators – families, groups of youngsters and gangs of middle-aged men out for a day on the beer – stood around the perimeter of the field to take in this magnificent spectacle and to proffer advice, mainly of a ribald nature, to the participants. That many of the mad ferreters had made a huge effort in their preparations was evident not only from their costumes but also in the ingenuity lavished on their ferret creations. After the mass record attempt Gary was to judge the best-dressed ferret competition. TV crews buzzed around capturing this background colour to the day's big piece of news, the announcement, due at 2pm.

Watching the festivities, Simon spotted Richard Tasker, who stood out from the crowd as he was wearing his normal business attire. However, as a concession to the leisure theme of the day he was accompanied by his wife and son. It was a most incongruous sight to see Tasker *en famille*. Simon went over to say hello. 'Nice to see you here, Richard – I take it you turning out personally is a good sign?'

Tasker made introductions to Debbie and Ben before turning to the main business of the day. 'Well, one can never be one hundred per cent sure of these things,' he said, 'but all the signs from Brussels are good. I'm quietly confident, that's all I'll say.' This was the most relaxed Simon had ever seen the man from Defra.

'Well, we'll owe a great debt to you if we get the nod,' said a magnanimous Simon.

Debbie gazed lovingly at her husband who had made all of this possible following his years of commitment and enterprise. Today would be his crowning glory and something their son Ben would remember for the rest of his life.

Simon was all politeness with Debbie, 'It's very nice to see you here, Mrs Tasker. What do you think of it all?'

'Oh, it's wonderful, but I must confess we're looking forward to the announcement most of all. It will be a big relief all round if – I mean, when – this is all over. He may not show it but I can tell you Richard's been like a cat on a hot tin roof for the past few weeks.'

'I can't disagree with you there,' said Simon. 'It has

been a bit stressful at times but nothing worthwhile was ever won without a struggle.'

'Having said that,' Debbie confided, 'he's been a new man this past week, so I wonder if he knows something we don't if you take my meaning.'

'I hope you're right,' Simon replied before adding, not for the last time that day, 'We won't have long to find out now.'

Richard Tasker had a final question over the plans for the announcement. 'Brandon suggested that I convey the result to the crowd when it comes through from our office – do you still want me to do that?'

'I think that would be most fitting. It's all set up with Brandon, I believe.'

'But he hasn't briefed me on what to say if the bid is unsuccessful.'

'I asked him the same question but he said we'd cross that bridge when we came to it. I think he's trying to keep us in a positive frame of mind.'

And with that, young Ben drew his father's attention to weightier matters as a thousand ferrets were inverted in anticipation of the countdown – 5, 4, 3, 2…

At the same time, in the Yorkshire Premier Lounge of Leeds Bradford Airport, Dave Rawson contemplated the fourteen hours and twenty-three minutes overnight flight to Milwaukee that lay ahead of him. It was a gruelling prospect, with changes at Amsterdam and Detroit, and he wouldn't arrive until 12.55 central daylight time the next day. Mervyn's secretary had been most insistent that this meeting had to take place immediately, giving Rawson less than forty-eight hours to organise a flight.

Rawson didn't need telling over the phone why he had been summonsed. He knew the game was up. By the time he arrived tomorrow, to be escorted from the airport to Mervyn's office, the EU announcement on Brim would be known. But he and Mervyn knew already that his days at Colton's were over; he'd screwed up big style and now he was going to pay the price. Maybe Mervyn would take his earlier achievements at Colton's into account and redeploy him elsewhere within the Monumental Breweries Inc. worldwide empire? It was unlikely, and in any event, did he really want that? His wife might welcome him being sent to a far-flung corner of the world but it was an outcome that held scant interest for him.

He ran through the arguments he could make for his defence – could he have done anything differently? Not really, he thought. If the EU was going to give Brim their geographical status, as looked likely, then the end result for Colton's would have been the same no matter what he'd done. At least he'd tried to railroad their bid; at least he'd been proactive in trying to influence the result. Plus, he'd captured nine years of Brimmer sales and stopped Brim from growing in that time. He'd done a bloody good job all told. Would the American see it like that? Would he heck. He knew Mervyn would focus on one thing only – he lost the game. And for good measure, he knew Mervyn would be less than sympathetic when it came to the scheme of trying to buy Brimdale Brewery. Mervyn would remind him how it had been obvious to him that Brimdale was never going to sell. He could hardly tell Mervyn what he'd done to try to make sure the deal went through – blackmail didn't figure too highly in the management toolkits so beloved of American business, where independent thought and creative thinking were outlawed.

No, he'd have to take his medicine and thank Mervyn for his time. Why was it, too, that Mervyn had to humiliate him by dragging him halfway across the world to administer the boot? Possibly, somewhere in that same management toolkit, it said it was preferable to dispense with an employee's services face-to-face – which would be a bit rich coming from the race that employed remote drones to take out its enemies. How Rawson wished they could programme a UAV to hit Colton's in Leeds and spare him the bother of this charade.

He had seventy-five minutes until his first flight. He needed a drink – sod it, he was the condemned man anyway. As he went up to the bar the young barmaid gave him a cheery smile. Before he could state his order she launched into the offer of the day. 'May I interest you in a free bottle of Brim, Sir? Today's the day they find out from Brussels if they can stop other people using the name and we're giving Brim away all day to wish them luck.'

Rawson peered back at her with a maniacal look on his face. 'I'll have a gin and tonic. Make it a double,' he replied.

Brandon wandered into the large marquee on the other side of the Festival green looking for Cora and her mother. He spotted them over by the stage chatting to Godfrey, who was due to entertain the crowds as soon as the 'Mad Ferret' had finished. Alicia, *sans* wheelchair, was dressed for the weather in a multi-coloured maxi dress that Brandon figured had last enjoyed an outing in the

1990s as, quite likely, had its owner. Alicia and Godfrey were getting on like a house on fire.

'It must be nerve-racking to go on stage in front of so many people?' Alicia ventured.

'Well, I'm not so bad; it's Bouncer who gets the butterflies. But I don't feed him so heavily beforehand now so he's a lot better,' replied the ex-cricketer.

Failing to recognise she was being teased the ever-inquisitive Academic followed up. 'And what, exactly, does the act consist of?'

'Act? It's no act. It's dead straight is this,' said Godfrey with a sideways wink to Cora. 'You'll just have to stick around and watch.'

Brandon's arrival saw them all asking if there was any news yet from the EU. On learning that it was still up in the air, each consoled the other with the mantra of the day: 'It won't be long now.'

Shortly, Godfrey announced he'd better attend to his last-minute preparations. Grasping Alicia's hand he shook it slowly and gently and said, 'It's been a pleasure to meet you, Alicia. I hope you're around for the rest of the day?'

Alicia, all of a flutter, could only say, 'Likewise, Godfrey. I'm sure we'll still be here for the announcement.'

As Godfrey headed backstage Brandon couldn't believe the two hadn't met before, with them both being long-standing residents of Brimdale and its environs.

'Curiously, no,' confirmed Alicia. 'I'm afraid we were very much immersed in the university world while Godfrey seems to have led a far more exciting life. He's very nice though, isn't he? Come on, Cora, let's get to the front of the stage – I don't want to miss this.'

Brandon laughed at her enthusiasm. 'Well, you can tell me about it later. I'm needed elsewhere.'

Brian was making sure Peggy was on top of things in the catering tent. They'd spent the past twenty-four hours preparing and setting up - Brian had actually been on site at 6am to turn on the hog roast ovens. Peggy had done every beer festival since the year dot but never on this scale and never with this level of enjoyment. She and Brian made such a good team, nothing was a problem. Brian kept on apologising as he was demanded here, there and everywhere by the press for interview snippets and photo opportunities and by the crowd for mobile phone snaps and autographs. 'Go on, Brian, we're all sorted here,' urged Peggy, proud that her man was so central to the day's proceedings.

Brian had been working his socks off for over seven hours when he decided to take a bit of a breather in the cool shade of the admin tent behind the main stage. As he stretched himself out in a welcoming deckchair he took stock once more of the remarkable transformation in his life these past few months. Salvation, realisation, proportion, love and a new purpose in life – not a bad shopping list he chuckled to himself. As he let these blissful thoughts wash over him he became aware of two people talking in the tent behind him. The voices weren't raised so it was difficult to make out exactly what they were saying but he discerned that it was Simon Backhouse and Brandon Todd in conversation. As Brian attuned his ears to pick up their drift he caught every second or third word with the result that he found himself trying to assemble the random words into a meaning, rather like gluing the pieces of a dropped Ming vase back together after an unfortunate accident.

Simon sounded weary and worried – maybe it was just the stress of it all. He could hear certain words – '*deception… Keldmire… catastrophe… close the brewery…*'

Brandon's tone appeared to be conciliatory and soothing – '*it's not going to get out… ingenious… have to protect the secret of the spring… can't turn back now…*'

What on earth were they talking about? Just then, his phone buzzed – a text from Peggy: *Can we start on hog number 3 yet*? He jumped up from the deckchair and scurried over to the catering tent. He shouldn't have been listening in anyway.

'Yorkshire,' shouted Sir Godfrey. Bouncer reared up straight and erect on his hind legs and appeared to applaud loudly with his upraised paws while emitting an ear splitting howl of approbation. The crowd cheered wildly at this most discerning, not to mention athletic, of canines.

'Lancashire,' came Godfrey's next command. Bouncer immediately assumed the attack position while issuing a fierce and threatening '*grrrrrrrrr*' from his snarled jaws. Spontaneous chants of 'Yorkshire, Yorkshire' issued from the boisterous audience.

'Let's see if you're good enough to field in the slips,' said Godfrey as he walked to the right hand side of the stage, leaving Bouncer in the middle. Producing a tennis ball from his pocket Godfrey skied it over Bouncer's head. The dog took two steps backwards and leapt high into the air to catch the ball between his teeth.

The marquee was packed, and Alicia, at the front, applauded and cheered along with rest, much to Cora's amusement. After 'best of three' on catching, Godfrey asked for a volunteer from the audience to help with the next trick. A young boy was selected and asked to go on hands and knees to form a hurdle. Bouncer duly obliged by vaulting over him, and before long Godfrey had four children spaced at intervals for Bouncer to attempt a relay. At the end of the trick, Godfrey encouraged Bouncer to give each of the children a high five to thank them for their support. The festivalgoers were lapping it up.

Alicia, unable to contain her glee at such unknown pleasures, turned to Cora. 'This is amazing, darling. I can't quite believe we're at a beer festival watching dog tricks. What would your father have said?'

Cora wondered the same, but then so many things had changed recently.

Godfrey was announcing it was time for the drinks interval. Bouncer dutifully sprang off stage left and returned five seconds later with a can of beer in his mouth. Godfrey took the can and looked sternly at the dog and shook his head. 'This isn't right, is it?' he said as he showed the can of Brimmer to the crowd. A huge 'boo' went up, and Bouncer collapsed to the floor with his head buried in his paws in a gesture of shame. Godfrey gave the can back to Bouncer who ran off again, only this time to emerge with a can of Brim in his mouth. Godfrey opened the can and took a sip before pronouncing his verdict – 'perfect'. The crowd laughed as Bouncer pawed his master for his share of the beer.

Godfrey was working up to the climax of his show.

'Ladies and gentlemen, for Bouncer's final trick he has something very special to share with you, but he's going to need your help. Can you do that?'

A huge 'y-e-s' came back from the floor.

'You know the sign an umpire makes when giving a wicket? Yes? Well, on the count of three, we're all going to give Bouncer that sign and see what happens. On the count of three – 1, 2, 3.'

A thousand index fingers were raised overhead pointing in the direction of the Border Collie. As Godfrey held the microphone to the dog's mouth Bouncer uttered, in a clear and unmistakeable tone, two syllables: 'Howzat'.

One man in the crowd turned to his companion and said, 'Shouldn't the given out sign come after the "Howzat"? That's the wrong way round.' There was just no pleasing some people.

Behind the main stage was now gathered the hundred-strong Brim choir who had been rehearsing *Salicin Shandy* for days. They were going to be belting out the campaign anthem for the crowd immediately after the announcement, hopefully in celebration rather than as a symbol of fighting on. All activities on the festival site had stopped for this moment and it seemed like the entire population of Brimdale was now crammed in front of the empty stage.

The people backstage were no less expectant or tense. Brian and Bouncer, fresh from their triumph, stood in line with Gary and Howard while Brian and Peggy kept up a patter of small talk to ensure silence didn't foster defeatist thoughts in these final moments. Simon secretly prayed their efforts would prove sufficient, for him as much as for Brim and Brimdale.

Cora and Alicia looked on approvingly as Brandon delivered the final briefing. 'As soon as we get the nod that Defra has heard from Brussels, I'll give the signal and you'll all file on to the back of the stage; there's a blue line marked on the floor – stand behind that. I'll then introduce Simon and Richard Tasker and tee up the "live" call that Richard will take from his office. Richard will then announce if it's a "yes" or a "no". If it's "yes", the screens will flash the news, there'll be a brief firework display and we'll play celebration music and bells over the PA. I'll then interview Simon and Richard on what it means to the brewery and the town, then we'll have the Salicin Shandy choir.'

Everybody nodded. It was left to Debbie Tasker to ask the question nobody else dare raise: 'What if it's a "no"?'

'We've got that covered, too,' confirmed Brandon. 'Sad music, a "thank you for your support" message on the screens but still with interviews and the choir. We're not thinking about that though – keep positive.'

At that, Richard Tasker's phone rang. It was his office with the news that they had received the official decision. Brandon ushered the *Brimerati* on to the stage. Not long to wait now.

CHAPTER TWENTY-NINE

The next afternoon the Fountain Head was transformed for the nuptials, as were the bride and groom. Peggy had opted for white – it was her first time after all – while Brian had decided that a smart lounge suit would be the order of the day, it being his second time around the block. Peggy had stuck to her promise to mainly invite a few regulars but it seemed to Brian that the pub was better supported than ever as he surveyed the throng of well-wishers gathering in the lounge – or wedding room as it said on the invite. Brandon had managed to work yet more magic on the media by keeping the ceremony a secret – how they would grumble when they found out they'd missed it. When the couple first asked Brandon to ensure no press crashed the party Brian thought Brandon would insist on using the occasion for further publicity for Brim but he simply told them that part of the job was done. He even felt that they'd receive more public support for the marriage and the restaurant if they didn't act like a couple of publicity-hungry desperadoes. As Brian said to his intended, 'You can never tell what's right and wrong with this PR game, can you?' Still, they were relieved.

Spirits were high as the guests arrived. A harpist

plucking away in the corner lent an ethereal air to the proceedings, causing Godfrey to conjecture whether he'd popped his clogs overnight. Alicia had made a big effort for her first formal outing in years, having rescued her wedding outfit – a bright pink two-piece topped off with an outsized hat – from the wardrobe where it had lain undisturbed since the days Charles was still getting on with Diana. Mrs Amos and Mrs Merriweather also sported vivid sunny outfits, as if to compensate for their customary absence from the establishment in which they now found themselves. It was noticeable how quiet Howard and Gary were in the presence of their spouses. As for Cora, to Brandon she looked as radiant and as beautiful as any woman he'd ever seen; his heart swelled with pride that she was accompanying him to this private and intimate gathering. He was going to enjoy this day.

The ceremony itself took place on the stage that had been bedecked and dressed in a forest of white flowers. As the bride and groom exchanged both vows and rings under the gaze of their friends the scent of love and goodwill intermingled powerfully with that of the pollen. Mrs Amos, once more parted from her husband who was attending to the wedding photographs, joined Gary and his wife, at least giving Mrs Merriweather someone to talk to about the frocks, flowers and frivolities of the day.

Afterwards, as they seated themselves in the newly decorated restaurant for the wedding meal, the guests were taken aback at the simple and tasteful splendour on display. The once dowdy room now shone and glistened with its linen, silver and glassware. The white flower cascade that started in the lounge continued its course into the dining area, exuding its seductive scent over all present. In a blatant effort at pairing up, Godfrey had been seated next to Alicia on the same table as Brandon, Cora, Simon and Regina Backhouse. Brandon marvelled that, in Brimdale at least, it took a wedding to flush the wives out but certainly the table couldn't help but be charmed by Regina who proved to be a very knowledgeable, witty and engaging addition to the company.

To Godfrey's obvious delight, Alicia was still enthusing about his and Bouncer's performance at the Festival the day before. 'Really, Godfrey, it was quite remarkable and put me very much in mind of Samuel Johnson.'

'Did he train his dog up, too? I never knew that.'

Alicia, by now getting used to his sense of humour, giggled. 'Godfrey, you are incorrigible, really. What I meant was, when someone told him that he'd heard a woman preaching, Johnson replied that a woman preaching was like a dog walking on its hind legs. "It is not done well, but you are surprised to find it done at all".'

'I like the sound of this Johnson fellow. Did he play for Yorkshire too?' ribbed Godfrey, feeling very much like he'd found the ideal opening bowler partner to prop up the Kirkstall Lane end.

After the guests had tucked into a three-course wedding repast of watercress and smoked salmon tart, shredded lamb infused with rosemary and mint followed by summer berry pudding – classic Brian recipes - it was left to Godfrey to voice the judgment most felt on the quality of the food: 'I reckon that Brian might have a future in this cooking lark.'

His culinary credentials still intact, the groom stood up to say a few words. 'If someone had told me six months ago how wonderful, rewarding, joyous and full of possibilities life could be, I'd have bashed them with my cleaver.' A fresh wave of warmth swept the room. 'As I look around today, everything a man could want is here. Friends and friendship. Genuine togetherness. People who are prepared to help each other out. And, of course, my beautiful bride.' Brian paused until the spontaneous applause died down. 'That I could meet, never mind marry, someone so special seems a miracle to me, and until I'd set foot in Brimdale I'd not really been one for miracles.'

A chorus of 'ahs' erupted from the guests.

'But here we are today, me and my amazing, gorgeous, brave Peggy, ready to share the rest of our lives together. We make a great team. I, for one, am going to relish every moment with her from this day on.'

As more applause broke out, Mrs Merriweather leaned over to Gary and whispered, none too quietly, 'You never say anything like that to me.' Mrs Amos made a mental note to take up the same point with her husband when he finally put his camera down.

'So, in closing, I'd like to propose a toast to the bride. Peggy, darling, my wife, my partner, my miracle.' Each of the guests rose and raised their champagne glasses which had been filled with Brim for the toast. He didn't have to say why.

The formalities over with, the atmosphere became even more relaxed as the guests retreated to the function room. Godfrey, to use his own expression, was 'up on his toes' as he entertained Alicia. Cora and Brandon exchanged numerous glances as Mrs Songhurst senior continued to burst out with laughter at the old cricketer's endless commentary and observations.

Regina appeared remarkably well-informed over what had been taking place on the Brim campaign as she probed Brandon on his thinking and planning. He realised how much Simon, too, must confide in his partner and he felt pleased that such a strong union was in place between her and her husband, not least because he knew how heavily Simon sometimes carried his load. It also struck Brandon that she must have enquired of her husband at some point: *what exactly was that sound of running water emanating from the basement of their house?*

Simon, however, had other duties to perform this day as he excused himself to go and set up the band equipment. On hearing the news, Godfrey couldn't resist chipping in with, 'Remember it's a wedding, Simon. Do you know anything upbeat?' Indeed, he did, as before long the small space in front of the stage was host to some enthusiastic, if rather rusty, dancing displays.

At the top table Peggy and Brian were now able to relax a little, the official part of the day having been successfully negotiated. Their happiness knew no bounds.

'It was lovely what you said in your speech, Brian. You know I feel the same, too.'

'I've never meant anything more in my life, Peggy.'

She gave him a kiss on the cheek. 'Well, here we go. We've only got the rest of our lives ahead of us.'

Brian raised his pint of Brim to Peggy in silent toast and said with a grin, 'Can't wait.'

'What a few days; what a few months,' exclaimed Peggy as she tried to take in all that had taken place in such a short span of time.

Brian suddenly recalled something that had been playing on his mind. 'Actually, there's a question I meant to ask you but forgot in all of the excitement.'

'This sounds intriguing,' Peggy joked.

'It was just that I was behind the admin tent at the Festival yesterday and I couldn't help but overhear a conversation between Simon and Brandon that sounded, well, a bit weird. I know I shouldn't have been ear-wigging, but I couldn't help it.'

'Never mind that,' said Peggy eagerly. 'What were they saying?'

'Well, I didn't catch it all but from what I could piece together, it sounded like they were talking about the spring at the brewery. I got the distinct impression that they were saying that the water for Brim doesn't come from here at all, but from Keldmire.'

'Oh, Brian. What are you like with your big ears?' she teased. 'You've got be very careful when you overhear things.'

'Well, it sounded like that right enough but I must have picked it up wrong.'

She looked around to make sure no one could hear her and then whispered into her husband's ear. 'Well, now we're married, we shouldn't have any secrets. Yes, it's true; the spring does rise in Keldmire and more folk than should around here know about it. Keep it under your hat, though. It would be a shame to spoil it for everybody.'

Shortly afterwards, Peggy took to the stage. 'Bloody hell, it's not last orders already is it?' shouted Godfrey.

'It might be for you if you don't watch it, Godfrey,' the landlady replied. 'I just wanted to say a few words myself. My husband and I...' A chorus of 'ooohhhs' rose from the floor. '... want to thank you for your wonderful support and love today. It's been the most fantastic day I can ever remember. I've been told that successful marriages are based on compromise. So I'd like to share the first trade-off of this union with all of you here tonight.' More 'ooohhhs', but more questioning in tone this time. 'So, for the first, and the last time, please welcome my other half and a song that he's rehearsed especially for the occasion.'

As the band launched into a jaunty intro, Brian leapt on to the stage and gave his bride a hearty hug before taking up the mic and launching into the first verse:

I can't eat my dinner
I can't sleep at night
I go out in the evening
Looking for a fight
Because my baby
She just told me everything
She was a lady wrestler
'Til she got banned from the ring

DIGESTIF

As Simon Backhouse entered the brewery this fine September morning he had a renewed spring in his step and his head was bursting with positive and exciting thoughts. The past few years had seemed never-ending, a torture to be endured as he'd hung on in there. Now, like a Formula One racing driver he'd seen the last of the five red lights extinguish and he could roar into action with a fresh set of warmed up tyres and a full tank.

He sat at his desk and skimmed his emails – there were hundreds of 'well dones' and congratulations swelling his in-tray. He allowed himself the smile of the victor as he flicked through the file of news coverage on Brim's stunning achievement in finally landing the EU's blessing for its bid for geographical exclusivity.

Finally, he tackled the pile of mail left on his desk by his secretary. One item caught his eye – an official looking registered envelope that someone on reception had signed for. He ripped it open to reveal the contents. As he speed read the accompanying letter he couldn't comprehend its meaning at first but then caught his breath as its import dawned on him. He seized at the enclosed papers and, in a rising panic, tried to convince himself he must be wrong.

No, the communication was clear enough. Keldmire Town Council was building a new bypass around the town and was serving the brewery, as the owner of Grange Manor, with a compulsory purchase order. In 24 months the family home and its secret spring would be six feet under and providing the bedrock for the new road, all to ease the travel strain for white van men and geriatric Sunday drivers.

He buried his head in his hands. He was going to need a miracle to get out of this.

Acknowledgements

I'd like to raise a glass to the following for their help and support in coaxing Trouble Brewing out of the taproom and on to publication: Mark Beaumont of Dinosaur for cover design; Chris Sharp for illustrations; Glenn Jones for setting up the www.paulcarrollink.co.uk website; Nina Webb of Brazen PR for marketing support; my beta readers Nathalie Bagnall, Catherine Barrett, Patrick Carroll, Liam Ferguson, Brendan Gore, David Hargreaves, Peter Jones, John Kelly, David Lomax and Gerry McLaughlin for invaluable feedback. Especial thanks to David Lomax for providing an extra pair of eyes at manuscript checking stage. Finally, a standing ovation for composer Brendan Gore for allowing use of the lyrics to 'Lady Wrestler' (check out the song clip at YouTube by searching Lady Wrestler/Gags).

The Author

Paul Carroll has been drawn to ink and the written word for as long as he can remember. Born in a pub in Leeds (really), Paul studied English at the University of Manchester before going on to run his own successful PR consultancy for a number of years. Nowadays Paul concentrates on his writing. *Trouble Brewing* is his third novel following *A Matter of Life and Death* (Matador, 2012) and *Written Off* (Matador, 2016).